DO OVER

DELANEY DIAMOND

GARDEN AVENUE PRESS

Do Over by Delaney Diamond

Copyright © 2018, Delaney Diamond

Garden Avenue Press

Atlanta, Georgia

ISBN: 978-1-940636-61-0 (Ebook edition)

ISBN: 978-1-940636-62-7 (Paperback edition)

www.gardenavenuepress.com

CHAPTER 1

"Good evening, Horace," Ella Brooks said to the doorman as she breezed through. She walked into the brilliant foyer of Presidential Commons, an exclusive building in Atlanta that housed condos and apartments occupied by some of the city's most affluent families.

The doorman's craggy gray brows lifted in surprise. "Miss Brooks, I didn't expect to see you back so soon."

She paused her stride across the floor. "I decided to take full advantage of the kids being with their father and take a couple of days all to myself." That wasn't entirely true, but she didn't need to burden the doorman with her personal problems.

"May I help you with those, ma'am?" The porter, whose dark hair was cut down to a buzz, stepped forward, his gaze encompassing the rolling suitcase and matching bag over her shoulder. James started working at the building only a few weeks before, and so far, everyone appreciated his friendly personality and attentiveness.

She smiled at him. "No, I've got it. Good night, gentlemen."

Ella made her way to the elevator, currently letting out a few occupants. She nodded at her neighbors and stepped in. As the doors closed, she leaned back against the wall, and the smile faded from her face.

Why did she bother being polite to her ex again? Oh right, because of their two daughters.

She'd become adept at hiding her true feelings for the man who fathered her children. Ever since he was dismissed from her family's business, Wayne complained constantly about not being able to take care of Hannah and Sophia in the same fashion Ella could afford. He complained about the small apartment he was forced to live in and the fact that he couldn't take them on nice trips the way she did. Never mind they didn't care, but because of his constant whining, she booked a couple of suites at a resort in St. Barts and leased a yacht for them to sail around the island.

She only joined them because she herself wanted to get away. But Wayne started a fight, and rather than let their daughters see them argue, Ella disembarked and flew back. Hannah and Sophia were disappointed, but she'd see them in a couple of days when they returned.

Wayne made it hard to be the bigger person. She'd thought about being spiteful and bringing the girls back with her but didn't want to be the kind of ex who limited her children's time with their father. Considering she was the custodial parent, she could make his life a living hell, but that would hurt her children, and she didn't want to do that.

She entered the penthouse, and as the door swung closed, Ella paused. The recessed hall lights were on. Did she forget to turn them off when she left? Unless the staff, who she'd given the week off, returned while she was out, she certainly did forget.

Shaking off her unease, she laughed softly. "You're getting forgetful in your old age, Ella," she muttered to herself.

She hung her coat in the closet near the door and made her way to the back of the penthouse, her suitcase rolling along the wood floor. She'd just turned the doorknob on the bedroom suite when the closet behind her opened. She didn't have time to react before a strong arm clamped around her neck and the bag on her shoulder dropped with a thud. She let out a short cry and writhed frantically, squirming in a futile attempt to escape the intruder.

"Keep still!" The man's gruff voice preceded his arm tightening so painfully, he temporarily cut off her air. She gasped and stopped moving, grasping at his thick forearms, her beating heart slamming over and over against her ribs. Oh dear God, he was going to kill her. She would never see her babies again.

"Be good and you won't get hurt."

Flashbacks to self-defense class rushed through her brain. *Get away. You have to at least try.*

With renewed vigor, Ella slammed her foot on top of the intruder's, grinding the stiletto heel with all her might. The man howled in agony. Gripping the arm around her neck, she did a quick sidestep and slammed the side of her fist into his crotch.

"Fuck!" When he bent at the waist, dragging her with him, she immediately followed up with an elbow to the nose. He hollered louder and collapsed to the floor.

She leaped over his crumpled body, noting the dark suit and tie, black gloves, and black ski mask. Panicked, she raced to the front door. Within feet of it, she was tackled from behind and sent sprawling to the floor. Her elbows collided with the hardwood. Blinding pain shot into her arms and shoulders, and she grimaced, barely preventing her chin from hitting the hard surface.

What was happening? This was a different man, dressed the same but smaller. He'd come out of nowhere.

How many of them were there?

The assailant grabbed her ankles and dragged her away from the door.

Ella realized she'd been so terrified and concentrating on getting away, she'd forgotten to scream. But she did so now— blood-curdling, hysterical cries—tears of panic and dread filling her eyes as she was hauled by her stomach deeper into the apartment. Her manicured nails clawed the floor. She prayed someone heard her. For the first time, she hated the thick walls and despised the quiet, tomblike quiet afforded by the expensive address.

Back in the hallway leading to the bedrooms, the dress she wore was bunched up under her chest and flipped up at the back to expose her ass in a lacy thong. She was exposed and vulnerable to these strangers.

The Dragger yanked her to her feet and slammed her face first into the wall. Pain radiated from her cheek all over the side of her face.

"Cover her fucking mouth!" the one she attacked earlier said in a loud whisper. He clutched his abused nose.

When the smaller man did as he was told, she bit a gloved finger, and he snatched away his hand.

"Bitch bit me!" He slammed her head against the wall again, harder this time. So hard she saw stars and became temporarily disoriented.

Each man gripped her by an arm and swung her in the direction of a third man who walked up. He was taller than the others and dressed in all black, too. Ella opened her mouth to scream again, but he pressed the cold barrel of a gun to the middle of her forehead. The scream died a sudden death in her throat, replaced by silent terror.

Tears blurred her vision. "P-please don't kill me. I have children. Two little girls."

"Then keep your mouth shut and you won't get hurt."

She heard a fourth guy come from her bedroom. "Shoulda never come back early, sweetheart."

"Well, she's back," the one with the gun said. He must be the leader. He spoke with quiet authority. "And having her here makes things easier." He stepped real close. "All you have to do is answer a few questions and behave yourself, and your kids won't become motherless. Got it?"

The horror of her situation set in. Her knees buckled, and she would have collapsed if not for the two men holding her up by the arms. She hung her head and let out a helpless sob, tears streaming down her cheeks. They could do anything. Rape her, beat her, kill her.

4

"Miss Brooks, I need you to confirm you understand the terms of our agreement. Behave yourself, and everything will be fine. Understand?"

"Y-yes." She choked out an answer, afraid that if she didn't, they would hurt her again.

"Wonderful."

They used duct tape to bind her hands in front of her and forced her to open the safe behind a false door in her dressing room. They scraped out all the documents, cash, jewelry, and other valuables and dropped them into briefcases. They did the same to the necklaces, rings, and fine pieces in her jewelry box, as well as taking her daughters' necklaces and bracelets from theirs. They removed the earrings and rings she wore when she entered the penthouse, and a gold bangle from her wrist.

When they finished, The Dragger pushed her into her bedroom. He stuffed a sock in her mouth and sealed it in place with duct tape. He positioned her in the middle of the bed and using twine, secured her still-duct-taped hands to the metal bars above her head. When he produced a red scarf taken from her dressing room, she shook her head vehemently, screams muted behind the gag. A lock of hair fell out of the top knot on her head and blocked one of her eyes.

He smiled, evidence of his maliciousness crossing his lips right before he covered her eyes, knotting the cloth with undo force. Then he closed the door and left her alone.

Ella sat in darkness for a while taking loud, deep breaths, arms stretched above her head. She said a quick prayer of thanks that the girls hadn't come back with her. The thought of them going through any of this made her weep silently. They were safe with their father.

How did these men, four of them, get up here? Presidential Commons was supposed to protect against this type of thing happening.

The door opened and she tensed, listening. Heavy feet tread across the floor, and then the bed depressed beside her.

"Hey," a soft voice said in her ear.

She discerned right away that the person speaking was the first guy. He had an accent, like someone from Boston. Not too strong, but enough that she detected it.

He ran a finger down the side of her face and she moaned, shifted to get away, winced at the awkward angle that stretched the ligaments in her arms.

"Maybe you and I can have some fun."

Oh god, he was going to rape her.

Ella whimpered, weeping quietly as he shoved the hem of her dress higher and stroked the inside of her thigh. If she survived this ordeal, she'd have to burn this dress. She jerked in an effort to get away, but he was persistent and at an advantage. She couldn't see. She couldn't get away. She couldn't even scream. Helplessly, she twisted against the restraint and openly wept. Her fingers and toes curled in distress as this strange man touched her inner thigh with his gloved hand, edging slowly higher.

"What the hell are you doing?" a loud voice barked from the door. The Leader.

"What? I'm having a little fun with the pretty lady."

"That's not why we're here. Leave her alone."

"Oh, come on, man."

"I said leave her alone. Get outside and help the others. We've been here long enough. It's time to go."

The bed moved as Boston Accent stood up.

The room was quiet except for Ella's heavy breathing, but she knew she wasn't alone. Finally, The Leader came to stand beside the bed. "It's okay."

She continued crying.

"We have a deal. Nobody's going to hurt you."

His hand touched her thigh and she jerked, kicking and screaming in her head.

"Relax. I'm pulling down your dress. If you don't relax, you're going to start hyperventilating."

Slowly, she did as he said and slowed her breathing.

"Easy. That's it. Stretch your legs out."

Gulping, Ella straightened her legs and eased back into the original position.

"Good."

His hand touched her thighs again, but this time she didn't pull away. He straightened her dress, pulling the hem down below her knees.

"We're leaving in a few minutes. I would untie you, but I can't risk you calling the police before we've had a chance to get way."

The door clicked closed. That was the last Ella heard from any of them.

* * *

ELLA WAS EXHAUSTED. She'd dozed off and spent the night in the same position, which was not exactly conducive to restful sleep. Her arms and shoulders ached, but she was alive. That was the important thing. All the cash and valuables could be replaced, and soon she'd be able to give her daughters hugs. She moaned and twisted to loosen her stiff muscles.

The sound of movement somewhere in the apartment caught her attention. Angling her head, she listened. Were the men back? No. There was no reason for them to come back. It must be morning, which meant that was Mrs. Newcomb, the housekeeper. Ella asked her and the chef to come back early. The chef would be there shortly with the week's groceries and to prep tomorrow's meal.

Ella made as much noise as she could, rattling the bed and kicking her heels. *Help me! Help me!* she screamed silently.

The vacuum cleaner came on. She tried not to cry from frustration, but it was hard. She waited. Eventually Mrs. Newcomb would come back there and see her. She just had to be patient. She'd spent the entire night in this condition. A few more minutes wouldn't hurt.

What felt like hours later, the door clicked open.

Mrs. Newcomb screamed. "Miss Brooks! Ohmigod. Miss

Brooks!" She rushed over and tugged on the twine but couldn't get it loose. "Ohmigod, ohmigod, Miss Brooks." She removed the blindfold, and Ella squinted against the brightness of the morning.

Mrs. Newcomb's eyes were wide in her brown face. "Going to get a knife to cut you loose. I'll be right back. Don't move. I mean…" Tears filled the older woman's eyes and she dashed off, leaving Ella alone.

Mrs. Newcomb returned with a serrated knife, which she used to cut the twine and the tape. Finally freed, Ella collapsed against the chest of her servant. With trembling fingers, she removed the tape from her mouth and spit out the sock. The maid held her as if cradling a child.

"It's going to be all right, ma'am. It's going to be just fine," Mrs. Newcomb said. With shaky fingers, she dialed 911.

CHAPTER 2

"So what time is the swim meet?" Detective Tyrone Evers swiveled away from the computer and the report he was in no mood to write anyway. One of the few things he hated about his job, the hours spent documenting every little detail. A necessity, but one he despised with a passion.

At the cubicle behind him, Martin Chu answered. "Nine o'clock on Saturday morning. You coming?"

"Thinking about it. Gotta support my girl whenever I can."

Pinned to the cubicle wall was a photo of Chu's eight-year-old daughter, Tyrone's goddaughter, grinning broadly with two gold medals around her neck. He'd been to a couple of her meets, and since last year she'd racked up more accolades on the swim team. This weekend was a big deal, an end-of-summer championship, and he wanted to be there to support her.

Not like he had anything else going on. Divorced and with no children of his own, the only schedule conflict would come from work, and since he had the entire weekend off, that wasn't even an obstacle. Maybe he'd bring some of the kids from the boys' club where he volunteered to come and cheer her on.

"Coach said she's a prodigy," Chu said. Pride filled his voice.

"I'm not surprised. She already broke the record in her age group. Next thing you know, she'll be trying out for the Olympics."

"Wouldn't that be great?"

"Believe it. Put it on your vision board or something." Tyrone stifled a laugh. He couldn't resist teasing his friend.

Chu frowned at him. "You joke, but a vision board is a great idea, and I'm glad my wife suggested I create one. The board is no different than writing down your goals. It helps you visualize what you want and focus your time and energy on achieving it."

"Uh-huh. Your wife tell you that, too?"

"Man, fuck you."

Tyrone laughed so hard, he almost doubled over. Chu rarely cursed, but when he did, it was hilarious for being so out of place of his personality.

"Evers!" a loud voice bellowed from way across the room.

Grimacing, Tyrone turned in the chair to see Sgt. Cross coming toward him, barreling past an officer taking a complaint from a woman perched on an old plastic chair. At six foot five, his peanut-toned skin remained perpetually damp because he was always stressing about one problem or another. His hair was cut low on his head, and he sported a handlebar mustache straight out of the eighties. He stopped at Tyrone's desk, deep scowl on his face.

"We've got a problem, and it's a big one. Got a call about a burglary over at Presidential Commons, and I need you to head over there pronto."

Tyrone flicked his eyebrows upward. "I've got to finish my report on the Denton case."

"Save that for later. This takes priority, starting now."

Noting the stress around his boss's mouth, Tyrone frowned and stood. "Who the hell got robbed that I need to drop everything I'm working on and head over there? The damn mayor?"

"Close enough. A friend of the mayor's. Actually, the daughter of the friend of the mayor. Ever heard of Ella Brooks?"

Tyrone shook his head. "Nah. Can't think of who she is."

"You'll know her if you see her, but I'm sure you know her mother. You've heard of Sylvie Johnson, right? She's related to the Johnson family that owns Johnson Brewing Company and a chain of restaurants. Sylvie owns a fashion house and some other shit I don't care about."

"Yeah, I know her. They're all billionaires."

Sylvie Johnson had a reputation for being a diva. She occasionally made the local news for her philanthropic endeavors, and her face was splashed across magazines for her charitable work as much as her work in film, fashion and furniture design. From all accounts, she was a no-nonsense businesswoman, and as a member of the Johnson family clan, known for keeping a lock on her privacy better than Janet Jackson kept a lock on her marriages.

"Those are the ones. Ella Brooks, her daughter, came home early from vacation last night. Four masked men were waiting for her. They emptied her safe of all jewelry and valuables, blindfolded her and tied her up."

"Is she all right?" Chu walked over to where they stood.

"Shaken up but essentially unharmed. Her mother and father were on their way out of town, but as soon as they received the news, turned the jet around."

"Private jet I take it? Must be nice," Tyrone muttered.

"Don't go off on one of your I-hate-rich-people tangents, Evers."

"I don't hate rich people." He didn't, but they received advantages poorer people didn't. Helping the less fortunate, those often overlooked by the system, had become a mission in his life.

"Right. Anyway, the mayor wants my best guy, and that's you. Chu will provide backup as needed, but today I want you at the apartment before Miss Johnson arrives. I want them to know we're on top of this case."

Much as he loved his job, working high-profile cases could be a real pain in the rear. As if there wasn't enough pressure to get the work done, the added pressure of having the higher-ups breathing down his neck for results because of an impatient celebrity or well-known personality didn't help.

"I get that Miss Johnson is a very important woman, but why does the mayor feel the need to get involved?"

"Let's just say, if it weren't for Sylvie Johnson, he wouldn't be mayor. She was a major donor to his campaign and organized private fundraisers with her rich acquaintances on his behalf. Mayor Simpton is adamant we give this case our best effort. Go over this thing with a fine-tooth comb and close this case as quickly as possible."

As if that could happen just because he said so. A burglary took place approximately every fifteen seconds, and even though most of them occurred during the day, only a low thirteen percent resulted in arrests. Those were terrible odds, which meant he was going to have to work his ass off for the next few months, chasing down every single lead, no matter how unlikely, to prove they were working the case. Even though they knew the chances of catching the perpetrators was almost impossible. All because a crime had occurred to one of the wealthiest and most influential families in the country.

"What kind of resources are available to me?"

"Anything you need, name it."

That was good, at least. "All right. I'll head over there now."

Sgt. Cross handed him a piece of paper with the name and address of the victim. Tyrone frowned, as a thought occurred to him. How in the world did four masked men get in and out of Presidential Commons without anyone noticing? They at least had a doorman and other types of security. Didn't make sense.

"Evers, I need you to give this your best shot."

Tyrone shoved his arms through the sleeves of his jacket and straightened the lapel. Flashing a grin, he asked, "When have I ever done anything less?"

* * *

PRESIDENTIAL COMMONS WAS TEEMING with police officers when Tyrone arrived. Right away, he assessed the lobby. Everything glittered and glowed. The Italian tile shined like glass, and amber-colored light fixtures on the wall gave an intimate, soothing effect to the cavernous interior.

He made a quick note of the staff on duty—two porters and a doorman. Were they always here or only during the day? After a flash of his badge and a quick greeting to the attending officer, he took the elevator to Ella Brooks's penthouse.

The first thing Tyrone noticed upon entering the home, after noting the officers collecting forensic evidence, was the understated opulence. The decorating wasn't overdone. Simple sophistication showed off her wealth without being gaudy.

He walked into the living room where an officer sat on the sofa beside a woman he assumed to be Ella Brooks. His boss was right. He didn't remember her name, but he certainly recognized the face.

At first glance, she looked like someone getting ready to go to work in a pair of dark slacks and a white shirt. The forensics team had probably already bagged her clothes.

Dark hair, parted in the middle, was pulled back from her face and secured at her nape. There was very little make-up on her narrow face. She appeared normal enough, but his discerning gaze picked up the cues to her night of terror. Her shoulders were slightly hunched as she observed the people milling around, and her arms were crossed over her midsection, a defensive move that indicated she still didn't quite feel safe.

She looked fragile and worn, and beneath the make-up, an unhealthy pallor stained her chocolate skin, and a purple bruise discolored her right cheek. She nodded at something the officer said, and when Tyrone ambled closer, her gaze flicked to his. Momentarily, he was taken aback by the light shade of her brown eyes, the color of dark topaz. Then he remembered her mother had the same color eyes. With the eyes, complexion, and shape of her face, she bore a startling resemblance to Sylvie Johnson.

Being in this line of work meant he'd seen a lot and had to steel himself from getting too attached to victims. His job was to get the facts and catch the perpetrators. But for some reason, this slender, beautiful woman got under his skin. The dullness behind her eyes shouldn't be there, and he sensed the light had been snuffed out long before last night. Something primitive unfolded in his chest. He literally had to fight the urge to pull her into his arms and comfort her.

"Miss Brooks?"

"Yes," she answered softly.

"I'm Detective Tyrone Evers."

Before he could follow up with any relevant information, a loud voice came from the hall. "Where is my daughter?"

An older version of Ella appeared in the doorway, with mahogany skin and hair pulled into a tight bun. Sylvie Johnson— billionaire, philanthropist, and entrepreneur. Same narrow face. Same high cheekbones and elegantly dressed in a silk blouse, slacks, and fine jewelry. She wreaked of money and class.

Tyrone straightened his spine.

"Mother!" The words were whispered, but at the same time sounded like a cry for help.

Ella jumped up from the sofa and into her mother's arms and collapsed into tears. Both women then sank into the chair.

"Mother is here, my darling. Mother is here." Sylvie comforted her daughter, rubbing her back and murmuring to her as Ella hid her face in her shoulder, body shaking from powerful sobs.

As a defense mechanism, a victim often remained stoic and strong in the face of questioning and trauma. Then, as soon as comfort came along, their defenses crumbled, and they allowed themselves to release pent-up emotions in the safety of a familiar face, usually in the form of a spouse, friend, or in this case, motherly love. Having seen the same scene play out numerous times before, Tyrone stepped back to give them room and a semblance of privacy. He signaled to the officer, who in turn stood and eased out of the room.

"I'm Oscar Brooks, Ella's father."

Tyrone had been so preoccupied with the women, he hadn't noticed the man who entered right after Sylvie. He took the hand extended to him. The father seemed less refined, and his appearance suggested he might be biracial.

"Detective Tyrone Evers."

"Do you know who these people are? Who could have done this to my daughter?" His face tight, Oscar spoke in low tones. He looked like a man barely containing his rage and the helpless frustration parents often experienced when they couldn't help a child.

"We're working on finding out. We—"

"Can you tell if it was an inside job? Someone watching her in some way?"

"That we don't know. It's too soon to answer those questions, Mr. Brooks."

"Do you know anything?" Sylvie snapped from the sofa. She still held Ella in her arms.

"Sylvie," her husband chastised in a weary voice.

"We need answers. How in the world do four men in ski masks enter the building without detection? There are cameras all over this building. Have you issued a warrant for the videos before they are erased?"

"We're working on all of that, ma'am." The conversation was not going well, but Tyrone kept his voice calm. He understood the frustration and the need for quick, tidy answers.

Assistance came from an unexpected place. Oscar walked over to his wife and whispered in her ear. When he straightened, she nodded, blinking rapidly, and pressed her lips together, but not before he saw them tremble.

She stood, pulling Ella with her, and they left the room.

Oscar ran a hand over his curly hair, jaw tightening in frustration. "Let's talk candidly. What are the chances of finding these men?"

"You want brutal honesty?"

Oscar nodded.

"Not great, but Miss Johnson makes a good point about the videos. We'll scour every minute of them, and as you can see, we're gathering as much evidence as we can." Giving a worried father the sobering burglary statistics was not wise, no matter how ready the man believed himself to be.

"Do you have a card?"

Tyrone lifted one from the inside of his jacket pocket.

Oscar glanced at the card and then looked into Tyrone's eyes. "Listen to me, you *have* to find these people."

"We'll do our best, sir."

CHAPTER 3

*E*lla sat quietly, knees together, as she listened to the detective review the facts of the case in gentle tones. They were seated in her bedroom suite, both of them in straight-backed chairs facing each other. At the detective's request, she'd excused her parents during this part of the conversation so they could talk candidly. She'd done so without hesitation because she didn't want to worry them, particularly her mother, with the details of what happened to her the night before.

Her fingers clenched around a damp Kleenex. The situation could have been worse, but that didn't stop her eyes from leaking when fresh memories of her ordeal resurfaced.

She'd already made a call to her ex-husband and told him to keep the girls for an extra couple of days in the Caribbean while the police continued their investigation. She wanted them to have full rein to go through the entire house and collect as much evidence as they needed, without having the girls underfoot or having them worried. She did, however, spend a few minutes chatting with Hannah and Sophia via video. Seeing their adorable little faces had made her tear up, and then she'd had to explain that she wasn't crying because of sadness, but rather because she loved them so much and was glad to see they were having a good time.

"I understand they were dressed in ski masks, wore gloves and dark clothes, but can you think of anything else besides their height and estimated weight, which you did a very good job of relaying, by the way, that might help us find these guys?"

Ella shook her head. "They were completely covered. I couldn't see anything."

"No tattoos or anything like that?" he prodded.

Ella shook her head in frustration. "No. Nothing. I wish I could offer more details, but I can't."

"That's all right. You never know, a detail might come to you later. If so, I want you to give me a call." He handed her a card, and she made a mental note to plug his number into her phone.

"Thank you." She took a deep breath and let it out slowly. "You said there are no signs of forced entry. That means they have a keycard to my home." A trickle of fear ran down her spine.

He nodded. "You should have the door re-programmed right away."

"Detective, what are your chances of finding these men?"

"We'll do everything we can," he said evenly.

"You do realize that's not a real answer?"

"Yes, I do." He smiled then, and the change in his appearance was like night and day. His hardened features softened drastically.

Under the circumstances, she couldn't figure out why she noticed, except the transformation went from a stern, almost mean appearance to one that was more approachable. He was good-looking but not her type. A bit rough around the edges, unrefined, with his tie askew and a little too much swagger in his walk. As if he owned the place and everything in it.

Initially, she couldn't figure out how to describe his skin, but seated across from him, the perfect description would be golden. Dark-gold, that was the color. His skin practically shimmered, and she idly thought he either had an amazing skin regimen or that glow was all-natural.

A fine beard covered his lower jaw and chin and framed a wide mouth with lips that weren't just full, they curved in such a way that made her suspect they were soft. Probably a good kisser with lips like that.

Despite the ruined make-up after she burst into tears, and what she otherwise suspected was a demeanor that screamed helplessness, a spark of interest lit his eyes when they sat down together. Ella knew that look. She'd seen it often enough from the time she hit puberty. Most of the time, she didn't care. Most recently, she'd been married, and though divorced for two years, she hadn't been on a real date in forever. That might explain the slight thrill she experienced at his suspected interest.

"Anything else you can think of?" Detective Evers asked, pulling her back into the conversation.

Ella went over and over in her mind what she could've done differently last night. When she noticed the light was on, she should have stepped back into the hallway and called for security to come up. Despite telling her it wasn't unusual for people to override their intuitive senses, she still beat herself up over her lack of awareness of her own surroundings. Something she learned in self-defense class and should have been anticipating.

"No, I can't think of anything else," she said.

Detective Evers stood. "I think that's enough for today. We'll need a full account of everything that was stolen. Make a list of all the valuables taken from your safe and elsewhere."

Ella joined him in standing. "I'll get you what you need, but my jewelry's all insured, so I'm not too worried about it. I'll get another copy of my will from the attorney, and all the other paperwork they took can easily be replaced. But there is one piece I hate to mention because it seems rather materialistic, but I had a string of pearls in my safe. They were handed down to me by my mother, which was a gift to her by her mother. I expected to give them to my firstborn daughter one day when she got married. If there is any way you could bring those back to me, I would greatly appreciate it. The sentimental value makes them irreplaceable."

"I understand. I see this all the time. For some people it's photos, it might be jewelry, it might be something as simple as a piece of clothing or as significant as a military medal. None of them hold any value to the criminal but have special value to the victim. If you have any photos of the items, that would be helpful."

Ella nodded. "I do. I'll make sure you get them right away."

"Excellent." He walked toward the door.

"Oh! I just thought of something." Ella rushed after him and grabbed his arm. The muscles there immediately bunched, and she pulled back, shocked. An electrical surge, like lightning, bolted through her palm. "Sorry. I didn't need to grab you like that."

"Not a problem. What did you think about?"

He appeared completely unaffected, but her hand still tingled.

"You asked me if I remembered anything distinguishing about the men, and it just dawned on me that two of them had very neutral speaking voices. Maybe a Midwestern accent, but I'm not sure. The other two had very distinct accents."

He whipped out his little notebook. "Go on."

"The small wiry one, the one who dragged me back down the hall…" She swallowed. "He, um, he spoke with a southern accent. South Georgia, maybe? The other one, the one who grabbed me first, sounded like someone from the New England area. Boston, maybe?"

He nodded as he wrote in the notebook. "That's good. Anything else?"

She bit the corner of her lip. His eyes followed the movement, and again she perceived his interest. A charge, slight but tangible, filtered across the short distance between them before he shifted his gaze back to her eyes.

"That's all I have for now. Does it really help?" she asked anxiously.

"Everything helps." They stood in silence for a moment, and then he cleared his throat. "I'll see what's going on out here. If you think of anything at all, you have my number. Don't hesitate to call me, all right?"

"I won't."

"Anytime," he said firmly, looking steadily into her eyes.

"Understood, detective," she said softly.

He nodded and left the room.

Ella remained behind and looked at the card in her hand. Despite the hard set to his face, she saw compassion in his eyes. But he was no softie. He was the kind of man who'd kick your butt and then explain to you why he needed to, hoping to educate you enough to avoid another butt-kicking in the future.

Detective Evers was certainly intriguing.

CHAPTER 4

"*I*'m outta here," Detective Chu announced.

"Later," Tyrone said, not turning around.

"You're staying late again?" Chu asked, walking over to his desk.

"Yeah. I have a few things I need to sort out in my head."

"Don't stay too long. It's almost nine o'clock, and you been at this all day." He patted Tyrone on the shoulder and walked out.

Tyrone stifled a yawn. His buddy was right, but he couldn't leave yet. He was missing something.

He rocked back and forth in the squeaky chair at his desk, tapping a pencil against the armrest. He'd been on the job almost fourteen hours today, reviewing the tapes from the building and questioning staff. Perusing his notes, he contemplated everything he'd learned over the past few days.

Miss Brooks returned early from her trip, surprising the burglars. Based on what he'd seen on the tape, the perpetrators appeared to be three white males and one black male. There were cameras in the elevators, but not on the individual floors, so he saw them exit onto Miss Brooks's floor. The footage showed them entering the building. The doorman was outside with one of the building's guests, a Mrs. Nolan. Once a week she arrived at the same time with a dog carrier. She shared custody of a Bichon Frise with her ex-husband and kept the dog four days out of the week. Horace, the doorman, always helped her get the animal from the car and made sure one of the porters assisted Mrs. Nolan to her apartment.

The men entered the building around that time and one of them gave the porter a slight nod as they walked purposefully through the lobby, as if they belonged there. And they looked like they belong there. They each wore dark suits, two carried brief-cases, and one lugged a rolling suitcase behind him. They looked like any number of businesspeople who stayed in the building's corporate housing, coming in from a long day at work. The men didn't set off any alarm bells because corporations often rented temporary space for their executives in Presidential Commons, so they easily blended in.

They also did a helluva job keeping their faces hidden from the cameras. They knew where the cameras were and how to angle their heads to avoid a good shot of their faces. Closeups didn't provide distinguishing tattoos or moles, and they were all clean-shaven. They blended in well and didn't leave much of an impression, so the descriptions offered by the porter and doorman were dodgy at best. These guys could be anyone.

They were good. They'd either done this before or had done an exceptional job on their first run. They left the same way they came, walking and talking and keeping their faces averted from the lens of the cameras in the lobby. The bank across the way showed them going down a side street and disappearing into the night, leaving Ella bound to the bed upstairs.

Tyrone flipped through the photos of the stolen merchandise. The men carried out designer purses worth thousands, jewelry, and cash in the suitcase and briefcases. The luggage was also prob-ably used to hide the masks and gloves, which they donned once inside Ella's apartment. The gloves he understood, to avoid finger-prints. The masks surprised him. He didn't want to think about what would have happened to Ella if they didn't have those masks on. His stomach knotted up as he considered the very real chance the case could have been turned over to homicide instead of burglary.

But something was still off. If they knew she was out of town, there was no chance anyone would be able to describe them after they'd entered the apartment, so why the masks? Was it an extra precaution in case someone was at home or showed up unexpectedly, or...

Tyrone stopped rocking the chair and sat up straight. The masks were a precaution, but the only reason they had them on when she entered the apartment was because *someone tipped them off.*

He flipped open his notepad and looked at his notes. The doorman, Horace, had recommended the new porter for the job at the building, and both of them were working that night. Either of them could have called upstairs and warned the burglars that she'd arrived unexpectedly.

Tyrone jumped up from the chair, grabbed his phone, and started dialing Miss Brooks's number on the way out.

* * *

"I'm working on a little project. Something to keep my mind off what happened," Ella said as she led Tyrone into the sitting room. She looked better tonight, more upbeat. And either the bruise was fading, or she'd done a better job with her make-up.

Her hair was much longer than he realized. Tonight she wore it pulled back into a sleek, low ponytail that remained stationed in the middle of her back and fell to bra-strap length. His nostrils picked up the scent of perfume, which she hadn't worn the first time they met. The light fragrance made his dick twitch.

Damn. He was here for work and couldn't help thinking of her as more than a case. He definitely noticed Ella was a woman, wondered what it would be like to have all that neatly arranged hair spread out in disarray on his pillows, lips parted and releasing soft pants of air, long legs wrapped around his waist—

"Have a seat." She gestured toward a sofa.

The sitting room was smaller than the living room, and despite the two-story high windows that dominated one wall, this room had a cozier feel. Perhaps because unlike the larger room, it wasn't a showpiece. The colors in here were neutral, with tan-colored furniture and a glass table with a wood base in the middle of the grouping of soft-looking chairs. The orb-shaped object that hung from the ceiling looked more like a piece of art than a light fixture, and the piano suggested that relaxing nights were spent in here listening to music.

"You play?" he asked, to keep his mind off screwing her.

"Yes. I took lessons when I was younger. I'm hoping my daughters will eventually enjoy it as much as I do, but so far..." She shrugged.

Tyrone scanned the pile of photos on the table and the half-empty page of an album she was in the process of filling. "You have a lot of pictures," he remarked.

"I like to capture special moments, especially the ones with me and my daughters. They're growing so fast. Just the other day they were babies, and now..." Her voice trailed off with a shake of her head.

The pictures appeared to be taken at different vacation spots around the world. Most of them did appear to include her daughters, but he also recognized her parents in a few of the photos, and a light-skinned man who was probably the girls' father.

Tyrone's gaze settled on two pictures of Ella, radically different from the somber woman before him. In the first, she wore a high-cut, one-piece white bathing suit, frolicking on the beach. Her frizzy, windblown hair whipped around her head, but she looked gorgeous. No make-up, no embellishments, only natural beauty shining through as she laughed into the camera. Another photo showed her standing on the bow of a yacht, an expanse of blue water twinkling beneath the sun behind her. He couldn't read her eyes because of the dark sunglasses, but the tilt to her lips suggested she was flirting with the camera, or the person behind the camera.

Tyrone sat on the sofa and picked up another photo. It caught his eye because of the enormous white Christmas tree behind Ella and her daughters. The three of them were wearing matching onesies and smiling.

"This is a nice photo." He turned it so she could see. "How old are your girls?"

Her features softened. "That picture was taken a year ago, but Sophia is four and Hannah is two. I admit I love the holidays. Spending time with family and other loved ones around that time of the year is very important to me."

She sat in the chair across from him and crossed one leg over the other. His eyes jerked over her crossed legs in cream pants and the way the short-sleeved, cashmere sweater molded over her breasts. She appeared regal and relaxed but with faint bags under her eyes. Like someone who hadn't been sleeping well.

She noticed him, too, though she tried to play it off as simply paying attention. During their first interview, he'd observed the way her eyes drifted over him and her startled reaction when she touched him to get his attention at the end of the conversation. She'd been shocked, the same as he, at the sudden spark that heated the exact spot where they touched.

If they'd met under different circumstances, and he didn't have to worry about the ethics of dating a victim in a case he was working, he'd take great pleasure in removing the veil of sadness from over her eyes and do everything in his power to prompt a proper smile to her lips.

"When Sophia was little, I started a tradition where we wear matching onesie pajamas and open our presents. Last year Hannah joined in the fun."

"Is that something you used to do with your mom?"

Ella burst out laughing and his gut clenched. Damn. Her features lit up, like in the photos.

26

"No," she said firmly. "My mother would never be caught dead in a onesie. I'm not sure she even wore one as a baby. She might disown me if she finds these pictures."

Tyrone chuckled, settling into the chair. "Come on. Your mother strikes me as one of those people who comes across meaner than she really is, but she's actually a sweetheart, isn't she?"

Her eyebrows climbed higher. "Not exactly, and if that's your perception of her, then I have to be concerned with your detective abilities."

"Should I be insulted for me or insulted for your mother?"

Her eyes crinkled at the corners when she smiled again. "My mother will be fine, trust me. She's exactly the way she comes across. My father can handle her, and he's the only person she listens to. She doesn't even listen to us, her children, when we ask her to stop meddling in our lives. Whenever he sees her getting too far out of pocket, he reels her back in."

Tyrone laughed again. "Sounds like my father and mother, only they're the opposite. My mother is the one who has to do the reeling, except with one thing. My parents dress alike. That's all my mother's idea, and there's not a thing my father can do about it." Tyrone used to think it was corny, but not anymore. Maybe age was changing him, but now he thought it was kind of cute. "Dad hates it, but he says marriage is about compromise, so he lets her dress them in matching outfits." She smiled, and more than anything, he wanted to see her do another full-on laugh. "How many siblings do you have?"

"I'm the oldest of four. My sister, Simone, is next, and I have two younger brothers, Stephan and Reese."

"I'm the oldest, as well. I have a younger brother who practices law in Macon, and a little sister who's only nineteen and in college. We call her the 'oops' baby."

Her eyes widened. "That's terrible."

He didn't know why he'd shared that personal detail. Something about Ella made him want to find out more about her and share more about himself. He smiled and shrugged. "She's tough, believe me. With two older brothers, we made sure my sister was ready for anything the world had to offer before she left the roost."

"Tough love? If she could survive her family, she could make her way in the world?"

"Exactly."

"Hmm, interesting. So why are you here, detective? You didn't say over the phone."

He needed to remember why he was there. He had a job to do. Tyrone removed the small notepad from the inside pocket of his jacket. "I need to get a better sense of how many people knew you left on vacation, and who knew you were coming back."

"I've told you everything I remember," she said.

"Tell me again." Asking a question more than once sometimes yielded new information.

She breathed a heavy sigh and tilted her head toward the high ceiling. "Let's see, the only people who knew my whereabouts were my personal assistant, my family members, my staff here, my ex-husband, Wayne, and of course his family would know."

"That's a lot of people. What about the building staff here?" He decided to tiptoe around his thought instead of alarming her.

"Yes, they knew I was gone. We have to let them know, and Horace knows to hold any packages that arrive while I'm gone."

"So you always tell Horace when you're leaving town? And he knew you'd be gone for a week?"

Ella nodded.

"But he didn't know you were coming back early." He fell quiet and let the words sink in.

"No. I left St. Barts suddenly. Only my parents and my personal assistant knew."

"Could your parents or your assistant have mentioned your unexpected return to anyone else?" he asked, trying to cover all the bases.

She frowned, a fine wrinkle furrowing her brow. "What are you suggesting?"

"Those men were wearing masks when you arrived, which

leads me to believe that someone, perhaps a member of your staff or the building staff, or a family member, told them you were coming."

Her eyes widened, and her mouth fell open. "I assure you no one in my family would do such a thing. No one in my family would steal from me. My goodness, we're all so close, and I trust them implicitly."

"What about your ex-husband? How's your relationship with him?"

The frown deepened, and she glanced away for a split second. "What would he have to gain? I don't know...I just don't know." She shook her head, as if to dislodge the idea of his guilt.

Tyrone circled back around to his original thought. "How well do you know Horace and James?"

"Not very well, but they're both kind and James offered to help me with my luggage when I arrived. I brushed him off since I only had two bags. I decided to travel light this time. Are you suggesting Horace and James had something to do with the break-in?" She rubbed her hands up and down her bare arms, as if the temperature had suddenly dropped.

"I'm not trying to scare you, but everyone's a suspect until proven otherwise." Tyrone's fingers tightened around the pen, fighting the urge to go over to the chair and pull her into his arms and ease her fears. What was wrong with him? This was his *job*, which he did all day almost every day. Yet this was the second time he'd wanted to hold and comfort Ella Brooks. "I don't think you should stay here alone."

She lifted an eyebrow. "I'm not alone."

"I understand you have staff, but perhaps being around family, people who love you and can offer support, would be better."

She uncrossed her legs and stared at the photos scattered on the table and seemed to fall into deep thought. "My mother suggested that I come to their house and stay for a while." She looked at him, as if to gauge his reaction. "She thinks it would be better for me,

29

and it would make her happy if I were closer so she could keep an eye on me."

"I can understand why she would feel that way."

Her light brown eyes took on a flinty appearance, and her delicate jaw hardened. "This is my home. I don't want to give these people the satisfaction of chasing me out of my own home."

He nodded, understanding the desire to maintain some level of control.

"You're looking at me with concern, detective. Maybe skepticism? There's no need for that. I'm a big girl, and I can take care of myself."

"I have no doubt you can take care of yourself. But, if you would allow me to say so, I suspect you need more than what you're getting here at the penthouse."

"Excuse me?"

"These guys aren't coming back, so I didn't suggest you go somewhere else because I was worried about your safety. How have you been sleeping?" he asked gently.

Ella averted her gaze and rubbed her hands together.

"I don't mean to pry," Tyrone said.

"Then don't," she replied coolly. She tilted her head higher.

"Miss Brooks, I can tell—"

"Did you have any more questions about *the case*? If not…"

"Miss Brooks—"

She stood.

After a moment's pause, Tyrone stood, too.

"Maybe it would be better if you called the next time you need additional information or have an update."

"I didn't mean to upset you."

"You didn't. I'm just throwing out a suggestion." She smiled tightly.

Tyrone tucked the notepad and pen into his jacket pocket. "I'll see myself out."

She kept the same tight smile on her face and didn't speak another word as he left the room.

CHAPTER 5

*E*lla sank onto the chair after Detective Evers left.

Who did he think he was, getting all up in her business? She folded her arms and stared at the spot he'd vacated. So what if she'd hardly managed more than a few hours of sleep since the break-in. Her sleeping patterns were none of his concern.

The doorbell rang, and she jumped.

"I'll get it, Miss Brooks," Mrs. Newcomb called out.

Ella breathed a little easier. The damn man had her on edge.

A few minutes later, her father appeared in the doorway.

"Father!" She rushed over and melted into the warm, tight hug he gave her. Oscar Brooks gave the best hugs.

He stepped back, taking her in. A slight frown crossed his face. "How are you?"

"Doing well," she lied. "To what do I owe the pleasure?"

"I thought you and I could talk for a bit."

"Okay." Ella searched his face. "You look worried."

"I can't help but worry. My daughter was attacked in her home, and there's nothing I can do about it. Our homes should be safe." Oscar paced over to the piano and dragged a finger along the shiny surface. "You need to come stay with your mother and me."

Ella's mood deflated. "We've already discussed this."

She was tired of the conversation. Her family acted as if she needed to be coddled, when all she wanted was to be left alone and allowed to stand strong on her own. Her mother was the worst, calling several times during the day to make sure she was all right. Yesterday Sylvie even took off work to spend the day with her until Ella finally told her she was fine and should go back to the office.

Her sister, Simone, called from overseas, promising to come back right away until Ella talked her out of it. The work she was doing in Asia was much too important. Her sister worked tirelessly as an ambassador for the family foundation, and Ella would not allow her to come back simply for the sole purpose of giving her a hug. Her brothers Reese and Stephan were in France, and she told them not to worry and she'd see them when they returned at the end of the week.

As if having concerned family members wasn't enough, dealing with her neighbors was an added strain. She went out earlier in the day and grabbed a bite to eat at one of the nearby restaurants. The pitying looks she received from a couple of the neighbors she ran into, as well as Horace, made her wish she'd stayed home and ordered in.

As far as Ella was concerned, there was nothing to worry about. Security had been kicked up at the building, and all the residents were on high alert, as well as the staff. Presidential Commons had never been safer. She wished everyone else understood that.

"I know we discussed you coming to stay with us, but your mother is worried sick. She wants you to come."

"I'm fine," Ella said gently.

"If anything had happened to you." His voice thickened, and he shook off the gravity of the thought. "If anything had happened to you, I would've torn the city apart myself until I found those people and ripped them limb from limb with my bare hands."

Of both her parents, Oscar was the most rational and easy-going. Those were words she would've expected to hear from her mother, who tried to control every outcome in her life and her children's lives. At times it drove Ella crazy and was part of the reason why she didn't want to stay with them. Sylvie would become overbearing and try to micromanage every aspect of her life.

Ella took a good look at her father. His olive-toned skin showed more pronounced lines, as if he'd aged ten years the past few days. The worry etched into his features tugged at her heart.

She put an arm around his waist and settled her head against his shoulder. His heart beat erratically beneath her palm. "I'm okay."

Oscar squeezed her tight and kissed her forehead. She was accustomed to getting loving bear hugs from her father. He was a very affectionate man, but the energy of this particular hug was stronger and more powerful.

Smoothing a hand over the hair at her temple, he said, "Do this for your mother, okay? With the girls coming tomorrow...well, you know how Sylvie can be. She's stressed about the three of you being here, even with staff. She's worried, and she's intolerable when she's upset." His voice trembled.

Perhaps she should stop thinking only about herself. The aftermath of the break-in affected not only her, but her parents, too.

"Okay. I'll do it for Mother, because I know she's probably giving you hell," Ella said, knowing full well his appearance tonight and the strain in his voice indicated he was just as distressed as her mother. "We'll come over after the girls get back."

"Good. Sylvie will be happy," Oscar said quietly. Relief emanated from his pores as he patted her back.

He left soon after, and Ella stared at the photos before she called the housekeeper and told her to prepare suitcases for her and the girls for a two week stay at her parents'. They might not need to stay that long, but she wanted to be prepared. She loved her daughters so much that the thought of any harm coming to either of them physically hurt. That was the other reason she accepted her father's invitation.

Because she understood.

* * *

ELLA AWOKE SUDDENLY and sat up with a jolt in the bed.

She heard something. Quiet movement. A rustle in the dark. Had she really heard anything, or was her imagination torturing her yet again?

Mrs. Newcomb slept in a room on the other side of the penthouse. Was she walking around?

Her heart rapped against her chest cavity as fear crushed in from all sides. The shadows in the dark appeared bigger and more ominous as panic crowded in. She stared at the door of her bedroom, locked and with a chair pushed under the doorknob, an extra precaution she wouldn't admit to anyone but had taken so she could at least fall asleep.

Ella squeezed her eyes shut, as tentacles of fear wrapped her entire body in chills. "Relax," she whispered. The danger had already passed. The men would not come back.

The phone rang and she screamed, wound so tight her head pounded with fright. Her eyes focused on the offending device on the nightstand. After two more rings, she picked it up.

Detective Evers.

Dizzy from relief, Ella answered the phone.

"Hello, Miss Brooks. I hope you don't mind my calling again so soon after I left. I was walking to a spot near my house to get takeout."

The shadows receded at the sound of his soothing voice coming through the line. She heard cars going by and the impatient honk of a horn.

"Hello, detective. Getting a bite at this hour?"

Ella's heart gradually went back to its normal rate. She turned on the lamp beside the bed and settled into the mound of pillows stacked against the iron headboard. She drew her legs up under the blankets so that her knees pointed at the ceiling.

"Unfortunately, yes. Other than some crackers from the vending machine at the precinct, I haven't eaten anything since lunch. Jim's Diner is nearby, open, and has excellent food. Breakfast food, but large portions and very hearty. When I get home, I'll make a pot of my world-famous coffee to go with the meal, and I'll be in heaven." Pause. "I called because I, uh, wanted to check on you."

"Do you call all your victims to check on them?" she asked, genuinely curious. She didn't think the police made these types of calls.

A few seconds passed with only the sound of traffic going by in the background.

"Every case is important to me," the detective replied.

"So no special treatment because of my family name or status?"

"Each case I work gets my undivided attention and one hundred percent of my efforts."

"You're very adept at avoiding answering questions directly," she pointed out.

He laughed softly, and she imagined his face softening. His laughter warmed her heart, and she relaxed. "And you're very direct."

"Touché." She couldn't help but smile. "I appreciate the call. After you left, my father came by and we talked, and he convinced me to go and stay with him and my mother. The girls return tomorrow. I didn't want to, but I do think it's best."

"You have to do what's best for you."

She nodded and plucked at the sheet. "I owe you an apology. Your question about how I was sleeping hit close to home and made me angry. Before you called a few minutes ago, I woke up in a panic. I thought I heard someone in the house, and...it terrified me." Her voice had dropped low. She laughed softly, embarrassed.

She felt like he could see her weakness, and she hated it. Hated being seen as weak, even though that's how she felt. Not only because of this experience, but in general. She wasn't sure how or when it started happening, but she no longer stood up for herself.

She didn't like this person she'd become during the course of her marriage and subsequent divorce and wasn't sure how to become strong again.

"You have nothing to be ashamed of, and you don't owe me an apology."

"Thank you." She swallowed. "Of course, you didn't help by suggesting Horace and James might be involved."

"I didn't mean to scare you, but we have to follow up on all leads."

"Of course. That's what I want you to do."

Neither of them spoke for a few seconds.

"There's nothing wrong with seeking help if you need it," Detective Evers said.

"I suppose. But when you want to be strong…" Why was she sharing so much with this man?

"You went through a traumatic experience. Your fears in the aftermath are perfectly normal, and you need to give yourself enough time to heal. Healing won't take place overnight. Have you thought about talking to someone?"

"You mean, like a professional?" The thought did cross her mind.

"Yes," he said gently. "I've seen residual fear in victims manifest in various ways. Some people suffer from panic attacks, others develop obsessive tendencies like constantly checking the doors are locked, some can't sleep, and the list goes on and on. Not everyone is in a position to get the help they need. You are."

His examples hit close to home. She'd become obsessive about locking the doors and already had them reprogrammed three times to put her mind at ease. And sleep, well, a good night's rest had become a luxury she couldn't afford yet.

"I'll think about it." She agreed to move in with her parents for the sake of the children, but she needed to be at one hundred percent. Like he said, take care of herself. "Detective, how old are you?"

"Excuse me?"

"How old are you?"

"Thirty-five. Why?"

"Because you're doling out advice like an old wise man."

He chuckled, and the flame of heat flickered in her belly.

"Thanks, I think." Pause. "And how old are you?"

"Thirty-two and counting."

"And you don't look a day over twenty-five."

She laughed out loud, shaking her head. "You, sir, are a liar. But I will gladly accept that compliment." She tucked a strand of hair behind her ear.

"Please do."

There was silence for a moment, but not the awkward kind.

"We're going to find out who's involved and make them pay," the detective said in a firm tone.

Ella dragged the long strands of her hair over one shoulder and sighed. Her eyes drifted to the drawn drapes that shut out the night. She used to leave them open but hadn't since the attack, as if someone could scale the walls of the building, peek in, and hurt her.

"You don't know that. These men could be anyone and anywhere."

"I do know that, because I'm on the case."

His reassurance did make her feel better, and she had no doubt he was good at his job. Nonetheless, she asked, "Isn't it a bad idea for you to make a promise like that? Especially when you don't know for sure if you can keep it?"

"This promise I intend to keep. It's a solemn oath. I won't rest until these bastards are brought to justice."

She smiled. "I want to believe you. Do you have a habit of keeping your word?"

He laughed softly, in a self-deprecating manner. "Not to the people that matter, but you can count on me."

She felt as if he had revealed quite a bit about himself in that short sentence. How had he failed in his personal life? Who had this man, so steadfast and strong, disappointed before?

"I'm going to sleep better tonight," she said. "Detective, thank you for calling. You have no idea how much I appreciate it."

"No problem. I'm happy to know I made a difference." He cleared his throat. "By the way, you can call me Tyrone."

She arched a brow, wondering if he normally encouraged victims to call him by his first name. Or was she special?

"All right, but only if you call me Ella."

"I can do that...Ella." He said her name as if he were trying it out.

Her toes curled under the covers, and she bit into her bottom lip. "Good night, Tyrone."

"Good night, Ella," he whispered.

She hung up and sat quietly for a minute. She wanted to say his name again and feel the texture of it. Roll it around on her tongue. "Tyrone."

Saying his name aloud sent a skitter of excitement across her shoulder blades. She pressed her palms to her warm cheeks and shook her head, laughing to herself.

He was different, that's all. Different than the rich men she encountered in her usual social circle. Not unlike her ex-husband, and look how that had turned out. The smile wavered. She knew better than to get involved with another man who didn't understand her world. They didn't fit.

The smile wiped completely from her face.

Ella glanced at the closed drapes. She'd had them specially made for the large window, in the same ice blue and soft brown that matched the decorations and linens in the room.

She reached into the nightstand and pulled out the remote that controlled the drapes and electronics in the room. Taking a deep breath, she pressed the green button and opened the drapes a few inches, not all the way. Enough so she could see a little bit. That would do for now.

She turned out the light and settled under the covers, and for the first time in a while, fell asleep with the moon peering in through the window.

CHAPTER 6

$\mathcal{W}$ayne arrived in the early evening with the girls, four-year-old Sophia and two-year-old Hannah.

"Mama! Mama!" they squealed.

Ella dropped to her knees before them and took all their hugs and kisses and planted way more than normal on their little round faces. She squeezed them so tight that Hannah complained.

"Mama, you hug too hard."

Ella kissed her plump cheek. "I'm sorry, sweetie. I just missed you so much and I'm happy that you're home." She snuck in one more hug and then stood, taking one hand in each of hers.

"I catch a big, big fish, Mama," Hannah said.

Ella smiled. "You did?" she said, opening her eyes wide.

Hannah nodded vigorously.

"Me, too, Mama. Daddy helped me bring it in," Sophia said.

"Oh my goodness, I hope you have pictures."

"We do! We do!" Hannah bounced up and down, bursting with excitement.

Wayne, standing at the door, came further in. The nanny, Tracy, stood behind. She was tall and thin, with short curly red hair and freckles.

Wayne, at over six feet, drew the eye, not only because of his looks, but he was clean-cut and gave off a positive energy. At least he used to. Over the course of their five-year marriage, he'd become more and more withdrawn, less energetic, more sullen, and less enthusiastic about them as a couple.

Both girls had inherited the fairer skin tone from his multi-ethnic background, milk with a smidge of coffee mixed in. And though their marriage hadn't lasted, she couldn't deny he was an excellent father, and the enthusiasm lacking in their marriage had been transferred into an enthusiastic relationship with their daughters.

"How was everything?" Ella asked.

"Fine. A few extra days were okay. There was plenty for the girls to do at the resort." He shoved his hands into the pockets of his chinos, seeming at a loss at what to say. Normally he didn't come upstairs when he dropped the girls off. He let the nanny bring them up, or Ella met him downstairs to get them.

"Are you all right?" he asked stiffly, eyes settling on her right cheek where makeup hadn't completely covered the bruise.

"I am. Been better, obviously."

He frowned. "You're not planning to continue staying here, are you? The girls—"

"I'm going to my parents' on Friday, and I'll be there for a couple of weeks."

His lips flattened into a line of displeasure. Before he could speak his thoughts, Ella caught Tracy's eye. "Could you please take the girls in the back and start getting them ready for their bath? And make sure they have everything they need for the stay at my parents'." She looked down at her daughters. "How would you like to go and stay at Poppa and Nana's house for a little while?"

The girls jumped up and down, squealing with excitement. They didn't know what was going on, and she intended to keep it that way. For them, it would just be an extended sleepover with their grandparents. Nothing out of the ordinary, except she would be staying there, as well.

They disappeared down the hall with Tracy, and Ella faced her ex, hands clasped in front of her. She didn't invite him further in because she didn't want him to stay any longer than necessary. He wouldn't, anyway. He'd long ago made it clear he couldn't tolerate spending time with her.

"How am I supposed to see my daughters over the next couple of weeks?" Wayne asked. "You know your mother hates me. She's going to make sure I don't see the girls."

"My mother doesn't hate you, and she's not going to stop you from seeing the girls." Only the second part of that sentence was true. "I needed somewhere to go, and Mother invited us to stay with them. It's perfect, because the girls love being there."

"And you're absolutely not doing this to get back at me?"

"Get back at you for what?" He thought everything was about him. She was exhausted by his paranoia.

"Because of our argument in St. Barts and the fact that you left early."

"Oh, for goodness sake."

"You have a lot of money, Ella. You could afford to stay anyplace you want, so I don't understand why you need to stay at your parents' penthouse."

"I don't understand why you don't understand why I *want* to stay at my parents'. You know what, I'm not going to have this argument with you. The decision has been made, the bags are packed, and we're going. That's final."

His eyes widened in surprise, probably because she didn't usually stand up to him in that way. In the past, she'd always try to be accommodating because of his fragile ego. But quite frankly, she was tired and didn't want to deal with this right now. What she needed more than anything was support, and that was the last thing Wayne was going to offer. Staying at her parents looked more and more attractive, because at least there she knew she would have her family around her and their support offered without asking.

"Well, I see you've already made up your mind," he said nastily.

"If there's nothing else…" Ella waited for him to respond.

He turned around with a huff and yanked open the door. "You always have to have your way, don't you?"

"That's not true and you know it." Her stomach muscles tightened with doubt. *Don't give in.* "Do you really need to pick a fight with me right now?"

"I understand you went through a trying ordeal. I'm not completely insensitive."

Really, I couldn't tell, she wanted to say, but she stayed quiet.

"I do feel sorry for what happened to you, but let's not forget about my personal situation. I used to have a job, which I no longer have. I'm living in a little apartment because I can't afford a bigger place. And why can't I? Because I was unable to get anything but a very small settlement in our divorce. And after your mother made sure that I was fired from the company, I could only get a job as an assistant manager at a local diner. Not exactly what I'd call prestigious. I wonder why that is. With all the experience I had as regional manager, you would think I could get something better."

Every conversation was always about him and what she'd done to destroy his life and emasculate him.

"Maybe you're overqualified for the positions you're applying for. Or it's just that the economy is tough right now."

"Or I've been blackballed. But that's not your problem, is it?"

"What do you want me to do?"

"In a perfect world, I'd get my job back. I was damn good at my job."

Actually, he wasn't. The truth was, his work record was not exactly stellar. He did fine as a general manager, but he got the promotion to regional manager because he was married to her. She'd nudged her cousin in Seattle, Ivy, who ran the restaurant group, to give him the promotion. Either he slacked off because he didn't think he had to work as hard anymore, being married to a family member, or he simply sucked at overseeing multiple stores. At any rate, staff covered for his mistakes and lack of oversight.

When he cheated and left her only months after Hannah was born, Sylvie made sure to call Ivy and insist he be fired. It didn't take long for them to have enough documentation to justify getting rid of him. He sued for wrongful termination and easily lost that fight.

"You're not going to get your job back."

"It's not that I want that job back. I just...wish I hadn't lost it."

And I wish you hadn't lied so many times about having to work. I wish you hadn't cheated with the woman across the street.

"Forget it. I'll call you when I'm ready to pick up the girls again." Wayne slammed the door on his way out.

Ella wrapped her arms around herself and leaned back against the wall. Typical Wayne, never taking responsibility for his actions and quick to blame her for everything wrong in their marriage. But she'd tried. She'd tried so damn hard when she realized she was failing, and she hadn't wanted to fail, because to fail meant that her mother and his father had been right. Sylvie said she shouldn't have married someone 'below' her station in life. She swore a man like Wayne couldn't handle being with someone as wealthy as Ella.

Wayne came from a traditional household, where the man was expected to be the breadwinner and head of the house. At first, she liked what she saw as his good qualities. She wanted a confident man who could lead. But his father warned Wayne that their marriage couldn't work because the natural order had been disrupted.

Ella had tried hard to stop the demise of her marriage and changed in the process. She became more conciliatory and less confrontational. She quit her job working at her mother's company so she could devote her time to tending to her family's needs. When they attended engagements, they appeared to be the perfect couple. Behind closed doors, they barely talked, and sex, infrequent, had become a chore.

But Hannah was the final straw for Wayne, completely unexpected and another bind that tied them together. All the irritation he'd been hoarding unleashed in an angry tirade when he told Ella, only months after their daughter's birth, that he was leaving her for another woman. He gave up on them, and she'd been trying so hard.

Ella shook off the memories and went to the girls' room. Tracy stood in front of one of the dressers with the drawer open, Hannah on her hip in her underwear and Sophia standing beside her tossing the contents of a drawer.

"I wanna wear this one." Sophia held up a nightshirt with Princess Tiana on it.

"Tracy, I'll take it from here." Ella walked into the room, and Hannah practically leaped into her arms. "Are you going home tonight or staying in the guest room?" Sometimes the nanny slept over instead of leaving and coming back first thing in the morning.

"I'll leave if you don't need me."

"That's fine. Like I said earlier, day after tomorrow we're going to my parents'. That's where the car will drop you off in the mornings."

"Got it."

"Did you enjoy St. Barts?"

"I *loved* it." Her green eyes brightened. "I would love to go back."

"We'll have to do that again soon." Ella looked at Hannah. "Tell Tracy goodnight. She's going home, and you won't see her for a few days."

"Night-night."

Tracy gave the little girl a kiss and did the same to Sophia. "Good night." She left the room.

"All right, my loves. It's bath time!"

Ella bathed the girls in the huge jetted tub in her bathroom, and for dinner, the three of them ate grilled cheese sandwiches and tomato soup, courtesy of Mrs. Newcomb. By bedtime, after traveling and their full bellies, the girls started getting drowsy. Instead of putting them to bed in their room, Ella took them into hers. With a hand to their little bottoms, she boosted them up on the bed. They scrambled across the mattress, she climbed in between them, and they snuggled up close to her.

"Night-night, Mama," Hannah said. She held tight to a teddy bear her uncle Stephan had given her which, unfortunately, had recently lost one of its eyes.

"Night, baby."

Before long, her daughters' even breathing was the only sound in the room. She glanced at the window, where the drapes were opened wider tonight so she could see some of the buildings and the night sky better.

She wondered if Tyrone would call tonight. She almost wished he would. Hearing his soothing voice would be nice right now. She was almost certain he wasn't the kind of man to have the same insecurities as Wayne, but one could never be sure. She never suspected Wayne would become the man he did, bitter and paranoid and angry almost all the time.

She gently rubbed Sophia's back when the little girl shifted against her.

Ella wouldn't sleep well tonight with the two of them in the bed twisting around all night, but she wanted them close. Tonight she'd listened to their laughter and excited voices as they talked about the trip and all the fun they had with their dad. Nothing was more beautiful than the sound of children's laughter, especially her own. Nothing was more comforting than getting a hug and kiss from them.

She didn't need Wayne. She didn't need any man. She had everything she needed right here in her arms.

CHAPTER 7

A change of setting gave Ella her first night of uninterrupted sleep since her ordeal, and on Saturday morning, she and the girls joined her parents for breakfast in the dining room. Trevor, her mother's house manager, looked particularly pleased to have the girls present. With the gray hair on his head, he was like a grandfather to them. He teased them lightly so they giggled and made sure they had plenty of orange juice, and Sophia received extra cheese in her eggs the way she liked.

Halfway through the meal, her siblings arrived. She hadn't expected them all to show up, but they knew she and her daughters were at their parents' house. They burst into the dining room with a bit of commotion, Stephan leading the pack, followed by Reese, and Simone pulling up the rear.

Both Reese and Stephan had inherited their father's lighter complexion, and Simone's skin tone fell somewhere in between both parents.

Her younger sister rushed over and flung her arms around her neck. "Are you all right? I'm so sorry I couldn't get here sooner." Her long hair brushed Ella's cheek.

"I told you not to come, remember? And I'm fine." She shot a glance across the table at her daughters, to give Simone the signal that now was not the right time to talk about the break-in.

Stephan, the oldest of her two younger brothers, didn't see the look and launched into a new question. "What's the status of the investigation?" Like her, he'd inherited their mother's light brown eyes.

Sylvie set down her fork and knife and cleared her throat. "Hannah and Sophia are present."

The three newcomers received the message right away, and Stephan went over to kiss on his nieces and tickle them until they begged him to stop. In the meantime, Trevor and Reese brought in extra chairs so everyone could sit.

"Breakfast for you all?" Trevor asked.

"I'll take something," Stephan said.

"Toast for me, and coffee," Simone said.

"Same. I'm not very hungry," Reese said, folding his arms on the table.

"How was Asia, darling?" Sylvie asked Simone.

From then on, the conversation settled on neutral topics such as business and the latest going on in that realm. Simone was an ambassador for the family's Johnson Foundation and worked primarily on children's issues. She traveled a lot, and with her husband waiting for her to come home, Ella was especially grateful that she chose to stop there first to see how she was doing.

Reese worked for Sylvie's company under the chief information officer for now. It was Sylvie's hope that when her CIO retired, Reese would take over that role in the company. He hadn't expressed much interest in doing so, and Ella wondered if he might strike out on his own one day. His trip to France had been to attend an international conference on information systems and advances in technology that could potentially help Sylvie's company.

Stephan had joined him in Paris because France was one of his favorite places to visit and he spoke French fluently. He didn't have anything else to do, so he tagged along and hung out and partied while Reese worked.

After the meal, Trevor herded the girls into another part of the house and cleared the dishes with help from another servant. It was finally time for the adults to talk, and talk candidly. Ella told her siblings everything she knew, and they listened quietly as she recounted her ordeal and summarized what the police had done thus far.

"So you're satisfied with the progress on the case?" Reese asked.

Ella nodded. "I trust Detective Evers—Tyrone—and feel like he's dedicated to the investigation and doing everything in his power to catch these guys."

"You're on a first-name basis with this man?" Sylvie asked. She lifted a white coffee cup to her lips.

"It's not a big deal, Mother. Neither one of us saw the need for formalities."

"It does seem rather familiar to me, but if that's your preference..."

Sylvie's shrewd gaze drifted away from Ella as she made to address the entire table. "I've been contemplating a few things, and I think the police might need some assistance with this investigation."

"Some assistance?" A sense of foreboding came over Ella.

"Yes. Your cousin Cyrus gave me the name of a company I think would be helpful. The Cordoba Agency is a private security firm that includes a private investigation branch of their business, and I've talked with Cruz Cordoba, the owner, about hiring his firm to provide backup for the police officers."

Silence fell over the table. Ella knew all about the firm. They were the ones who helped her cousin's husband locate his family. Whatever the task, they got it done, but they were a shadowy firm cloaked in mystery and had nothing to do with law enforcement.

"Mother, I don't think that's a good idea," Ella said carefully.

She knew her mother meant well, but no way the police would go along with this. "They could jeopardize the investigation."

"They will be working with the police officers, not against them," Sylvie said.

"They'll get in the way. It's only been a week. We have to give the police time to do their job." She wondered what this development would mean for Tyrone and how the additional bodies would affect his investigation. Furthermore, she didn't want him thinking this was in any way her idea or that she condoned what her mother planned to do.

"Having the Cordoba Agency involved will speed the investigation along. Which is a good thing. The sooner we get these thugs off the street, the better for all of us. We don't know if these people are targeting our family specifically, and even if they aren't, they are out there and able to do harm to other families. As far as I'm concerned, it is not only in our best interest to get them off the street, it is our civic duty to do so if we are in a position to do so." She looked at the other end of the table. "Your father agrees with me."

All heads swung in the opposite direction.

Oh no.

If Oscar agreed with Sylvie, there was no way Ella would be able to talk her mother out of this. Once her mother got her mind set on a plan of action, she always followed through. The one person they could count on to talk her out of an idea was their father. However, if he was on her side, then her mother would definitely steamroll over the investigation by hiring this outside entity to "assist" the police investigation.

"I agree with your mother."

Darn it.

Oscar stroked his hair-roughened jaw. "We've discussed the idea at length and agreed the additional manpower is the best decision right now. We have every confidence in law enforcement. However, we do know that they work under certain restrictions. These restrictions are not there for the Cordoba Agency. They have the ability to follow up on certain leads and apply other types of…" He paused, searching for the right words. "They have other avenues open to them that the police don't, and I think we should take advantage of that."

"And what if they jeopardize the investigation?" Simone asked, making eye contact with Ella, expressing her sister's silent reservations.

"They won't. These men and women are professionals," Oscar said.

"Can I say anything to talk you out of it?" Ella asked.

"You can try, darling, but the decision has already been made." Sylvie placed her porcelain cup in its saucer.

"On Monday, your mother is going down to the precinct to talk to the sergeant in charge. At that time, she'll inform him of the contact at the Cordoba Agency and let them know that they will be assisting in the investigation."

Ella groaned inwardly.

"I've also decided to hire new security for all of you," Sylvie added.

A series of grumbles and arguments erupted around the table from the rest of her siblings. Sylvie allowed them all to talk for a few minutes and present their arguments before she lifted a hand. Silence descended on the room.

"My dear, dear children, this is not up for debate. We do not know who these people are, and we do not know if they are targeting our family specifically. Ella's building has excellent security, yet they were able to get into her home. I cannot in good conscience allow any of you to suffer the same fate. Until these people are caught, all of us, myself included, will have to be more diligent and more self-aware, and we will all have additional security."

"This is going to be very expensive," Ella pointed out.

"I would spend my last dime to protect you all, and then I would borrow more," Sylvie said firmly.

No one said a word.

Additional security sounded like a good idea, but it meant less privacy and more inconvenience. It also meant more nondisclosure agreements, which did not guarantee your personal life would not be shared with other people. Despite the use of NDAs, no one ever wanted to have to enforce one because it meant your privacy had been compromised. The chances of a contractor or employee sticking to one were practically nil without an innate sense of loyalty in the relationship. Despite the fact that people said they didn't talk, they did, and it was nearly impossible for them not to at least discuss what they saw with close friends or family.

"I know you don't like this. Believe me, I don't, either. I hate that we have to live like prisoners in a free society, but there are dangerous individuals out there, and I refuse to take any chances with the most important people in my life. I really don't care whether you like it or not, this is what's going to happen until these men are caught."

Essentially, that was the end of the conversation, and there were no more arguments to be made. Both her parents had decided, and Ella understood why. She would do the same for Sophia and Hannah. Anything, absolutely anything, to ensure their safety.

She placed a hand over her mother's, which had turned into a fist on top of the table.

"Thank you, Mother," she said.

Sylvie turned over her hand and clasped Ella's firmly in hers. Her face softened as she smiled into her eldest child's eyes.

A chorus of *Thank you, Mother* went up from the other three.

And that was the end of that.

CHAPTER 8

"I didn't know you were coming."

Ella hopped up from the sofa in her mother's sitting room and gave her cousin a hug. She had been waiting for the men from the Cordoba Agency to arrive when Trevor announced her cousin's arrival.

Cyrus Johnson, Jr. was the eldest of her deceased uncle's children and the CEO of the family's beer and restaurant conglomerate based out of Seattle. Of his siblings, he was the one who most closely resembled Cyrus Senior physically and in disposition. So much so that for years they'd called him Number Two. His angular face tended to be set in unyielding lines, except when his features lit up around his young daughter and son.

"These guys are good, but I wanted to make sure everything went well myself and take a good look at you."

"So you're staying the night?" Ella asked.

He shook his head. "I'm flying back after the meeting."

"May I get you something to drink, Mr. Johnson?" Trevor asked.

"I'm fine. Thank you, Trevor."

The house manager nodded and left them alone.

Ella waved Cyrus to a chair. "Mother should be out in a minute." She sat down.

Cyrus undid the buttons on his jacket and took a seat. He studied her for a few seconds. "How are you?" he finally asked.

Ella smoothed the hair at her temple. "Much better."

"Aunt Sylvie said the police don't have any leads so far."

"It's too soon. They're working on questioning everyone." She needed to follow up with Tyrone. "How are Lily and Michael?"

"Keeping us busy. Michael is taking his big brother role very seriously and insists on helping Dani feed Lily." Cyrus smiled faintly. He and Daniella hit a rocky patch some years ago and separated for a while, but the family was ever so grateful that they reconciled. Daniella and the kids were good for him.

"I wonder where in the world he gets the protective big brother thing from." Ella quirked a brow.

Cyrus chuckled, and at that moment, Sylvie entered. Cyrus stood to greet his aunt.

"Hello, darling. How was your flight?" Sylvie gave him a hug.

"Uneventful. I got some work done on my way here. I also spoke to Cruz." Cyrus glanced at his watch. "He assured me they'd be on time."

"We still have a few minutes. Sit, sit. How is your mother?"

Another brief conversation ensued as Cyrus gave an update on his mother and other family members in Seattle. Soon, Trevor announced the arrival of the security team, and when Ella saw them, she barely managed not to gape.

The two men who entered were intimidating, both with jaws that appeared to be made out of brick. The head guy, Cruz Cordoba, was tall with dark eyes and a solemn face. The suit he wore couldn't hide his massive build. Well over six feet, his hard-muscled physique showed loud and clear that this man was powerful and not someone that n'er-do-wells should tangle with. The black man standing next to him looked equally intimidating. Ball-headed, not as tall, but also solidly built.

The two men came further into the room and shook hands

with Ella and her mother. Then they sat next to each other on the sofa, both of them taking up all the space available on the furniture.

After a few minutes spent over pleasantries, Sylvie got down to business. "I reviewed the website and contracts you sent. I'd like the gold package for my family."

Cruz raised an eyebrow. "Miss Johnson, the gold package is usually for people under imminent threat. I believe the bronze package would suffice. That would place two bodyguards with each member of your family, twelve hours per day as they travel around the city, and on an as-needed basis as you see fit."

"I agree with my aunt. The gold package is best for now."

Cruz turned his attention to Cyrus. "If you like, but you know how we work. My men are well-trained."

"It would put my mind at ease," Sylvie said. "Frankly, I'd rather not have Ella move out of here until we capture these monsters, but I'd be holding her against her will."

"And I'd stop speaking to you," Ella added.

Sylvie sighed dramatically. "By hiring you, I can have my way, just a little bit. The gold package and add a driver for her."

"Understood." Cruz nodded.

They finalized the particulars. By the time the men from the Cordoba Agency left, they'd agreed to touch base with Sylvia the next day to sign the contracts.

"Anything else?" Cyrus asked, looking at Ella.

She shook her head.

"Well, on that note..." Cyrus stood.

"You should stay for dinner," Sylvie said. Her brow wrinkled.

"Another time."

Ella gave him a hug. "Tell Daniella I said hi, and I'll give her a call next week."

"I will."

"Have a safe trip back, darling, and thank you for coming." Sylvie gave him her cheek, which he dutifully kissed before disappearing.

With the men gone, Sylvie stood with her hands on her hips and looked at her daughter. "Well? What do you think?"

"I think you're overreacting, as usual. I wish you would listen to them, because they're the professionals. If they think the bronze package is enough, that should be enough. You're spending extra money for no reason."

"Please let me handle this."

"Yes, Mother," Ella said sarcastically.

Sylvie pressed her fingers to her forehead and sighed. "Why do I have such difficult children?"

Ella went to her mother's side and took her hand. "Thank you." She kissed Sylvie's cheek.

Sylvie squeezed her hand, eyes observant as they scoured Ella's face. "You're still not back to one hundred percent, are you? I can see it in your eyes. I want you to take a spa day tomorrow. Relax and spend a few hours not worrying. Your father and I will watch the girls."

That sounded like an excellent idea. "I'll take you up on that offer."

"Good. Mother knows best."

AFTER HER SUNDAY afternoon visit to the spa, which left Ella rejuvenated and feeling less stressed, she rushed across the parking lot to the front door of Sweet Treats Bakery, hoping to catch them before they closed. She'd promised Hannah and Sophia strawberry cupcakes, and whenever she made them a promise, she liked to keep it.

Pushing open the door, she was hit immediately by the tempting aroma of cookies, cakes, and other baked goods. Her gaze swept the almost-empty retail space, and her heart jumped a little when she saw none other than Detective Tyrone Evers in a black Atlanta Falcons hoodie and matching sweatpants.

He peered into a cake box and nodded. "Looks good. I'll take it," he said to the woman behind the counter, who watched him with a tad bit more adoration than appropriate.

"Hello, Tyrone." Excitement zinged through her when she said his name aloud.

In the process of pulling out his wallet, he swiveled in her direction. His eyebrows climbed higher, and his features softened into a smile. "Ella. Fancy meeting you here."

His gaze ran over her, something she noticed he did a lot, and she wondered if it was an automatic thing he did because of his line of work—checking people out, assessing them. The swift perusal made her nipples throb and awakened the spark that burned between them and fanned it into a hotter flame.

"What's the occasion?" She nodded toward the cake.

"Oh…birthday cake for, um, a kid I mentor."

He half-shrugged, removing his wallet and handing over a credit card to the cashier. He acted as if he didn't want to say who the cake was for, as if he might be embarrassed to say that he was a mentor. How odd. Some people bragged about their volunteer work, as though they should receive a trophy. In fact, in her circle, the more people knew about your charity, the better. They held ceremonies and handed over large amounts of money in a type of competition to see which person or family was the biggest donor.

But she got the distinct impression Tyrone preferred to keep that part of his life quiet. A humble man, which made him more intriguing.

"That's very sweet of you."

"Nah," Tyrone said with a laugh. A hint of color entered his cheeks. "He turned twelve. It's a big birthday, and his mom couldn't afford to buy him one, so…" Another shrug. "What about you? What are you doing here?"

"Picking up cupcakes for Hannah and Sophia, my daughters. I spent a couple of hours at the spa and made them a promise. I dare not turn up empty-handed. And not any cupcakes will do. They have a discerning palate, my kids, so they'd know if I purchased them from anywhere else but Sweet Treats."

"That explains it," Tyrone said.

"Explains…?"

"The time at the spa. You're glowing." The cashier handed back the card, and he signed the receipt. He acted as if he hadn't paid her a compliment and made the temperature of her skin spike higher.

The cashier turned her attention to Ella, and Tyrone waited as she pointed out three cupcakes, deciding to get one for herself. He waited while the woman boxed them and Ella paid, and they both left the bakery with desserts in hand and strolled through the parking lot.

"I start therapy this week," she said.

"You do? When?"

"Wednesdays and Fridays."

"Good. I'm glad to hear that."

Her assistant had found a therapist whose specialty was working with victims of crime. She looked forward to the first meeting with nervous anticipation, but hoped the doctor could help her overcome her fears.

They stopped at her silver Mercedes coupe.

Tyrone whistled. "Nice car."

"I needed something to get around in when I didn't want to call my driver or use a car service."

"I know what you mean. Sometimes I feel guilty about calling my driver, too, so I prefer to tool around in that five-year-old Sentra. My Porsche is in the shop, by the way."

Ella giggled. A man with a sense of humor was darn near irresistible. "You're terrible."

Tyrone sobered and cocked his head at an angle. "How often do you use a car service?"

She blinked at the shift in the conversation. "Not often," she said slowly.

"Did you use a car service when you left for your trip to St. Barts?"

"Yes."

"And when you came back?"

"Yes." Ella licked her dry lips as they stared at each other. "Are you suggesting what I think you're suggesting?"

He frowned, all business now. "We leave no stone unturned and need to follow up on every possibility. Did you already give me the name of the company?"

"No. I didn't even think about it. I completely forgot about the car service."

"It might lead nowhere, but I need their information."

"Yes, of course. As a matter of fact." She set the box on top of the car and dug into her purse. Pulling out a card, she said, "Here you go. That's the owner. I'm sure he'll be happy to answer any questions you have."

Tyrone studied it. "Good."

"I should warn you, by the way, that you're going to hear from my mother. She's stopping by the precinct tomorrow."

He lifted an eyebrow. "Sounds ominous."

"It can be."

"Why is she coming by? Is she dissatisfied with something we've done?"

"She has an idea on how she can help, but I'll let her explain when she gets there."

"Huh. Okay, thanks for the heads-up."

They stood awkwardly for a moment, and Ella said, "Well, I'll let you go to your birthday party celebration."

"And I'll let you handle your cupcake situation."

She smiled, and he smiled back.

She removed the cupcakes from the top of the car and slid behind the wheel of the vehicle. She waved at him before pulling off. Leaving the parking lot, her eyes flicked to the rearview mirror. Tyrone was still standing there, watching her drive away.

CHAPTER 9

*T*yrone's stomach sank.

Like Ella warned, her mother had arrived at the precinct, which couldn't be good. He was accustomed to complaining citizens, but high-profile ones like Sylvie Johnson added an extra layer of difficulty to his job.

He saw where Ella got her style from, because the apple didn't fall far from the tree. Using the center aisle as a runway, Sylvie strutted through the bullpen with her nose in the air and an expensive-looking purse—probably Hermes or some such brand—in the crook of her arm. At the other end, Sgt. Cross opened the door and she swept inside. He immediately closed the door behind her and the vertical blinds covering the window that gave him a full view of their work area.

Three minutes later, the phone on his desk rang and he was called in to talk about the Brooks case. He stood and pulled on his jacket.

Chu rolled back on his chair. "Good knowing you."

"Ha, ha." Tyrone shot him the finger and plodded to the sergeant's office.

Inside, Sylvie Johnson sat across from Sgt. Cross, who mopped his damp face with a handkerchief, looking decidedly ill at ease, as if *he'd* been called into *her* office. The look she gave Tyrone was lofty, a result of good breeding and decades of a no-nonsense attitude meant to intimidate and get quick results.

"Please, have a seat, detective," Sylvie said, taking command of the room.

Sgt. Cross cleared his throat and straightened his tie. "Ms. Johnson would like an update on the case."

Tyrone took a seat and then pulled out his notebook, launching into what little they knew so far. Upon conclusion, he snapped the notebook closed and stuck it back into his jacket pocket.

"Do you have enough people working on this case?" Sylvie directed the question to Sgt. Cross.

"We do, but Tyrone is the lead detective, and he's our best. His close rate is the highest in the precinct."

She smiled, and it struck him that she was one of those people who smiled while quietly tearing you down.

"But is he enough?' she asked, clearly implying he wasn't.

"Ms. Johnson, I've worked in the Atlanta precinct for thirteen years, with eight of those in burglary. As the sergeant said, I have the highest close rate in the precinct, so if anyone can catch these guys, which there's no guarantee, I'm your man. I'm working with detectives in other counties, cross-referencing similar cases in the database, and we have a number of resources at our disposal. I understand the need for urgency, but these things take time."

Quiet fell in the room. Sylvie looked at the sergeant and then at Tyrone. The silence went on so long, Tyrone shifted in his chair and was about to speak when Sylvie spoke.

"Do you have children, Detective Evers?" she asked.

Taken aback, he didn't immediately answer. His gaze shifted to his boss, who nodded imperceptibly, before returning to the woman beside him. "No, I don't."

Not that he didn't want any. He'd wanted a least one. Boy or girl, didn't matter. But he'd asked Nyla, his ex-wife, to wait. He didn't want to bring a kid into their marriage until he felt he had enough time to devote to him or her. Even though their marriage didn't last, he regretted that decision, especially when he spent time with his brother's kids.

"Nieces or nephews?"

"Yes. Both."

"And I'm sure you love them as if they're your own?"

"Yes," Tyrone answered again, wondering where the line of questioning was headed.

Sylvie nodded her satisfaction. "And you, Sgt. Cross? Do you have children?"

He nodded. "I do. Three. Two boys and a girl."

"Wonderful. Conversations are so much easier when you're speaking to people who understand you. Ella is an adult, but she is still *my* child. I still see her little tear-streaked face when she fell and skinned a knee. Or the joy in her eyes when I gave her a toy she'd wanted. I love all my children dearly. I have always, and will always, do anything to make sure they are safe and protected. Even as adults. Right now, my daughter does not feel safe in her own home, and she's staying with me. I want my daughter and my granddaughters to not only feel safe again, I want them to *be* safe. I won't be satisfied until those thugs are apprehended."

Sylvie stood, and both men stood with her. She removed a card from her bag and placed it on the desk in front of Sgt. Cross. "I would like you to call these people."

The captain lifted the card, and his brow furrowed. "The Cordoba Agency?"

"They're a private security firm that also has a private investigation division. They're very thorough and very discreet. I have already paid them a handsome retainer to get started. They will not get in your way, detective. They have been hired as security and to consult with you and move this case along."

Tyrone's blood boiled. Who the hell did this woman think she was, bringing in an outside entity to interfere with his investigation? "With all due respect, Ms. Johnson, I—"

"Er, what Detective Evers means to say, ma'am"—Sgt. Cross shot Tyrone a warning look—"is that we have everything under control. It's been less than two weeks, and these things take time. Bringing in a firm to consult will only complicate the investigation and more than likely slow it down."

Sylvie's spine straightened. Considering her already superb posture, Tyrone didn't see how that was possible.

"Sergeant, are you telling me, that if harm came to either of your three children, you wouldn't do everything in your power to make sure justice is served? Are you telling me that you would be satisfied with *taking time* to reach a resolution, when those monsters could strike again? Not only at your child, but at some other parents' child? Perhaps the detective's nieces and nephews?" Her laser-like glare was as lethal as the sharpened edge of a sword.

"Ms. Johnson—"

"Is that what you're telling me, Sergeant? Are you suggesting that I'm being unreasonable to offer you additional manpower and resources at no cost to your department?"

Tyrone's gaze swung between the two of them, but it didn't take long for the battle of wills to result in a victor. He saw the moment his boss caved. His shoulders dropped, and he stared down at the card in his hand.

Shit.

"No, Ms. Johnson. I'm not suggesting that at all," Sgt. Cross said.

"Wonderful. I'm glad we were able to come to an understanding. I knew you were a reasonable man. I knew you wouldn't force me to go over your head. It would spoil our relationship and can be so awkward, can't it?" A last warning that she had the mayor's ear, and all said with a smile. Sylvie returned the bag to the crook of her arm. "I'm sure you'll keep me posted on the progress." Not a question at all. A demand disguised as a statement.

"Of course."

She shot one last glance at Tyrone. "Good day, gentleman." She left the same way she arrived—nose in the air and back ramrod straight.

Sgt. Cross collapsed into the chair. "That woman scares the hell out of me. I was holding in my gut and didn't even know it." He blew out a heavy breath. "I'm not afraid of much, but for some reason she intimidates me, and I'm not ashamed to admit it. She's a ball buster. Feel sorry for her husband."

"I wouldn't worry about him. He seems perfectly capable of handling her." Tyrone recalled how Oscar had spoken quietly to her the first time they met and how she'd nodded and then taken Ella from the room.

Sgt. Cross handed Tyrone the business card. "Meet your new partners."

"You don't really expect me to work with these guys? I don't know who they are or what they do. This is bullshit."

"I'm sorry, but were you in the same meeting as I was? You don't have a choice, Evers. The mayor has already been riding my ass. Every couple of days I have to give him an update. What do you think will happen if she complains to him? She's his biggest donor, and the fundraisers she organized with her wealthy friends helped to get him elected."

"You told me that part already."

"Well hear it again, because maybe you forgot. He expects her support for the re-election campaign." He ran a hand down his handlebar mustache. "Figure out how to work with these guys and solve this case. The sooner the better."

"I'm not jeopardizing my case by being hasty."

Sgt. Cross stood. "Listen to me. I don't care what you do or who you talk to. Turn over every stone, contact every snitch. *Find these guys.* Sooner, rather than later."

"Repeating the same words won't make this any easier."

"Does it make you feel better to mouth off to me? You heard Ms. Johnson. Her daughter's not even in her penthouse anymore. She's staying at her mother's. Ms. Johnson probably wants her privacy back."

"Doubt it."

"What?"

"I said, 'doubt it.'"

"How would you know?" Sgt. Cross's eyes narrowed.

"She's the one who asked Ell-Miss Brooks to come stay with her."

"And you know this how?"

"She happened to mention it to me when I was giving her an update, all right?" Tyrone tapped the card on the edge of the desk. "Anyway, I'm glad she finally left her apartment. I felt sorry for her, staying there by herself."

"She's not some poor little orphan. She went from one penthouse to another and could have moved from day one if she wanted to."

"I get the impression her family wanted her to, but she refused. Said she wasn't going to let those criminals scare her out of her home."

"That was either brave or stupid," the sergeant muttered.

"I thought it was kind of brave."

Sgt. Cross's eyes narrowed again. "You have a soft spot for this chick, don't you?"

Heat crawled across his scalp, and Tyrone snorted. "What? No way. I admired her a little bit for sticking it out, that's all. A few high-profile guests moved out right away, but there she was, the victim, still hanging in there."

"Listen, don't go getting any ideas about this woman. Stay in your lane."

"What?" Tyrone laughed. "Come on, man. I said she was brave, that's all."

"Yeah, yeah, I heard you. But it's the way you said it, with a goofy look on your face."

What would happen if he punched his boss?

"Women like Ella Brooks don't lower themselves to messing with guys like us. You need fat pockets and the right pedigree, pal.

Since you have neither, you'd just be wasting your time thinking about her."

"Okay, we're done here. I'll let you know how things go with my new partners." Tyrone stalked out of the office and barely managed not to slam the door.

CHAPTER 10

*T*yrone stepped out of the building, tugging up the collar on his jacket as the wind kicked up in downtown. His footsteps slowed when he saw Ella walking toward him, two big, muscular guys in suits walking several steps behind her. He imagined nothing but a giant boulder could crush the men, and even that was debatable.

"I was on my way to get you," she said. A warm smile graced her features, and those eyes of hers shown like little brown gems.

She wore her hair pulled back, with no jewelry in her ears or elsewhere on her person, which made him wish he could solve this case faster and retrieve not only all her possessions, but the one piece she wanted, the pearl necklace.

"Why's that?" he asked.

"You had to deal with my mother."

"The meeting was interesting, but you don't owe me anything."

"On the contrary, I do. I love my mother to death, but I know how she can be. She probably dominated the meeting and ran all over you and your sergeant. Am I right?"

Tyrone shoved his hands deep into the pockets of his jacket and laughed softly. "Something like that."

"In that case, I definitely owe you."

Huh. If he were reading the situation correctly, Ella had come up with a bogus reason to spend time with him. He couldn't deny his attraction to her, right from the beginning. She wasn't really his type. Too prim. Too proper. He liked his women a bit more down to Earth, but he found himself drawn to Ella and imagined doing all kinds of *im*proper things to her. He wanted to fuck her every way imaginable. Turn miss hoity-toity inside out, curl her toes, and find out how nasty she could get.

"Okay. So what can I expect?"

"I have to admit to being a little selfish. You spoke so highly of your meal at Jim's Diner that one night you called me, now I'm curious to try their food. I thought we could go there, and I'd try your favorite meal."

"You? At a diner?" His gaze flicked quickly over her plaid boucle jacket, dark slacks, and stilettos.

"Is that really so hard to believe, Tyrone?" She tilted her head in a playful manner, and a brilliant smile crossed his face. Quite a difference from the woman he'd first been introduced to, sitting with slumped shoulders in the living room of her penthouse, face drawn and eventually sobbing into her mother's shoulder.

"I admit, I'm surprised."

"Don't be. Is there somewhere else you'd rather go? We can go anywhere you like."

"Much as I'd like to go to Jim's, the diner isn't open right now. How about Pancake Shack?"

Her brow wrinkled. "Honestly, I've never been there."

"What? Oh man, then we need to go for sure. I'll introduce you to the best patty melt you've ever eaten."

She laughed, and the sound sent shivers racing up his spine. "How can I resist? I hope you don't mind if we take my car, and I also hope you don't mind the bodyguards." She jerked a thumb over her shoulder. "This is only temporary."

She spoke as if she expected to interact with Tyrone after the case was solved. Perhaps Ella was thinking ahead, something he'd found himself doing, as well. The only reason he hadn't moved on her was because they were in the middle of an investigation, and being under the microscope on this particular case meant treading more carefully than usual. Having lunch with her, considering his attraction to her, hovered dangerously close to crossing a line, at least in his mind. However, if he played his cards right, there could definitely be more contact after the case was closed.

"I don't mind at all. It'll be nice to travel in style for a change."

Her smile broadened, as if his answer had pleased her greatly. They walked to the limo, shadowed by the two men.

"I'm still getting used to having so much security," Ella murmured, as they settled onto the leather seats. Her security jumped into a dark sedan behind them.

"I assumed people like you traveled with bodyguards all the time."

"Oh, no. Hardly ever, to be honest. Only during special engagements and when we're traveling overseas, depending on the country. Under normal circumstances, it's not necessary."

Tyrone gave the driver the location of the restaurant, and they took off.

"Nothing new, I suppose?" Ella asked.

He could tell her that this morning former rapper DJ Terror's condo had been robbed while he was out of town. Once again, the thieves did an excellent job of hiding their faces. Four men, all dressed in suits with gloves. Just like with her case, they hauled out the loot in luggage and briefcases. He didn't bother, though, instead, shaking his head that he didn't have any more information, which he really didn't.

Before long, they pulled up outside the Pancake Shack, and the people inside stared out the windows at the limousine. When they entered the building, all eyes followed them, and Tyrone couldn't help but feel like a bug under a microscope at all the blatant looks they received. Ella, however, seemed unperturbed by the attention. Either she was used to it, or she'd learned to ignore the stares.

They took a booth at the back. One of the guards sat at the counter, and the other slid into a booth two tables down.

After the waitress came over and took their orders, Tyrone rubbed his jaw, as he watched Ella across the table.

"So, you don't always travel with security, and no entourage, either?"

"I'm not a celebrity."

She removed her jacket to reveal a pale silk blouse underneath. The high neck covered her completely, but his sharp eyes snagged for a second on the matching lace camisole underneath.

"I gained a little notoriety because of the break-in, but most people don't know who I am," Ella continued. "Did you, before you were assigned to my case?"

"No, I didn't," Tyrone admitted.

She nodded. "I don't court the spotlight and have no interest in being famous. That doesn't mean I don't have some level of notoriety because of who my family is. As for an entourage, you'll only ever see me with a driver. I admit to hating to drive, and it's so much easier to have someone at my disposal who's willing to take me wherever I want to go." She shrugged, as if embarrassed by the admission, dropping her gaze for a second. "Anyway, I don't want to discuss any of this, if you don't mind."

Their iced teas arrived, and soon their meal did, too. Ella bit into the toasted bread, and Tyrone waited for her reaction.

When she finished chewing and swallowing, she said, "Not bad. It's really good, actually."

"Then my job here is done." Tyrone bit into his sandwich.

Time slipped by as they chatted about the case, and he gave her a quick update on who they were in the process of questioning, as well as the contacts he'd made with officers in other jurisdictions. Somehow, the conversation turned to her kids.

"Honestly, I worry about spoiling my girls. Right now, they're adorable, but I know how easily that could get out of hand, and I don't want them to be the kind of spoiled, bratty kids who are in the tabloids for embarrassing reasons."

Ever since he got involved with this family, Tyrone started doing more research about them online. Initially, he searched for information on Ella, to get a sense of who she was. But there was plenty of information out there about her siblings and cousins. One of her siblings in particular, Stephan, seemed to court controversy. Clearly the kind of spoiled, entitled person she worried her children would turn out to be. Stephan already had a few brushes with the law and scandal. Nothing had come of any of them, and Tyrone suspected that was all thanks to coverups by the family.

"It all depends on how you handle their formative years," Tyrone said.

"True," Ella agreed, nodding. "I hope I'll be a better mother than I was a wife." She grimaced.

"Are you suggesting you were a bad wife? I find that hard to believe." She seemed too gracious and elegant, but maybe there was some hidden flaw he didn't know about.

"You're being kind, but I think everyone looks back on past relationships and wonders what they could have done differently. You're divorced, too. Aren't there things you wish you could have done differently?"

The conversation entered territory he hadn't anticipated, and it took a while for Tyrone to answer. He sipped his tea to buy time. "There are things I wish I would have done differently."

Like paid more attention to his wife's late night out with "the girls," which turned out to be lies. Or a weekend trip to recharge, which was really a trip to the mountains with her lover. Right under his goddamn nose. He was a detective and hadn't figured out what she'd been up to, with all those clues. Oh, the irony.

"Me, too. Sometimes, I wish I could have a do-over."

Tyrone's gut clenched, and he set down his sandwich. "With your ex-husband?"

"No. That ship has sailed." Ella's brow wrinkled. "When I think of a do-over, I don't mean getting involved with the same person. I want to use the lessons I learned from my first relationship to do a better job with someone else."

Tyrone nodded.

"So you're thinking you would like a do-over, too?" Ella asked lightly.

Tyrone had been with a few women since his divorce. Nothing too serious, usually just to have someone to keep him company, kill the boredom, and satisfy the biological urges of his body. He was in no rush to get married again, but he understood her desire for a do-over. He sometimes wondered if he took the plunge again, he could do the marriage thing better the second time around.

"Yeah, I think I'd like a do-over, too."

"Maybe we'll both get a chance one day," she said.

He nodded. "Yeah, maybe."

The conversation turned to other topics, and as they talked, he realized how much he enjoyed listening to her. She had an easy-going personality, and not only that, she seemed nice. Genuinely nice, not pretending or displaying a facade to fool him into thinking she was a decent person. Which made him curious about why her marriage hadn't lasted.

They finished up the meal, and she dropped him off at the precinct.

"Thanks for lunch. I should return the favor some time."

"That's not necessary. Besides, I was doing this because I owe you, remember?"

"Right." He slipped out of the car and ducked his head to add, "I'll call you and give you an update tomorrow." He didn't need to update her so frequently and didn't do it for anyone else.

"That would be nice. Thank you."

He shut the door and walked into the building with an extra pep in his step.

* * *

"Evers!" Tyrone flinched, turning to watch the sergeant come

71

charging down the middle of the room. "What the hell is this?" He shoved his iPad in Tyrone's face. Right there on the screen was a photo of Tyrone and Ella having lunch at the Pancake Shack.

Damn, that was fast. He'd had lunch with her only a few hours ago.

"That's me and Ella Brooks having lunch."

"Is that such a good idea?"

He lifted an eyebrow. "I had no idea you were so interested in celebrity gossip."

"Don't be a comedian. Since our victim is from a prominent family, people tend to send me information to make sure that I'm aware."

Tyrone shuffled some papers on his desk. "There's nothing to be aware of. We were talking about the case. She took me to Pancake Shack for lunch so that we could discuss it. The end."

"Listen, I don't want to ride your ass any more than I like having mine ridden, but I've got both her parents on my ass, and then her cousin in Seattle called for me today, too."

"Her cousin?"

"Yeah, the unofficial male head of the family, I guess. Someone named Cyrus. The CEO of the whole fucking conglomerate."

"Well, well, well, aren't you Mr. Popular."

"Yes. It's been swell. I need you to stop playing footsie with this woman and get me something fast. So we'll at least look like we're working on the case. Call somebody in for questioning or something."

"Every lead I have ends in a dead end. There's not a whole lot to go on in this case. I'd have to bring someone in on trumped-up charges." He was kidding, but his boss's expression suggested he was open to the idea. "No way. Let me keep working it, and you keep fielding calls so I can get my work done."

Arm on the edge of the cubicle wall, Sgt. Cross leaned in toward Tyrone. "Remember what we discussed. Don't get caught up with this woman. Keep your head on straight."

"Aye-aye, captain." Tyrone did a mock salute.

Sgt. Cross breathed heavily through his nose, shook his head, and marched away.

Tyrone pulled into his desk and buried his face in his hands. He needed a break in this case, but nothing had worked out so far. Questioning Horace and James had been a bust, and he was no closer to finding out who any of the four men were.

He swiveled back and forth in his squeaky chair.

"Would you cut that shit out?" Chu shouted at him. "Or use some WD-40 on that thing!"

Tyrone shot his co-worker the bird and continued to swivel.

CHAPTER 11

"On my father's side, my grandmother is Brazilian and my grandfather is African-American. My daughter Sophia is named after my grandmother." Phone to her ear, Ella walked through the penthouse in an oversized nightshirt carrying a glass of red wine as she explained her family background to Tyrone. "They met when my grandfather, quite the adventurer in his day, went down to Rio. According to him, the minute he saw my grandmother in the crowd, he knew she was the one. She's very pale, and because of anti-miscegenation laws, they couldn't get married at first. So, they played up the fact that she was a foreigner and had wavy hair, said she was a mixed-race black woman, and they got married."

"Your grandfather was a determined man." Tyrone laughed.

"He was determined to marry her by any means necessary."

Ella had never grown tired of hearing her grandfather recite that tale. He was dead now, but she imagined how much he must have loved her grandmother and all they suffered back in those days. Their determination to be together made her think long and hard about the passion lacking in her own marriage, and how much she'd wanted to experience that type of ardor, to have someone want you so much they'd do anything to hold on to you. They treated you with respect and love. Not blame you for all the problems in your relationship and cheat and leave when they got tired of pretending.

"My kind of man," Tyrone said. "Your turn."

"Let's see, have you ever shot anyone?"

"No, but like any good cop, I go to the gun range and practice regularly."

"Have you ever been shot?"

"No. My career is boring, boring, boring."

"Somehow I doubt that."

He chuckled. "Okay, that's not entirely true. But there's a hell of a lot of paperwork, which I hate, and the work comes in spurts. Some days are quiet, others busy as hell."

This had been their routine every night over the past week, ever since lunch at the Pancake Shack. Ella put her daughters to bed, then poured a glass of wine from her parents' collection and settled in to wait for Tyrone's phone call. Some nights he called later than others, but each time after working at least a twelve-hour day. The conversations began under the pretense of getting an update on the case, which lasted a grand total of three minutes or so. Then they spent the next hour, or two, talking about everything under the sun.

She couldn't pretend the conversations were completely innocent, at least on her part. She wanted to listen to him smile as he talked. She welcomed the opportunity to have a grown-up conversation without animosity and blame, and she liked the warmth that always settled in the pit of her stomach at the sound of his voice.

She'd learned a lot about Tyrone during these conversations. His parents were both entrenched in the justice system, his father as a defense attorney and his mother as a judge. His younger brother worked for a large firm in Macon, and he expected his sister to go into law, as well. Tyrone was the only one who'd decided to work as a police officer. When she asked why, he said he didn't care about the money, and while he took his job as a line of defense between criminals and law-abiding citizens very seriously, he also wanted to help as many people as he could before they had to stand before his mother. That admission made her admire him even more.

Still, he admitted there were 'bad people out there' and worked hard to keep an optimistic outlook, according to the 90/10 belief in law enforcement. Ninety percent of the people were decent. Some just made mistakes or fell on hard times. If he could help them before they entered the system, he wanted to. He believed that was part of his job.

"Okay, next question. Have you ever gotten a complaint against you?" Cradling the phone to her ear and balancing the glass, Ella climbed into bed. She stretched her legs under the warm down comforter and settled against the stack of silk-covered pillows.

Tyrone chuckled. "As a police officer, we get complaints all the time. Show me a cop with no complaints, and I'll show you a cop who never left the station."

"What's the weirdest complaint you ever received?"

"Let's see." He fell quiet, and she sipped wine as she waited. "I once had a woman complain she didn't like the way I looked at her."

"Are you serious?"

"Absolutely. Several times suspects accused me of not reading them their Miranda rights. Television cops arrest people and right away they read them their Miranda rights, but that's not how it happens in real life. We're required to read a suspect their rights only after they're in police custody and we've begun questioning them about an offense. We're not required to do it before, and some criminals don't understand that. Unfortunately, they believe the BS they see on TV."

"Count me in with the criminals watching BS TV. I assumed it was standard and you had to read them their rights immediately."

"That's what a lot of people think, and when we don't, they

think they can beat the charges. It would be hilarious if it weren't so sad."

"What do you love about the job?"

"When I worked patrol, I liked knowing I could make a difference in someone's life, especially kids. Meeting people in the neighborhood and winning their trust isn't easy, but when you do and develop a good relationship with them, it makes policing a lot easier. We can save lives and curtail violence that way. As a detective, it's rewarding to nab a bad guy, especially when I can give someone back a piece of their property that has sentimental value. Crimes are like one giant puzzle, and I can't lie, there's a certain satisfaction that comes from solving puzzles."

"What do you hate about your job?"

"Budget limitations, the scrutiny from citizens and media who don't understand what we do every day, how much pressure we're under, and people who think they can do our jobs better than we do. The demands on my time can sometimes suck. I've had to cancel plans at the last minute or flat out say I'm not available, which doesn't go over well. But I chose this profession, so I suck up the bad and concentrate on the positive."

"That's a good attitude to have. I used to work." Seemed so long ago, a period in the distant past when she was a different woman altogether. Bolder and more confident. Able to think for herself. What happened to that version of Ella?

"Oh, really?"

Ella nodded, though he couldn't see her. "I worked at my mother's firm, SJ Brands. She was grooming me to take over the company one day."

Sylvie had taken her multi-million-dollar inheritance and turned it into a multi-billion-dollar company with three divisions that spoke to her passions in life—a movie production company, a fashion and cosmetics line, and a furniture company, which marketed to female executives. The work had been interesting, and Ella missed being tested and challenged on a daily basis. She missed one-upping competitors and coming up with new products to expand their reach and market share.

"What happened? Didn't like it?"

"No," Ella said, letting the word drag out. "I left to concentrate on being a better mother and wife." Because her husband wanted her to, and she felt it was the right thing to do at the time. But it hadn't been. She did so much to make Wayne happy and make him feel comfortable, and none of it mattered. He only resented her more because she'd given up a career for him. He even resented the fact that she didn't work and was still getting a hefty allowance deposited into her account every month. The truth was, no matter how hard you try, you can't make someone love you if they don't. She'd learned that lesson the hard way.

"You miss working at the company?" Tyrone asked.

"A little. But I don't regret the time I've spent with Hannah and Sophia."

"I wouldn't expect you to. Your daughters sound like they're quite the characters."

One of her nightly rituals was telling him about their antics—climbing into bed with her in the morning, arguing with each other like sworn enemies, but making up with plenty of hugs and tear-streaked faces. As much as they argued, they loved each other, and where Sophia went, Hannah was sure to follow like a shadow. She idolized her older sister to the point that Ella often bought them clothes in the same design but different colors, so Hannah could dress like her sister.

"They are characters. Maybe one day you'll get to meet them."

"Yeah?"

She bit her lip. "Yes."

Where had that come from? She was getting a little too comfortable with Tyrone. Suggesting he meet her daughters was stepping over an invisible line and entering territory she wasn't sure she wanted to venture into.

Was Tyrone her type? She kept coming back to the fact that he was not from her social circle, and at the risk of sounding like a snob, there was good reason for her hesitation. After all, it hadn't worked for her the first time, had it? For years she believed she, her mother, and Simone were either jinxed or unlovable. But her sister was happily married to a nightclub owner, and though her parents split for a long time, they were back together, happy, and planning a wedding. So a relationship could work, with the right man.

She wouldn't mind dating again, but marriage wasn't a priority. It wasn't worth the heartache. Was Tyrone Evers the right kind of man?

"Ella, there's something I've been meaning to ask you, and man, I hope I'm not being too forward, but when this case is over, would you like to have drinks or dinner with me sometime?" Tyrone asked.

There it was. The invitation she'd been waiting for, yet dreading. Two years since her divorce, but was she really ready to move on, with two kids in tow? Except for a few times, normally when a man asked her out, she declined the invitation, and she absolutely refused to be set up.

She swallowed, excitement still present, but traces of fear creeping into her thoughts. "I'm not sure. Can I think about it?"

The silence almost made her take the words back.

"Sure," he said, disappointment coloring his voice, and knots of discomfort filled her stomach. "Take all the time you need."

"It's just that, I have two daughters and this case is still ongoing. I'm in flux at the moment, not knowing if I'm coming or going." She laughed to soften the blow, but the sound was hollow and mirthless, and she knew he could tell.

"You don't have to explain anything to me, Ella. The invitation remains open, for whenever you're ready to accept it."

"Thank you," she said quietly, grateful for his understanding.

"It's late. I better go."

She hated saying goodbye to him each night. A full day would pass before she spoke to him again, and twenty-four hours never seemed as long as when she had to wait for his next call.

"Have a good day tomorrow."

"Thanks. You, too."

Ella hung up and stared at the screen of the phone. She watched as 11:05 changed to 11:06. One minute and counting until she heard from him again.

CHAPTER 12

"*M*aybe those four guys on the tape weren't the thieves," Chu said.

Both he and Tyrone had come from the interrogation room where they'd questioned a potential witness. Another dead end. The crooks had covered their tracks too well. The longer they went without arresting someone, the colder the case became, and that meant memories would be tarnished. They'd put a rush on the fingerprint analysis but came up empty-handed there, too. They were running a trace on the suit fibers, but he wasn't optimistic. Those were off-the-rack suits and could have been purchased at any local men's store.

"They were the thieves. Don't forget we saw the same guys on the tape from DJ Terror's place. They're the only ones who make sense, but they've managed to do a helluva good job covering their tracks." Tyrone was in a particularly foul mood because of his conversation with Ella a few nights ago. What was he thinking, asking her out? He'd misread her comment about her daughters, thinking maybe she wanted more than a friendship.

His phone vibrated, and he looked down to see a new message

from Cruz Cordoba, his unofficial partner and the owner of the Cordoba Agency.

I have some info for you. Check your email.

Tyrone fell into the desk chair and shook the computer mouse. He typed in the password on the screen and went straight to the email from Cruz.

"1010 Parker Avenue, Decatur," he murmured, reading Cruz's note.

He clicked open the attachment, and his mouth fell open when he saw the contents.

There was no sound, but the electronic file showed footage of the back of a home in the suburbs. The video was taken at night, with night vision enabled. The time stamp was the same night as Ella's attack. The most interesting aspect of the film was the men dressed in suits walking from a vehicle to the back door, carrying briefcases and dragging a suitcase.

Tyrone jumped up from his chair. "Chu."

His co-worker frowned over at him. "What?"

"Is Judge Becker back from vacation?"

"Yeah. Why?"

"We just got a huge break in the case, and we're gonna need a no-knock warrant."

* * *

"Look at what we have here." Using a crowbar, Chu had pulled up a loose floorboard in the dining room and found a stash of cash and jewelry.

It had only taken a few hours to get the warrant and have the judge sign it so they could enter the house on Parker Avenue. Using a battering ram, a group of six cops, Tyrone and Chu included, entered the home.

"Keep searching the house. This can't be all of it." Tyrone holstered his weapon. He wore a skull cap on his head and a bulletproof vest like the rest of the men and two women officers.

He sauntered into the living room, rubbing the sore underside of his chin. When they'd burst into the house, one of the men had taken off running. Tyrone tackled him, and they'd scuffled a bit before he was subdued. The sofa was occupied by three handcuffed men, two others were being led outside, and a sixth was being interrogated by one of the officers.

"What do you mean you don't know where any of this came from? Are you kidding me? This guy…" The officer jerked his thumb at the handcuffed perpetrator.

"I'm telling you, man, I don't know nothing about nothing. This ain't my house. I'm just visiting, and you guys are gonna be sorry."

His voice made the hairs on Tyrone's neck stand on end. "What did you say?" He focused on the handcuffed man.

"I said you guys are gonna be sorry."

Boston accent.

"Sure you're visiting. And I'm Mother Teresa." Chu, who had come out of the dining room, elbowed Tyrone.

But Tyrone was distracted and saw red. This was the guy. He was the one who terrified Ella in the bedroom. All he could think about was her recounting of how this man fondled her and threatened to rape her with veiled words.

"You piece of shit," he growled low in his throat. Before Tyrone could even think, he'd grabbed two handfuls of the guy's T-shirt and slammed him against the wall.

"Hey!" Boston Accent's eyes widened in panic.

"You get a kick out of hurting women? Women who are tied up and can't defend themselves?" He shoved his forearm into the man's neck.

"Hey, get off me, man!" he choked out. "Get him off me!"

Chu grabbed Tyrone from behind and pulled. "What are you doing?"

Tyrone didn't let go, shoving his arm harder against the thief's throat. "How does this feel? Handcuffed and helpless. Doesn't feel too good, does it?"

The man's face went red, and his panicked eyes shifted to Chu. "This is police brutality," he wheezed. "Get him off me!"

A female officer rushed over, and together she and Chu yanked Tyrone off the suspect. Chu shoved him into the dining room and got in his face. "What is the matter with you?"

"I'm filing a complaint. That was police brutality!" Boston Accent yelled.

Chu looked over his shoulder. "Shut him up. Shove a sock in his mouth if you have to." He returned his attention to Tyrone, who flexed his fingers continuously and restlessly paced the floor "Are you insane?"

"I'm fine," Tyrone said tersely.

"Or maybe you're too close to this?"

Another uniformed officer came to the doorway, looking at Tyrone with concern in his eyes.

Tyrone stopped pacing. "I'm fine."

"Listen, if you need a break…" Chu let the sentence trail off.

"No break necessary." Tyrone expelled a deep breath. "Let's figure out where the rest of the money and jewels are because I know this isn't all of it."

Chu hesitated, but he finally seemed convinced Tyrone was back to his normal self and set off down the hallway.

Tyrone braced both hands against the wall and bowed his head. He didn't know where that level of rage had come from. It shot up inside him with volcanic intensity. If Chu and the other officer hadn't pulled him off, he couldn't say for sure he wouldn't have done major damage to the guy, just to teach him a lesson.

Pushing away from the wall, he joined the others. They spent the next hour interrogating the men and located the additional stolen goods in two locations: a locked chest in an upstairs bedroom and a locked box underneath a loose floorboard in the biggest bedroom.

Crouched over the smashed-open lockbox was where Tyrone found what he thought was the pearl necklace Ella had told him about, and her other missing jewelry. He removed the photo she'd given him from his wallet and matched the necklace. Unless there was another one in the house like it, or worse, hers had already been sold, it looked the same. Only she could tell him for sure.

"That it?" Chu peered over his shoulder.

"Think so." Tyrone stood and shoved the necklace in his pocket.

"What are you doing?" Chu asked.

"This means a lot to her, more than anything else. Instead of making her wait to go through all the paperwork, I'm going to take it directly to her. And don't worry, it'll get written up in the report."

Chu threw up his hands and shook his head. "All right. As far as that's concerned, I didn't see anything."

"Fair enough." The decision to bend the rules was his own, and he didn't want to get his friend in trouble should there be a problem later.

Everything else, including the cash, was bagged and tagged and carted off. The thieves hadn't been at this very long. The other two occupants of the house were buyers. The police had found them just in time. If they hadn't, he might have lost his chance to secure Ella's property.

Tyrone walked out the front door. Police tape sectioned off the area, and the lights of the squad cars flashed on the homes nearby. He noticed a few people peeking through their windows, but the bolder ones stood at the outskirts of the scene with camera phones capturing the unfolding events.

Across the street, Cruz Cordoba leaned against his black SUV, wearing a pair of dark sunglasses with his arms and legs crossed. Dude was big as hell. At least six-five, his hard-muscled physique packed into a shirt that looked two sizes too small, showing off arms as big as hams.

Tyrone walked over to him.

"Care to tell me how you got that video? Looks like it might be footage from the house behind theirs."

"Nowadays, everybody has a camera, at the house, in the car.

Luckily, a lot of these videos are backed up to a cloud. That one happened to fall into our laps." He spoke with an accent. During their conversations, Tyrone learned he was Cuban.

"Just fell in your laps, huh?"

"Something like that." Cruz chuckled softly and straightened. "Looks like you're all done here."

Tyrone glanced over his shoulder at the house. "Pretty much. We're going to take these guys down to booking and let the forensics team finish up. And I have a report to write."

"I'm glad everything worked out."

"I appreciate your help."

Cruz shrugged. "There's only so much we can do."

"Same here." Although he couldn't see his eyes, he got the distinct impression Cruz was studying him.

"If you ever want to do more, let me know. We could use a good detective with connections on our team."

"How do you know I'm good?"

A mysterious smile crossed his face. "I know."

Tyrone shook his head. "Thanks, but no thanks. I'm happy with my work."

"Pays better than what you make now, and the hours are better, too."

"I'll pass." Stuck helping a bunch of rich people was not his idea of doing good. They could afford an elite service like the Cordoba Agency. He liked to think he helped those less fortunate by putting one hundred percent into every case he worked.

Cruz shrugged and opened the driver door of his vehicle. "If you change your mind, you know how to reach me." He hopped in, and before long, Tyrone was looking at his tail lights going down the street.

"Who was that guy?" Chu asked, walking up.

"The one who supplied the video."

"Oh." Chu hooked his thumb through the loop of his slacks. "I'm heading out. You ready?"

"I'm going to head over to Ell—Miss Brooks and give her the necklace."

"Oh, right. I forgot." Chu didn't question him. He understood where Tyrone's head was at.

"I'll catch up with you guys later," Tyrone said.

Chu went off toward his vehicle, and Tyrone fingered the pearls in his pocket. As Chu drove away, he went to his car and took off in the opposite direction.

CHAPTER 13

*E*lla did a last check of her reflection in the bathroom mirror. She had applied a light coat of make-up to her face, some lip gloss, and slipped into a purple maxi dress after she received the call from Tyrone. She didn't want to greet him too dressed up. It was, after all, the middle of the night. The girls would sleep through a tornado tearing the house apart, but she hoped she didn't wake either of her parents or Trevor as she moved around the house after midnight.

She tiptoed down the hall and waited anxiously in the vestibule for Tyrone to arrive. She'd called downstairs, so they should let him right up. She wondered what news he could possibly have that couldn't wait until morning. Did they catch the men who robbed her? That would certainly be wonderful news.

The elevator chimed, and her heart went a little faster. The doors opened, and her breath caught when she saw Tyrone in the cabin. Delicious-looking in a pair of dark slacks, a bulletproof vest over his button-down shirt, and a gun holster over his shoulder. A dark skull cap pulled down to his thick eyebrows gave him a rugged appearance.

Be still my heart.

He stepped into the dimly lit entryway, and she caught sight of a bruise beneath the sprinkling of hairs on his face.

"What happened?" She reached up and brushed a thumb over his skin, but snatched back her hand, finger tingling from where she'd touched. She didn't know him well enough to extend such familiarity. She interlaced her hands in front of her and fought the urge to reach for him again.

"Got into a little scuffle tonight. Nothing I couldn't handle," he said with a sideways smile, rubbing a palm over the same spot.

"What happened to the other guy?" Ella asked.

"He was handled," he said.

Oh my. She smiled, because she hadn't expected anything less. "I'm glad you're okay. You said you have an update for me? Is it good news?" She didn't want to get too excited but suspected only good news would bring him by with an update at this hour.

"Very good news." Tyrone pulled a string of pearls from his pocket.

Ella gasped and covered her mouth. "When did you get this?"

"Tonight."

"Does that mean what I think it means?" she asked tentatively.

"We got 'em. You don't have to be afraid anymore and neither does anyone else."

She let out a little scream and flung her arms around his neck.

For a split second he stiffened, then one arm closed around her, and she was enveloped in a firm, one-armed hug. She felt every one of his long fingers spread out against her back. She should let him go, but remained on tiptoe, the scent of sweat, no doubt from the night's difficult work, filling her nostrils. Heat singed her skin where his fingers spread low on her back, and her nipples tightened as her breasts pressed against the hard vest and his hard body.

Ella stepped back, arms falling to her sides, but Tyrone didn't release her. The same arm remained loosely around her waist, allowing space between them while still holding on.

She pressed a hand to her chest. "I don't know what came over me. I shouldn't have…" She didn't recognize the breathy sound of her own voice.

"It's okay." His voice sounded extra deep, and he watched her beneath lowered lids, his jaw tight.

"Anyway, I knew you'd catch them." They were so close, she saw the way his nostrils flared ever so slightly. She took another step back, and his hand fell away.

His Adam's apple bobbed up and down, and he glanced at the necklace in his hand for a second before returning his focus to her. "It would be nice to take all the credit, but we received some help from your guys at the Cordoba Agency. Don't tell your mother." He winked.

"I promise I won't." Ella laughed shakily and swallowed. "I'm glad they were helpful."

"Very. Cruz actually offered me a job."

"Are you considering it?"

He shook his head. "Nah. My heart and soul are in law enforcement."

She looked at the necklace. "Can I touch it?" Goodness, that sounded dirty.

"Of course. I don't know what I was thinking. Here you go. Can you confirm it's yours?"

He handed over the jewelry, and Ella took extra time examining it so she could collect herself. The electricity that reached across the space between them hadn't completely subsided yet.

"It's mine." She knew this piece of jewelry very well. Clutching the pearls to her chest, she said, "I don't know how to thank you enough. Of all the items that were taken, this was the most important, the one I wanted to get back more than anything. Mother will be pleased you were able to retrieve it. Where are the rest of the items?"

He appeared a little embarrassed. "Well, ah, to be honest, you shouldn't have the necklace yet. It should be in evidence at the police station, with the rest of the items. But I knew how anxious you were about recovering that piece and the sentimental value it held for you. We have to do our paperwork, but I couldn't make you wait to have it back in your possession."

"I don't want you to get into trouble."

"I won't. It'll make the report, which is the important thing. When you get it isn't relevant."

She doubted the truth of that statement. "Did you bend the rules for me?"

"Maybe." He angled his head and smiled at her.

Her heart fluttered a little faster. "I appreciate it."

"I didn't mind one bit."

They both fell quiet for a moment, and her heart fluttered even faster. She had a good view of his lips, as if the recessed lights shined a spotlight on his full, wide mouth. She wondered what it would be like to kiss Tyrone. His lips had fascinated her almost from the beginning, even when they shouldn't have and she should have been preoccupied with more important matters.

"I can't thank you enough for making a special trip over here to give me this." She racked her brain for something else to say to prolong the conversation.

"Not a problem. Not an inconvenience."

"So, the case is closed."

"Yeah."

The end. No more late-night conversations or humorous stories. She'd never get a chance to taste his world-famous coffee or eat breakfast at his favorite diner. She'd never have another excuse to call and shoot the breeze under the guise of wanting an update on the case. Ella's fingers tightened around the pearls as a sense of loss crushed her beneath its weight. His empathy and kindness had come along when she needed it most, making her strong when she was tempted to be weak.

Tyrone broke the prolonged silence. "I better get out of here. It's late, and I've got a report to write that will probably take all night. I can't let the other guys do all the work, no matter how much I'd like for them to." The corner of his mouth lifted into the semblance of a smile.

"This is it, then? I won't see you anymore." The thought of never seeing him again filled her with quiet desperation. She wanted him to stay, wanted to find an excuse to hold on to him and extend this moment, but she couldn't think of a single excuse to make that happen.

"Maybe we'll run into each other again, at a Pancake Shack or something."

She laughed through the ache in her chest.

"Goodnight, Ella." Tyrone turned back to the elevator and pushed the down button. The doors opened immediately. But instead of stepping in, he turned around.

Ella held her breath expectantly.

"Take care," he said.

"You, too."

He walked into the cabin.

Wait! her mind screamed.

The doors closed, and a wave of emptiness engulfed her. She felt as if a piece of her was gone. Silly, but true. During the course of this ordeal, he'd been as much of a rock to her as her family.

Clutching the pearls, Ella padded toward the back of the penthouse and stopped to peek in on her daughters. The night light offered enough illumination so she could see their little faces. Spread-eagled across their beds, their even breathing filled the room.

She shut the door and went to her room. Setting the jewelry on the nightstand, she climbed into bed. She felt lost, adrift on a sea of loneliness and sadness. Staring across at the abstract painting on the wall, she had absolutely no idea what to do with herself. No idea how to make the ache in her chest go away.

CHAPTER 14

*E*lla climbed into bed and tried to read but couldn't concentrate for thinking about Tyrone. For the past two days, he'd dominated her thoughts, and she missed their late-night conversations. She was relieved when someone knocked softly at the door.

"Come in."

Sylvie entered, her long hair around her shoulders and wearing a nightie and matching negligee belted around her waist. "Do you mind some company?" she asked.

"No, I don't."

Sylvie eased the door closed and came over to the bed. She made a point of tucking the blankets around Ella. "Comfy?"

"Yes."

She climbed onto the bed and opened her arms. Ella rested in her mother's embrace. Sylvie stroked her hair, and they sat quietly like that for a while, which was fine with Ella.

"When are you going back home?" Sylvie asked.

"Maybe on Sunday." She almost didn't want to leave. Funny, since she hadn't wanted to come in the first place.

"You know you can stay longer if you like."

"I know."

Sylvie sighed. "I worry so much about making sure you kids have everything you need. A roof over your head, the finest clothes, and anything money can buy. In spite of all that, I never truly considered how to keep you safe and secure, the way I did when you were children."

"I'm an adult. It's not your responsibility anymore."

"You will always be my responsibility." She squeezed Ella tighter. "If anything had happened to you…"

"Nothing happened." She lifted her head to look at her mother. "And, I'm really enjoying the therapy sessions. Talking to someone helps put my fears into perspective. I'm not as frightened as I was when this first happened, and being here helped. I didn't want to come, but I'm glad I did, and I appreciate you paying for the extra security."

"You know the money is negligible. I would go broke protecting you and my granddaughters. I wanted the best, and we hired the best. Now that those hooligans are caught, we can all sleep better at night."

Above and beyond her maternal instincts, she knew the additional reason her mother was so extra cautious. She lost both of her brothers under sudden and tragic circumstances. Ella could only imagine the fear Sylvie experienced when she thought about losing one of her own children.

"There's something else I need to talk to you about. Something I've been thinking about the past couple of days."

"What is it, dear?"

Ella took a deep breath. "I've been doing a lot of thinking, and I'd like to come back to work at SJ Brands."

Sylvia pressed a hand to her chest, and her mouth fell open. "Really? You're not just saying that?"

Ella laughed at her mother's dramatic reaction. "I would never joke about something like that because I know how important it is to you that I come back to the company. My only concern is, is there still a place for me?"

"My darling, of course there's still a place for you. There will always be a place for you, and I told you that when you left to take a break to be a mommy. You are a little behind the curve, but I know you'll pick everything up very quickly and easily. You're smart, and I know you can do it."

She should have known her mother would react in such a positive way. "Where do you see me fitting in?"

"Where you were before, of course. You'll be my vice president of operations."

It was Ella's turn for her mouth to fall open. When she started working for the company, she worked as her mother's right hand, learning the ropes about the operations of all her businesses.

"Surely you have someone else who's taken over that role."

Sylvie studied her daughter. "And who would that be? When I told you I would hold the vice president position for you, I meant it. It's still available. I have, of course, found ways to work around not having you there. I spread the work a little wider amongst the staff, and I have a lovely young woman working very closely with me now who I see as a possibility to aid you in the fashion side of the business. She's really been a godsend. So, all you have to do is come back and sit in your old office."

Speechless, Ella felt tears come to her eyes. "Should I be upset that you were so confident I would be back?"

"Mother knows best, dear. That's all you need to know." She patted Ella's hand.

Ella sighed. "I really screwed up, didn't I?"

"We all make mistakes. The question is, do you learn from them?"

"I intend to." Ella heaved a heavy breath. "I'd like to start back right away."

"Wonderful. I'd love to have you back right away. What are we going to do about the girls?"

"I'll start looking into nannies." Since she would be working, she would need someone to help Tracy. Her ex-husband would have a say in the final choice, but she didn't expect much kickback from him about hiring additional help.

"And how are you and Father and the wedding plans coming along?" Ella asked.

Sylvie blushed, something she didn't do often. "We're fine. As a matter of fact, your decision to come back to the company could not have come at a better time. You know how your father is. He's so demanding."

Ella hid a smile. It was funny listening to them talk about each other.

"He's told me that it's time for me to start slowing down, and with the wedding in early December, the sooner the better, as far as he's concerned. Of course, there's also a honeymoon to plan. He wants us to go somewhere and be alone for a period of time, just the two of us." Sylvie rolled her eyes as if that was the worst decision ever, but Ella knew her mother was excited about the prospect. "I'm going to do that to make him happy. Cutting my hours a little bit at the office will make him happy, too, and with you there I know the operations will run smoothly and trust that I will be leaving my business in good hands."

"Thank you for entrusting me with your company. I promise I won't let you down."

"I know that, my darling. I have every confidence in you."

* * *

THREE HOURS LATER, Ella still couldn't sleep. She paced the floor of the bedroom, pulling her lower lip between her teeth.

An online article divulged that three of the men involved in the burglary were chauffeurs, but the entire gang consisted of six men total. One of the six, who was not physically present for the theft, worked for the company she regularly used and had taken her and her daughters to the airport when they left for St. Barts.

The leader was a career criminal, adept at opening safes, breaking and entering, the works. He'd recruited the others with a plan to rob wealthy clients while they were out of town. Future plans had been thwarted by the arrests, and there were only three known victims—Ella, DJ Terror, and an actress who lived in Atlanta but worked in L.A.

James, the new porter at the building, was the younger brother of the leader. He'd tipped them off about Ella's return, and he'd also been the one to get them access to her penthouse by copying her keycard.

The good news was they'd caught the gang of thieves. The bad news was she couldn't talk to Tyrone anymore. Why couldn't she move on? They barely knew each other.

She picked up her cell phone and put it back down, eyeing the device like some dangerous foreign object. She'd deprived herself of enjoyment for so long, only attending charity events or animated movies with her children. The occasional meal out with family or friends was the extent of her social interaction. When was the last time she'd done anything for herself?

"Just do it."

She laughed, nerves trembling in her belly, and snatched up the phone. She dialed his number. Holding on tight, she listened to the phone ring and almost hung up, when he finally answered and his groggy voice came through the line.

Her heart kickstarted. "Did I wake you?"

He yawned. "It's kinda late."

Well after midnight, but she'd wanted to make the call while she still had the nerve.

"I assumed you'd be up late. I shouldn't have called at this hour. I'll call you back in the morning. Have a good night." The words rushed out of her.

"Whoa, whoa. Relax. Normally I'd be up, but I worked extra hours yesterday and today. I hit the bed as soon as I came home and fell asleep right away. To what do I owe the pleasure of your late-night call?"

Do it.

"I was thinking about the question you asked me last week."

Goodness, this felt strange, calling up a man in the middle of the night about a date. She stopped pacing and held the phone tighter.

"What question is that?"

Did he really not remember, or did he just want to make her say it?

Ella strolled over to the window and looked out at the city. "The question you asked about taking me out for drinks or dinner."

"Oh, that."

She heard sheets rustling and wondered if he wore pajamas or went to bed wearing less. Less, she hoped. It would fit her fantasy of imagining his firm, naked chest revealed by the sheets. Perhaps with a sprinkling of hair that disappeared into his pelvis. The direction of her thoughts made her blush.

"What decision did you come to?" Tyrone asked.

"I would like to accept your offer, if it's still open. You know, now that the case is closed."

"There was no expiration date on that offer." She heard the smile in his voice.

"Good." Ella squeezed her eyes shut and tried to keep the exultant excitement from her voice. "So, um...do you know when you'd like to go out? Friday night or Saturday night work for you?"

"Can't. I have plans."

"Oh."

"Birthday party for my goddaughter on Friday night." He yawned again. "And on Saturday I'm the detective on call. Which means I have to be in a position to drop whatever I'm doing when calls come through."

"Oh." Whew. She'd thought maybe there was someone else.

"Are you free next weekend?"

"Yes." She hoped she didn't sound too eager.

"Great. How about I come get you at seven for dinner, and then we can play it by ear from there."

"That sounds wonderful."

"All right." He yawned. "I better get back to sleep. Been a long week, long day, and I need my beauty rest."

Ella laughed. "I understand." She'd hoped to extend their conversation but couldn't very well expect him to lose out on his sleep because of her. "I shouldn't have called so late. Have a good night."

"Ella." Something in his voice held her attention. It was the firm, precise way he said her name. "Whenever you feel the need to call me, pick up the phone and dial. I told you that in the beginning, and I meant what I said. I'm glad you called. No matter what time you do call, I'm glad. Don't ever hesitate. Promise me you won't."

With typical Tyrone smoothness, he'd put her mind at ease. "I won't," she promised.

After they hung up, she pressed the phone to her chest and rested her temple against the cool window. Anticipation swelled in her chest. A date. What the heck was she going to wear?

She couldn't stop grinning.

CHAPTER 15

$\mathcal{T}$yrone checked his appearance in the mirror, brushed his hair, and straightened his tie. Pulling on a navy jacket, the third of the night, he rolled his neck and stepped back to survey his appearance. Damn, he was acting like he'd never been on a date before. Like a teenager again, which was funny because he hadn't been a teenager in over fifteen years.

The nervousness in the pit of his stomach reminded him of his first official date without any parent chaperone. He still remembered the girl's name. Beatrice Finch. Real sweet, glasses, and with legs for days. He'd always been a leg man. He'd been nervous as hell because he'd considered her out of his league. She was popular, but not for the usual reasons. She wasn't on the dance team and didn't play any sports. Beatrice Finch was smart as hell, nice, and everybody liked her. He'd been honored that her parents allowed him to pick her up, although most of the parents trusted him because at the time, both his parents were lawyers. He took Beatrice to the movies and then for ice cream afterward, and that night, they both had their first kiss.

Ella Brooks made him feel the same as Beatrice did that night. Not in the sense that his hormones were all crazy, although they were definitely all over the place since he'd been thinking about having sex with her for weeks. But in the sense that he didn't know what he was doing, and maybe he was in over his head.

He wanted to live up to whatever her standards were. This woman was probably used to being taken to the finest restaurants and wined and dined by men whose bank accounts far outmatched his own. Yet she had agreed to dinner with him. And right now he was feeling a little bit out of his depth.

He laughed at his reflection and shook his head. "Chill, dude. You're going on a date, not a reception at the governor's mansion."

Blowing into his palm, he checked his breath. Checked it again, and decided to pop a peppermint in his mouth. He tossed the tie, opened the top button of the black shirt, and checked his appearance again.

"Good enough."

On the drive to her penthouse, he bolstered his courage and reminded himself that she was a woman like any other. Yes, she was wealthy and beautiful and classy. But she was still a woman. And she had, after all, accepted his offer, which meant she had at least had *some* interest in him. If he was lucky, they'd get through the night and she would agree to another date. Because he had no doubt that he would want to have another one with her.

As she'd requested, Tyrone waited in the lobby for the doorman to call up to her penthouse, pacing the floor and rubbing his sweaty palms on his pants leg. Once again, he second-guessed himself. Maybe the suit was too much. Maybe the suit wasn't enough. Maybe he should have kept the tie.

When she told him about going to jazz at the High Museum, he'd simply said yes without knowing exactly what the night entailed. He'd never been before. He should have done more research.

The elevator doors opened, and the hairs on the back of his neck stood up. He held his breath as he watched Ella come toward him, chatting with another resident. He barely noticed the other woman. Ella held all his attention, moving with a sexy walk that mimicked those he saw from runway models. Long legs that looked longer in a pair of black high-waisted pants and a long-sleeved blouse with a high neckline that somehow managed to make her look sexy even though he barely saw any skin. Her long hair was secured on top of her head in a loose bun, and she traveled with a black purse tucked under her arm.

Elegant and classy. Yep, he was in over his head.

She waved goodbye to her friend, who gave him a curious nod before walking around him toward the door.

"Hi." She smiled at him, bright, even teeth exposed as her red lips turned up into an open smile.

"Ready to go?" he asked.

"When you are."

* * *

THE ATRIUM of the museum was packed when they arrived, with hundreds of patrons milling around. In a room full of eye-catching women, Ella stood out as a unique gem. After purchasing tickets, they went through to the area where the musicians, a band of four, were already playing, surrounded by a host of people sitting and standing around them. Tyrone looked out at the crowd. Seemed all of the tables were taken.

A young woman wearing a white shirt and black vest came up to them. "Good evening, Miss Brooks."

"Hello, Carla. How are you this evening?"

"Good. Your table is waiting for you."

"Thank you so much. I appreciate you taking care of that for me." Ella smiled, and to the casual observer, it looked like she shook the young woman's hand. But since he was standing close by, he saw the exchange of cash.

He followed Ella toward the back, where a table marked *Reserved* sat empty with two chairs.

"I haven't been here in a long time, but the musicians are

always excellent." Ella stood beside her chair and watched Tyrone sit down.

"I hope the food is good." He frowned up at her. "Is something wrong?"

"Um...no." She continued standing, looking at him expectantly.

Then he realized the problem. "Oh, shit, I mean, I'm sorry." Tyrone jumped up from his chair and pulled hers out. He wasn't used to this kind of thing and glanced around, hoping no one noticed.

"That's all right." When she sat down, he pushed in her chair and reclaimed his. "Thank you." She smiled warmly across the table at him.

They ordered a couple of appetizers—flatbread topped with vegetables and a cheese platter accompanied by artisan bread—while their drinks consisted of a beer for him and a dirty martini for her. To encourage conversation, Tyrone moved his chair next to her so they could easily talk over the sound of the music. Closer than he needed to, but she smelled good and he liked being next to her.

"What was it like growing up with a judge and a defense attorney as parents? That must have been an interesting upbringing."

She asked a lot of questions, which was nice, as if she were interested in him as a person.

"Oh, absolutely. My mother became a judge about ten years ago, so initially I had two attorneys as parents. One who handled defense and the other a prosecutor. Everything was an inquisition in my household. From a young age, I learned to only answer the question that was asked and no more."

Ella laughed. "It couldn't have been that bad. No worse than any other parents." She sipped her martini.

"I beg to differ." Tyrone popped a piece of cheese in his mouth and slid his arm along the back of her chair. He leaned in. She smelled like a rose garden. "Here's an example. One night, when I was thirteen, my dad stopped by my room. 'You finished that homework?' he asked. I hadn't, cause I'd been hanging out with my friends all afternoon and got in the house right before he did. So I told him I'd finished my homework."

"You lied?"

"Oh, yeah. Didn't you ever lie to your parents?"

"Rarely. Especially to my mother. I always felt she could see through me. My father was easier to get around, although it might have been he was kinder while my mother is more no-nonsense."

"Well, imagine having two parents like your mother, and that was my house. So, my father lets me think he accepted my answer and leaves. A few minutes later, he's back at my door, and he's got my backpack in his hand."

"Oh no. This doesn't sound good." She covered her mouth, amusement brightening her eyes.

Her reaction encouraged him to continue the tale. "He holds up my backpack. 'Is this your backpack?' I look at it and confirm that it's mine. 'We agree that this is your backpack?' he said. My heart is beating crazy-fast right now, and I'm thinking about how I can lie my way out of this and not get punished. I had plans to hang with my boys over the weekend, and it would be just like my father to ground me so I couldn't hang out with them. 'Yes, it's my backpack,' I replied. He opened my bag and pulled out my math homework. Two sheets of math problems with no answers."

"Oh, you were a bad, bad boy," Ella said, shaking her head.

A shiver shimmied down his spine. "So my father asked, 'Is this your homework?' I admitted that it was. 'Your unfinished homework?' he asked. By now, he looks pissed, because he knows I lied to him. So I start to explain, and I said, 'Well...' 'Is this your name across the top?' he asked me. I know I'm screwed by now, but a plan starts to formulate."

"You can't possibly get out of this."

They were sitting so close, leaning into each other, that he saw the different flecks of brown in her eyes. "I stood up, and with as much authority as I could muster, I said, 'If it pleases the court, allow me to explain. I have finished my homework. I finished yesterday's homework. You didn't ask if I finished today's homework."

"He didn't accept that horrible excuse, did he?"

"He looked at me as if I'd lost my mind."

"Something I would have done also."

"And said, 'Boy, if you don't sit your...' And then he burst out laughing. At that point, I figured he wouldn't punish me."

"But he did."

"Yep. He told me that was a nice try, but the law of the house had been broken. I was fully aware of the law, and I tried to cover it up, which often resulted in worse punishment. He used his judgment, however, and allowed me to go out with my friends, but I had the pleasure of cleaning the entire yard and the attic all by myself."

"Lesson learned." She patted his leg, and the muscles in his thigh tightened.

She quickly set her hand in her lap.

"I don't mind if you touch me, you know."

"You don't?"

"Nah. You can touch me all you want."

Ella tilted her head. "Are you being a bad boy right now?"

They hadn't taken their eyes off each other since he started the tale, and he almost forgot they were in a room full of people.

"Not yet."

CHAPTER 16

A round of applause went up from the group after the saxophonist finished his solo and ended the set. As people filed out, Ella and Tyrone remained at the table, entrenched in a conversation that used to bring her unspeakable pain. But she opened up to Tyrone in a way that surprised her. He was so easy to talk to, and she sensed no judgment when she answered his questions.

There'd been few lulls in the conversation, but during those moments, they'd simply listened to music. He was good company, funny, and he smelled good, too. There was nothing like a man who smelled good.

"Why didn't you leave him if you were unhappy?" he asked.

"This sounds silly, but I wanted to believe in us and break the curse."

"The curse?"

"The Brooks women curse. We always fall for men who—" She couldn't say men outside of their social circle. "Men who aren't right for us. I wanted to believe Wayne was different, that we were different. I genuinely thought we could work and hoped I wasn't wrong, because I wanted to prove my mother wrong. Especially since my mother warned me, you see. On more than one occasion she told me not to marry him. And I guess, ultimately, I wanted him to live up to my idea of the man I thought he was, the man I'd fallen in love with."

She tried harder, became more accommodating, became more generous, but her efforts only seemed to make him despise her more. He was no longer invested in the relationship, and nothing she did would make him love her again. The man she'd met and fallen in love with had disappeared.

"So how long were you married?"

"Five years. I wish I could say they were five glorious years, but our relationship was strained almost from the beginning."

"Why is that?"

Ella thought for a moment, considering how to choose her words so she didn't sound pretentious or offensive. "It's hard to explain, but I've always had a problem meeting men who were comfortable with a woman like me. I come from money, and some men can't handle that. My mother has always advised me and my sister that we should marry men of means, unlike what she did when she married my father."

"Ouch." He frowned.

"She didn't mean any harm," Ella said hastily.

"Was that her way of saying she wasn't happy with your father?"

"My parents are back together, but they're still divorced. They took divorce to a whole new level when they split. A low level. It was definitely not amicable. My mother has the uncanny ability to remind people of their shortcomings, and when she's correct, has no problem reminding you that she told you so. Anyway, despite all that, this is the happiest I've ever seen them."

"So, when you and your husband divorced, how did she react?"

"It was an opportunity for her to point out how very correct she had been and how I should've listened to her in the first place instead of marrying someone who worked for our family's company."

"Oh. He worked for the family business," he said, as if that explained everything. He took a sip of beer.

"Yes. I don't know if you know this, but in addition to owning a beer brewing company, my family owns a chain of restaurants. There's a high-end chain called Ivy's, and then there's The Brew Pub."

"I'm familiar with both restaurants but didn't know your family owned them, too."

"We do."

"I've been to The Brew Pub. The food is delicious. Now that I think about it, the only beer served there is Full Moon beer products." He sat back. "I should have known that."

"A lot of people don't think about it or realize it. Anyway, my ex was the general manager of one of the Ivy restaurants when we married. After we tied the knot, he was promoted to regional manager."

"Nepotism has its advantages," Tyrone said.

"And its disadvantages. Apparently, he was not very competent in his new role, but staff never complained and covered for him because he was married to me. After we divorced, they no longer felt the need to do that, and they let their frustrations be known. He was fired not too long afterward for his poor work. He sued the company for firing him, calling it retaliation after our divorce. It was a big mess, all fought out in court. The company won because there was plenty of documentation of his shortcomings, and he received ample warnings before he was dismissed."

"That had to hurt."

"I'm sure it did." She clasped her hands on the table, thinking back to that period. "I tried really hard to make my marriage work. Watching my parents hurt each other and knowing how their divorce affected me and my siblings, I did whatever I could to make him happy and make sure that my marriage lasted." She tried too hard, in retrospect. Her concerns about his fragile male ego caused her to shut down and avoid conflict as much as possible.

"How is your relationship with your ex now?"

"Not great. Partly because he can't find another job as prestigious as regional manager, and he seems to think my family has badmouthed him and prevented him from finding a job he's worthy of. The other day he told me he's "settled" for an assistant manager position at a local restaurant after leaving the diner he worked for, all of which he thinks is beneath him. I actually think he's much better suited to that role. He became complacent when he worked for the family business because he knew the chances of getting fired were almost nonexistence while we were married."

"If you don't mind my asking, what caused you to get a divorce?"

"He cheated on me. He used to tell me he was working late or couldn't make an event because of work." Her mouth twisted into a pained smile.

"I'm sorry to hear that." Tyrone let out a harsh breath. "I understand your pain."

"Don't tell me you're the victim of cheating, as well?"

He nodded. "My wife and my best friend."

"Oh no! I'm so sorry. That must have been devastating. As painful as it was having my husband cheat on me, I didn't lose a friend in addition to losing a husband. That type of double betrayal...well, I'm sorry you had to go through that."

All of a sudden, their connection felt deeper because they'd been through the same hurtful experience. She wondered if he felt the same helplessness, the same doubt as she did, wondering what she could have done differently. Was she partly to blame for the demise of her relationship? No matter how many times she answered no, doubts slipped through the cracks with the pain.

"I'm sorry I had to go through that, too." Tyrone laughed sourly. "I've known this guy since we were kids, so pretty much all my life. I don't know why, but eventually their relationship ended and my friend tried to reestablish our friendship."

"Wow. That's, pardon my expression, ballsy."

Tyrone chuckled. "I never expected that word to come from those lips."

She smiled. "You'd be surprised what all these lips can do."

"Oh yeah?"

She blushed then. "I'm being too forward."

"Not at all. I like it."

Her smile broadened.

"You said you have photos of your daughters on their last trip?"

"Oh yes. They went fishing and were so proud of themselves." She removed the phone from her purse and with a few swipes handed it over to him. "You can keep swiping. That entire folder is filled with pictures of my girls."

There were pictures of the girls, but also pictures of her and the girls on vacation, similar to the ones she'd been placing into the photo album when he turned up at her apartment weeks ago. He paused at a photo of her holding Hannah on her hip on the beach. She wore a pair of dark sunglasses and a sheer beach wrap around her waist, hardly covering up her curvaceous figure in the red halter-topped bikini.

"This is a nice shot."

"Oh, I forgot that was in there."

"I'm glad you did." He continued flipping through the photos. He finished and handed back the cell phone and removed his. "Okay, here you go. You can't swipe too far right. I'm not as orga-nized as you."

"Don't worry, I'll only look at a few."

She flipped through the pictures and stopped at one, turning the screen toward him. "Parents?"

"Yeah. That's Pops and my mom."

"You weren't kidding. They do dress alike." In the photo, they both wore khaki pants and denim shirts.

"Not all the time, but a lot."

She flipped through some more photos and stopped at one. "Where was this taken?"

Tyrone looked closely. "I hung lights out on the little, and I mean *little*, balcony outside my apartment. It's tiny, but there's a really nice view of the city from up there. Sometimes I just sit out there with a cup of hella good coffee and relax."

"And where do you get this hella good coffee?"

"I make it, of course. It's my world-famous coffee."

"Oh, of course." She handed back the phone. "I'm almost done with my drink. Do you have any interest in seeing the exhibits?"

"As long as I'm with you, I'd love to."

"You're turning into quite the sweet talker."

"You ain't seen nothing yet." He grinned, and the flash of teeth and unguarded interest took her breath away.

They went to one of the upper floors and spent the next hour viewing the European art collection, which included terra cotta sculptures, as well as Baroque and Impressionist paintings. By the time they finished, only a small fraction of visitors remained.

They went outside to the valet stand, where Tyrone handed over his ticket.

"Do you have big plans for the rest of the weekend?" Ella asked, as they waited.

"No. Do you?"

"No major plans. The children are with my parents, and tomorrow they're taking them to Miami to spend time on my father's boat. I have the morning and Sunday free to do whatever I want."

"I'm pretty free myself."

"It seems we're both free," Ella said. She couldn't look at him right then. Her face heated at the direction her thoughts had taken.

Tyrone looked at her. "So it seems."

Heart racing, she asked, "Do you live far from here?"

"Not too far. About ten minutes. Why?"

She swallowed. "I could use a cup of that really delicious coffee you make." She ventured a look at him.

"Oh yeah?" A slow smile came across his lips.

"Mhmm. And I was thinking...I wouldn't mind seeing the view you bragged about," she said quietly.

His gaze dropped to her mouth. "Coffee with a view coming up."

CHAPTER 17

*W*aiting on the elevator only heightened the tension between them. "This thing only works half the time," Tyrone said irritably. He jabbed the button, although it was already lit.

"We can take the stairs," Ella offered.

"No." He shook his head and pounded the button with his fist.

Finally, after several tense minutes, the elevator showed up and they entered the cabin. The ride up to his apartment was made in silence. During the short trip, Ella second-guessed herself a number of times. Perhaps she was moving too fast. Would he think she was easy? Would he respect her in the morning? So many thoughts ran through her mind that by the time they entered his apartment, her hands were clammy and she was on the verge of running back out the door.

"I'm a little embarrassed at the condition of this place. I should've cleaned up before I let you come up here." Tyrone opened the door and allowed her to precede him into the apartment.

Contrary to what he said, the place was not a mess, unless he counted the magazines tossed onto the coffee table, instead of being neatly arranged, as needing to be 'cleaned up.'

There wasn't much furniture. A small dinette set split the open floor plan in two. To the right led to the kitchen, and the left opened to a living room where two couches faced off across the coffee table.

The side table next to one of the chairs displayed a few photographs. A quick glance and she saw one was a group shot of him and his family. The second photo was of him and a little Asian girl. He had a hand on her shoulder, and she was wearing a bathing suit and wore a gold medal around her neck.

"That's my goddaughter. She's a champion swimmer," he said proudly.

Above one of the sofas was a framed Atlanta Falcons 2016 Conference Champions collage signed by a number of the players, pennants, and an Atlanta Falcons flag inscribed with the words "Man Cave."

Ella arched a brow at Tyrone. "Let me guess. You like the Falcons?"

"A little bit."

"All those times we talked and I didn't know how much of a fan you were?"

His husky laugh spread warmth low in her belly, like fingers sliding across her skin. "Blame my father. I got it from him. We can both get a little extreme, and I didn't want to scare you off." Little did he know, he couldn't scare her off. As a matter of fact, fanaticism was rather endearing.

"Have a seat."

"Thank you." Ella settled onto the worn, brown leather couch.

Tyrone went to the kitchen, which she could easily see from her position in the living room. He opened and closed the doors of a few cabinets. "You're not going to believe this, but I'm out of coffee. Can I get you something else to drink?"

She hadn't really wanted coffee but was so nervous, her throat had become parched. She couldn't figure out why she was so nervous with him. It's not as if she hadn't slept with anyone since her divorce.

"Do you have juice?"

"Orange juice in the fridge. Cranberry juice cocktail in the cabinets. I could drop a few cubes of ice in to chill it."

"Cranberry juice sounds perfect."

In short order, Tyrone brought out two glasses. He kept the one filled with orange juice and handed her the other filled with ice and cranberry juice. "I didn't deliver on the coffee, but I can deliver on the view. Right this way."

He seemed so at ease that Ella relaxed a little. She followed him out the sliding glass door to the balcony. The entire city lay before them, twinkling lights with the familiar building of Bank of America Plaza in the distance.

"This really is a lovely view," she commented.

"You can see the whole city from here." Tyrone took a sip of the juice and then rested his forearms on the metal railing. "The neighborhood might be a dump, the apartment might be a dump, but this view is everything."

Ella watched him from the corner of her eye. "It's not a dump. It's actually quite...quaint."

"Quaint, huh?"

"Yes." She sipped her cranberry juice and avoided his eyes.

Tyrone chuckled softly. "Normally you're direct, but you were being polite just then. You're used to nicer places than this."

"I can adapt. I'm not a snob or difficult to please."

"I didn't think you were."

They fell silent for a little bit.

"I have a confession to make," he said.

Oh boy. Ella's stomach tightened.

"I haven't had a real date in a long time."

She laughed, a combination of relief and understanding. "Me either," she admitted quietly.

"So what does that mean?" Tyrone asked.

"Nothing, really. Just two people who haven't dated in a while figuring things out together."

Tyrone stepped behind her, and she held her breath. He didn't touch her.

"I may be rusty on the dating scene, but there's one thing I'm not rusty on." He spoke into her left ear.

"Oh really? Had lots of practice, have you?"

"Some practice," he amended, laughter in his voice.

Tyrone dropped a cool, moist kiss on the side of her neck. "Nervous?"

She laughed shakily. "A little."

"Believe me, I understand. I can't tell you how many outfits I changed into before meeting you tonight."

His admission made her laugh out loud. "And there I was, thinking you were this confident, assured man."

"Oh, I'm confident and assured. Just not as much when I'm with you."

"So I make you feel…what, exactly?"

He turned her around so they faced each other and placed her glass on the table next to his. He looked deeply into her eyes. "I feel not so confident. Not so assured."

He lowered his head, and her heart raced when his lips brushed hers. "You taste like cranberry juice," he whispered.

"You taste like orange juice," she whispered back.

He kissed her again, this time with more passion. Cupping the back of her head, he pressed his mouth harder against hers, and she leaned into him, slipping her hands onto his shoulders. She angled her head to the right and tasted fully of his lips.

Goodness, he was a great kisser. Just the right amount of pressure. When he slipped his tongue between her teeth, she moaned. The invasion made her toes tingle, and she locked her arms around his neck.

The kiss ended when Tyrone released her mouth and looked down at her from eyes that were dark with passion. "Are you sure? You ready?" He breathed hard as he tugged her blouse from her pants.

"Yes, I'm positive." Ella stood on tiptoe and pressed her mouth to his again, anxious to get more of his taste and the pleasure of his kiss.

Tyrone groaned and splayed his hand across the bare skin of her back.

"I don't want you to think I'm easy. You know, the kind of man who puts out on the first date with every woman he meets." He nipped her bottom lip.

Ella smiled against his mouth. "I promise I won't judge you."

Tyrone cradled her jaw in his hands and gazed down into her eyes. "I feel like I'm the luckiest man in the world tonight."

Before she could respond, he kissed her again. Slowly but surely, desire spiraled up through her body. This time the kiss was soft and sweet. He guided the direction of it without making her feel any pressure at all. In fact, she suspected that he was holding back, so she pressed a little closer to let him know that she was all-in and wanted this as much as he did.

Her normal reservations simply dissolved with him, and besides, hadn't he seen her at her weakest point? Crying, vulnerable, and listened to her on the phone while he whispered encouraging words to make her feel better and help her feel less victimized. His words had given her strength, and right now his kisses made her feel more desired than she had in a while. There didn't seem to be any agenda with Tyrone.

Her arms slipped back around his neck. She kissed him thoroughly and hard, and he met her enthusiasm with a chest-deep groan.

His mouth lowered to her neck, and his hands fixed to her waist. Moving backwards slowly, he guided them inside the apartment. From what seemed like a faraway place, she heard the sliding glass door close, as he continued to drop tender kisses to her neck. He couldn't get very far, though, because of the high neckline of the shirt, and she cursed herself for wearing this outfit, one that she thought looked classy at the beginning of the night, but now proved to be a hindrance as they moved toward more intimacy.

He lifted his head. "It's much more comfortable in the bedroom."

"Then take me to the bedroom."

CHAPTER 18

$\mathcal{E}$lla could barely contain her excitement. Arousal licked between her thighs and swept heat over her skin. She unbuttoned her blouse and tossed it on the floor while Tyrone kissed her neck and the crests of her breasts. Multi-tasking, he lowered the zipper on the side of her pants, and with a gentle wiggle, they fell around her ankles. She kicked off her shoes and stood before him in her brassiere and panties.

"You're so beautiful," he whispered, his dark eyes growing darker, the pupils dilating as his gaze swept her body.

Tyrone stepped behind her and unclasped her bra. It landed in a pile with the other clothes at her feet, and he cupped both of her breasts from behind, holding the weight of them and squeezing them together. They became painfully erect, and the little tips pushed against the palms of his hands. Arching her back she moaned, angling her head to the left and letting him kiss her, harder this time. She sighed into his mouth, sucking on his lips and snaking her tongue in a sexy duel with his.

He hooked his thumbs on either side of her thong and dragged it down her thighs. The movement frayed her nerves and sent a tiny tremor bolting through her body. She'd never been this sensitive to a man's touch before. Every movement he made sent her into a frenzy of anticipation.

She stepped out of the underwear and he stayed low, running his hands up her calves to her thighs and squeezing her bottom. She bit her lower lip as he kneaded the flesh and groaned in his throat. Struggling to stay upright, she gasped when she felt his tongue. He licked his way from the curve of her left butt cheek up the middle of her back to her shoulder blades.

Ella turned to face him and pulled his shirt over his head. When his chest was revealed, she stopped for a moment to stare at him. Goodness, he was beautiful, golden skin sprinkled with dark hair and covering tight muscle that made her ache all over. The tips of her fingers ran through the soft hair at his nape and smoothed down his throat and over his chest. She let her fingers flick his hard nipples, and he grunted but didn't move, looking down at her as he allowed the exploration. Her fingers trailed over his pecs and the colorful tattoo of a coiled cobra on his biceps. He had an incredible body, very firm but soft.

He slipped his arms around her waist and pulled her in close, kissing her with passion and hunger, as if he hadn't already kissed her plenty already. His hands slipped down to her bottom and molded over her curves, tracing the line of her hips and back up her ribcage.

Ella reached for his belt, and he let her undo his pants, watching as she unzipped him, her fingers trembling slightly. When she was done, they both pushed, and his pants dropped, the boxer briefs with them. Her eyes widened, and she gasped when she saw his erection, urgent and solid, standing up between them.

He chuckled. "Thank you." He licked her mouth and she licked his back.

Fully naked, they fell onto the cotton sheets of the bed in an ungainly heap of arms and legs. While she lay on top of him, his hands smoothed down her back and the curve of her spine, down to her bottom where they came to rest and squeezed.

"I love your ass," he said, as if she couldn't tell.

Already wet, Ella rubbed her naked core against his hard shaft and listened to him groan.

"You shouldn't play like that." His voice had a rough edge to it.

He rolled her onto her back, fastening his lips over one breast. The nipple tightened in his warm mouth, and her lips fell apart on a silent cry as she angled her body higher into his. While he sucked her breasts, he stroked his hands down the middle of her chest, caressing her hips and pelvis, and finally finding the wet spot between her legs.

She gasped when he touched her, and her mind spun out of control as she burned with greater need. He kissed his way lower, covering every inch of flesh as if determined to know all parts of her. Wherever he touched, it singed her skin and made her body tingle. She couldn't recall the last time she'd felt this aroused.

Panting, trembling, Ella opened her legs as he went lower still and kissed his way past her abdomen to the strip of hair at the juncture of her thighs. The soft abrasion of his beard rubbed her inner thigh when he kissed her *there*, lightly teasing.

"Tyrone," she murmured, shutting out the ceiling by closing her eyes so she could focus on what he was about to do next.

He caressed the distended nub of nerves with his tongue, and she almost came right then. His mouth and lips imparted such exquisite pleasure that when he fastened his whole mouth on her slick flesh, she nearly catapulted off the bed, grasping the sheets and moaning aloud as he went to work on the most sensitive part of her body. He made love to her lower lips like a man who enjoyed putting in the work, sliding his tongue across her wet sex, while his hands squeezed her breasts.

Her legs moved restlessly, her toes curled, and she whispered his name in a frantic plea for reprieve. But he gave her none. He continued until spasms rocked her body, making her breasts shake and her entire body tighten under the force of the orgasm.

When he was done and she finally caught her breath, he came back to her breasts and squeezed them together. He sucked each one in turn, kissing and licking while she squirmed beneath him.

He was incredible. She wanted more. She wanted to give him more, some of the pleasure that he was giving to her.

Pushing Tyrone onto his back, Ella gave him a long, sultry kiss and then dropped kisses along his cheek and down his strong throat. She rolled her tongue around a nipple and listened to the harsh intake of breath and the guttural sound that emanated from his lips, as if he wanted her to stop, but she knew he didn't.

She eased her hand down his abdomen and clasped his erection. His body jerked. He was hot and hard, and she stroked gently, listening to the rumble emerge in his chest. He bit down on his bottom lip as she continued to touch him. Then she kissed her way down his body and offered the same attentiveness he did to hers. Her lips drifted through the soft hair that trailed below his abdomen. Her teeth grated along his inner thighs, teasing him before she gave what she knew he wanted.

She closed her mouth over the tip of his shaft and then took him all the way into her mouth, as deep as he could go. The tip bumped the back of her throat, and she hummed, watching as his body tightened under the grip of her mouth. A hand on the back of her head guided her movements as she continued to suck and lick him with enthusiasm.

"Fuck." He grabbed her by the hair and groaned, his face contorted into a grimace. When he could take no more, he stopped her movements and groaned. "Ella," he said hoarsely. "I want to be inside you."

Tyrone reached over to the table beside the bed and pulled out a condom. He quickly covered himself in protection and positioned between her legs. She lay back, legs spread as his hands lifted her hips. The first thrust that breeched her entrance left her gasping. He shifted to hold her arms above her head and drove into her with hard, measured thrusts. Ella crossed her ankles over his taut buttocks and rocked right along with him.

He nipped the underside of her chin and the sensitive skin at the side of her neck. "You want all this dick, don't you?" His husky voice painted warmth in her loins.

"Yes," Ella whispered, almost in tears because he felt so good. She breathed at an irregular pace as he pistoned into her, and she welcomed his invasion, straining upward to take more of him.

"That's it, sweetheart. Take all of it." Tyrone spoke through clenched teeth, plunging deeper.

Her cries became louder as his fingers tightened around her wrists and every stroke brought her closer to climax. She arched against him, taking each concentrated thrust, her heart about to jackhammer a hole in her chest. Her head thrashed against the mattress as he controlled her every movement, going slow one minute, then speeding up the next.

For her, this was not only a meeting of the bodies. It was a meeting of the minds and their inner beings. Noises of pleasure filled the room as they both strived toward ecstasy. Faster and faster. His lips covered hers, and his tongue forced its way past her teeth, resulting in a coordinated plundering of her mouth and body at the same time.

The orgasm built inside her, not like a rippling wave, but like a tsunami. It took hold suddenly, and she started to shake.

"Harder," she begged. Her voice was a trembling fragment of itself.

She spiraled into the heavens, drowning, drowning in sensation. From what seemed like far away, she heard a sound, a keening cry of satisfaction as the climax swallowed her whole.

Seconds later, his body arched violently, and with a deep-seated grunt, Tyrone collapsed beside her, spent.

CHAPTER 19

*T*yrone awoke the next morning, wound around Ella's back. For the longest, he'd told himself he needed to get curtains for the windows, but at the moment he was happy he hadn't. The light coming in from the outdoors illuminated the room and gave him an excellent view of her body.

She'd slipped back on her underwear, and he'd put on a pair of boxers to sleep in. His face was buried in her thick hair, which had come undone at some point during the night and lay between them like a pile of shiny black silk.

He took a breath. Her hair smelled crisp and clean, like lemon and sage. He imagined waking up like this every morning, with her as the first sight when he opened his eyes, wrapped around her—

Whoa. His mind skidded to a halt before leaping off a cliff of crazy thoughts.

He eased his arm, a little numb from where she lay on top of it, from under her. He liked Ella, a lot. But in all honesty, he hadn't considered a future with another woman since his divorce. Work was a priority, and marriage had left a bitter taste in his mouth after his wife's betrayal.

Carefully, Tyrone smoothed his fingertips down the soft, deep brown skin of her back, but he wasn't as careful as he thought, because she woke up. She stretched and looked back at him, squinting against the light. "What time is it?"

"Early. A little after eight," he replied.

She brushed hair out of her face, not the least bit self-conscious of the sheet that hung around her waist and exposed her breasts and dark nipples. Looking at her now, all he could do was remember how incredible she looked riding him the second time they made love, those same breasts jostling right before he grabbed them in his hands and plucked them one at a time into his mouth. His body still hummed from the memory of her hands and mouth on his skin. There was nothing reserved about Ella in the midst of lovemaking.

"I should get up," she said.

To be honest, she looked rather tired, as if she could sleep for a couple more hours.

Tyrone got up. "Why don't you stay in bed. I'm going for my morning run, and on the way back, I'll pick up breakfast for us."

"Are you sure?"

"Relax and go back to sleep. I'll be back in an hour and a half or so."

She plopped back down onto the bed and pulled the sheet beneath her armpits. "Well, if you insist." She giggled. "I always take advantage of the times I have alone. The girls sometimes come into my room early, before the nanny gets to the apartment. I'm going to take you up on this offer to sleep a little late."

Tyrone tugged on a pair of jogging pants and a sweatshirt, pulled on his tennis shoes, and then walked over to the bed. He trailed his fingertips through her hair, a wave of tenderness coming over him. The last time he'd had a woman spend the night had been months ago. He hadn't really wanted her to stay the night, but he would have been less than a gentleman if he asked her to leave right after they had sex.

With Ella, though, he wanted her to stay—the night, the morning. He would spend the whole day with her if she let him. Maybe he could convince her to spend the day in his company. He'd work on that when he got back.

"Don't go anywhere."

She smiled softly. "I won't. I promise."

He dropped a kiss to her nose and left the house. Instead of taking the elevator, he ran down the stairs and along the route he took on his usual morning run.

He jogged five miles round trip. The distance included running by the park and past buildings in different stages of rejuvenation as developers moved in and took advantage of the low prices to build new residential and commercial space. Pretty soon, he wouldn't know the place and probably wouldn't be able to afford living in the neighborhood. For now, it was all familiar territory. He knew the landscape and the people, and they knew him.

On the way back, he stopped at two places. The first was a local grocer to restock on coffee. The second was Jim's Diner, only blocks from his house.

When he first moved in a little over a year ago, after his divorce, he hadn't been used to making his own meals and cooking for himself. Having Jim's nearby where he could run in and get a cheap but filling meal had been a godsend. The place was owned by Thanh Ha, originally from Vietnam, and her husband, Jim.

Jim had fought in the Vietnam War and suffered from insomnia. According to Thanh, he would get up late at night and start cooking to keep himself occupied. Eventually, she realized that he needed an outlet, and that's when she suggested they open the diner. All they served was breakfast, from ten at night until ten in the morning. The place became a hit with folks leaving the clubs late at night or simply driving around looking for cheap but delicious food that was filling.

"Hey, Thanh," he called as he entered the small diner. He nodded at some of the familiar faces and waved at Jim through the window that opened into the kitchen. His head was topped by hair gone completely white.

"Hi, Tyrone. What are you having today?" Thanh asked, shoving her glasses higher on her nose. Waitresses handled the dine-in guests, and she took care of the take-out orders.

"Let me have a number one and number two," Tyrone said. He fished cash out of his pocket.

Thanh's eyebrows raised in surprise. "That's a lot of food for you. More than normal."

No point in pretending. Thanh was very perceptive. "I have a guest."

She smiled knowingly. "Ohhh. Good for you. You're a good man, and you need a good woman." She totaled the meals on the register.

"Who said anything about it being a woman?"

"So you prefer men?" Thanh asked. She gave him the total.

Tyrone laughed and handed her a few bills. "No, ma'am. I prefer the ladies. Always have and always will. So yes, my guest is a woman."

"I'll tell Jim to throw in some extra ham and bacon for you," Thanh said with a wink.

"Thanks, I appreciate it."

Ten minutes later, he was on his way with the food. When he entered the small apartment, he set the coffee and styrofoam containers on the kitchen table and found Ella in the bedroom, making the bed. She wore his black shirt from last night and looked better than he ever could in it. With her pretty chocolate skin and the color of the shirt combined, she looked like a dark angel. She'd combed her hair, and the long strands fell forward across her face as she worked, swishing and reflecting the sunlight that came in through the windows.

He leaned a shoulder against the doorjamb. "You don't have to do that. Half the time I leave the house without making the bed."

"I thought I'd be polite since I was the last to get up." She fluffed a pillow and set it against the headboard. "There. All done." Using her fingers, she pushed her thick hair out of her face.

Damn, she was beautiful, standing there, long legs on display, her face freshly washed and make-up-free.

"I brought breakfast. You hungry?"

"Starving."

He extended his hand, and she walked over and took it. He tugged her closer, unable to help himself. He needed to kiss her. Her lips were soft and malleable beneath his. He tightened his arm around her waist so that she was flush against his body. She slipped a bare leg between his, and his loins stirred.

"I better behave, or we'll be messing up that bed you just made."

Ella smiled, tilting her head back to look up at him. "That would be terrible, because I worked so hard on that. You have no idea. And besides, I told you I was starving, and you promised me food."

"True. I would be a terrible host if I didn't feed my hungry guest."

"Absolutely terrible. The worst."

He dipped his head and kissed her again, this time taking a gentle nip of her lower lip. "Stop tempting me." He let her go.

"I was *not* tempting you." She swatted his hip and scurried out the door.

Tyrone followed more slowly and pulled out a chair at the table. "Madam," he said with a flourish.

She giggled and took a seat. "Thank you."

"Now it's time for my famous coffee and a meal from Jim's Diner."

"Ooh, Jim's Diner. I can't wait."

"Trust me, the food is delicious."

Coffee was made, and Tyrone pulled down plates and produced silverware. They set the table and divvied up the pancakes, hash browns, ham, bacon, grits, and scrambled eggs.

"There's enough food here to feed an army," Ella said, eyes wide.

Despite her comment, she dug into the meal, moaning softly and giving the thumbs up. "You were right," she said, halfway through the meal. "This is so good. And so is the coffee. I'm glad I finally got a chance to taste it."

Tyrone rested his arm on the table and leaned forward. "You can come get coffee anytime you like."

She cradled a white mug in her hand, looking at him over the rim. "Don't be surprised if I take you up on that offer."

"I hope you do." The words were heavy in the air, and his chest became weighted down by the thought of more mornings like this, gazing across at Ella and having the opportunity to kiss and touch her at will. He dug into his scrambled eggs.

They finished the meal, eating every bite except for vestiges of hash browns left on Ella's plate.

"How about you spend the day with me?" Tyrone said. He'd been thinking about asking for the past few minutes as they chatted.

"I can't. I'm meeting my sister in a couple of hours for a spa day."

"Too bad. I thought you had the rest of the day off and we could...you know, hang out together."

"I only have the morning off," she reminded him. "Can I get a rain check?"

"Sure," he replied, hiding his disappointment.

They cleared the table and placed the dishes in the sink. He fully intended to let her go so she could get ready, but having her stand so close to him again, smelling sweet and wearing his clothes, sent a charge through him.

His arm slipped around her, and he pulled her close. "One more time before you leave," he said in her ear.

She didn't resist and didn't say no. She melted into him, and his mouth covered hers as he walked her backward into the bedroom. Turns out they did mess up the bed again. Her cries in the morning were as spine-tingling as her cries at night. Thrusting hard, Tyrone filled his memory for later—with the faint aroma of her flower-scented skin, the sensation of her soft thighs as he gripped them, and her delectable flavor as he licked her neck and sucked on the dark nipples that capped her full breasts. When they were done, he collapsed beside her, exhausted and satisfied.

Ella went into the bathroom to dress, and he went back out to the kitchen and drank a second cup of coffee, debating whether or not he should ask her out again. He certainly wanted to see her again, but the problem was, he didn't want to give the impression that he was looking for anything too serious. Because he wasn't. At this point in his life, he preferred to keep things casual. At least for a little while longer.

She emerged from the bedroom, her hair pulled back into a neat bun and wearing the clothes from the night before. The sensual, sexy woman had been tucked away beneath a high-collared shirt and long, black pants.

"Gimme a sec, let me grab my keys."

"You don't have to drop me off. I called my driver while I was in the bedroom. He should be here shortly."

"Oh."

She looked in her purse, but he had the distinct impression that she didn't really need anything in there. She was doing that to avoid conversation.

Any thought he had of following up died with her reaction. Even though he didn't expect a full-blown relationship, her reaction landed like a punch in the abs. He'd hoped to see her again. He'd hoped to slide between those legs again. Hell, he was still semi-erect from thinking about the sex they'd just had, and disappointment burned a hole in his chest.

Her phone beeped, and she looked at the screen. "That's him now." She tucked the purse under her arm. "I guess, I'll...call you."

"Do that."

She walked toward the door, and he followed her. Before stepping out, she turned and kissed him on the cheek, spreading warmth over his jaw. "Thank you for a lovely evening. And breakfast. And truly delicious coffee. I see why it's world-famous."

"My pleasure. Everything was my pleasure," he said huskily.

She smiled and then disappeared down the hall.

Tyrone watched until she turned the corner and then went back inside. He sauntered into the kitchen, picked up his coffee and took a sip. For the longest time after she left, he didn't move. He leaned against the counter, staring at the space where she'd sat at the table, hating the empty feeling of not knowing if he'd ever see her again.

CHAPTER 20

*E*lla had a few girlfriends, but her very best friend was her sister, Simone. With only one year between them, they had always been close. One of the activities they liked doing together was going to the spa, a tradition that started with their mother. When they were younger, she took them with her for a girls' day out. Sylvie no longer accompanied them, but Ella and Simone continued the tradition whenever they could, bonding over the latest news in each other's lives during hours of pampering. She planned to do the same with her daughters when they got a little older.

They bought the Signature Package today, which included four hours of massages, body therapy, facials, manicures and pedicures, and a pre-dinner snack. Upon arrival, they went their separate ways when Ella chose the seaweed mud wrap and body polish, and Simone opted for the herbal wrap and body polish.

Afterward, they both sat in a back room in white robes and slippers, hair pinned up and waiting for their masseuses. Simone flipped through a magazine while Ella sipped cucumber water, reminiscing about her night with Tyrone.

"Are you still going to therapy?" Simone asked.

132

Ella nodded. "The therapist says I'm doing a lot better, and I feel better. She thinks I'll be able to cope on my own in a couple of weeks." The twice-weekly sessions had helped her face her fears and see beyond the trauma of that night. Slowly, she was getting back to normal.

"You're going to make me ask, aren't you?" Simone said.

"About what?"

"About your date. How was it?" Her eyebrows shot higher in her round face, so much like their father's.

"The date went better than I anticipated." Heat spread over her skin.

"Are you ready to tell me who this man is now? You were so secretive about his identity, I was starting to think he didn't actually exist."

"He exists." Ella narrowed her eyes, which made her sister laugh.

"Happy to hear he's not imaginary. Now give me the details."

"His name is Tyrone, and he's the detective who was in charge of investigating the break-in at my place."

Simone's eyes widened. "Detective Evers?"

Ella nodded.

"When did this happen?"

"He asked me out, and after some thought, I said yes. We went out last night, like I told you."

"Why are you only now telling me your date was Detective Evers? I assumed he was someone Mother had introduced you to, or...oh, I know why."

"Why?"

Sympathy filled her sister's eyes. "Because you're worried about the curse. Because he's not wealthy, or from a prominent family, or a combination of the two."

Ella set the glass of cool water on the table in front of them. "I'm not embarrassed by him, if that's what you mean."

"I know you're not embarrassed by him, but you probably

didn't mention him just in case the date bombed. Because you thought it might."

Her sister knew her so well. Despite the late-night conversations with Tyrone, she'd held doubts about their compatibility. "You're right, but I'm also not in any rush to start a serious relationship, and I wanted to be sure, comfortable with him first before telling anyone. It's been a long time since I've gone on a date."

"You think you'll see him again?"

"I think so." She hoped so. She'd left his apartment a bit uncertain of his expectations and how to proceed.

"That sounds promising. So the night went well?"

"Very, *very* well." Ella ran a hand down the side of her neck at the memory of his guttural voice in her ear, and her private parts tingled.

Simone tossed the magazine on the table and crossed her legs in the direction of her sister. "Do tell. Did you have sex with him?"

"Simone, you are so—"

"Don't play coy with me. Did you, or did you not?"

Her cheeks burned, but she couldn't stop grinning. "Yes. But it wasn't planned," she added hastily when Simone squealed. "It just happened, and I was just having fun." Friendship, fun, all of which she'd been missing.

"And you should keep having fun." Simone rested her chin on her fist. "So, are you going to give me any details, or do I have to pry them out of you? On second thought, I can guess how *very* well the night went."

Ella blushed. She dropped her voice and leaned closer. "The sex was good. Really, really good. The same as with...do you remember Rupert?"

"Of course. He had you strung out."

"He did, didn't he?"

Rupert St. Clair was kind and proper, which hid the fact that he was a blonde-haired, blue-eyed beast in bed. One would never expect it from a buttoned-up suit who spoke in such formal tones he had a faux British accent, but the sex with him had been incredible. Even after they broke up, she couldn't say no to him. A few years ago, she saw in the society pages that he'd married a black woman from a prominent Louisiana family. With her marriage on the rocks at the time, Ella couldn't deny being a bit envious of his lucky, lucky wife. While she'd been going through the motions of sex like a debtor paying her dues, that woman had assuredly been screaming down the walls like a lottery winner.

"Being with Tyrone was like being with Rupert, but more intense." More carnal and raw.

"You have feelings for him. Strong feelings." Simone said the words as a statement of fact, not a question.

Ella hadn't wanted to examine what she felt too much, but she couldn't deny her sister was right. "I do."

"And that's probably why you enjoyed yourself so much. I strongly believe sex is better when emotion and feelings are involved."

"You might be right, but I don't want to get ahead of myself. Tyrone and I are getting to know each other, and I want to enjoy him for now. I'm not even sure what happens next."

"My advice is to let the relationship evolve naturally."

Ella nodded her agreement. "It's been so long since I've felt this kind of excitement."

"Feels good, doesn't it?"

"Yes. Like being stoned or drunk." She laughed at the analogy, but it was true. If she bottled the feelings Tyrone evoked, she could make a fortune getting people high.

"And isn't that the best feeling?" Her sister had fallen in love and married in the past year and transformed into a new woman. She consistently wore a smile as bright as the diamond on her finger.

For a long time, Ella thought she didn't need to be with a man or in a relationship. She had friends, family, and two little girls who were her world. Yet the fuzzy heat caused by Tyrone, the tingles, the heady anticipation for his call or touch, couldn't be ignored.

"Yes," Ella admitted. "It's the best feeling."

* * *

MONDAY MORNING, seated at her desk, Ella could barely concentrate on the words coming out of the workman's mouth, an older gentleman talking to her about the changes she wanted to make to her office.

Not once had she stopped thinking about Tyrone and the night in his arms. The human contact. The touching. The licking. The sucking.

She half-listened as the workman talked about the type of paint he'd use and how long the job would take. She doodled on a piece of paper, moisture seeping into her panties when she recalled how Saturday morning, Tyrone had taken her with the same passion as the night before, as if eating breakfast had given him a burst of energy. There'd been the same intensity in his voice when he demanded to know if she liked it. He hadn't even removed the shirt from her body. He simply undid a few buttons so he could suck her nipples and then lifted up the tail of the shirt and entered her with such a powerful thrust it took her breath away.

She relived that moment over and over. The way he'd gripped her thighs and wouldn't let up, not even to achieve his own orgasm, until she'd come again. With Wayne, she may or may not come, and her last lover had been careful and treated her like a delicate flower. When she'd hinted at wanting rougher sex, he'd looked at her askance, as if there was something wrong with her. But Tyrone held no such inhibitions. He made love, but he also fucked. Aggressively, the way she wished her last lover would have. He fucked hard, demanding, forceful, and made sure she knew who was in charge in that bed.

It was *so damn thrilling!*

Ella laughed out loud, and the workman paused and looked over at her. His brow wrinkled. "Did...did I say something wrong?"

Ella's cheeks flushed hot. "No, no, Vince. Please continue. My mind wandered for a minute. What did you say?'

Vince resumed talking, and Ella paid closer attention this time, interjecting questions and comments where appropriate. By the time he left, she was itching to call Tyrone. But she hesitated. Should she wait for him to call? What were the rules nowadays? Were there any rules?

One hand on her hip, she gnawed her bottom lip as she paced the floor, trying to work up the courage to move forward. She gave herself a pep talk. "Nothing wrong with calling him first. Women do that all the time. He'll probably be flattered."

Ella picked up her cell phone and dialed Tyrone's number. While it rang, she looped one arm across her waist and rested her bottom on the edge of the desk.

"Hello?" His warm voice came through the line, and she realized she'd called him without a plan and without having thought through what she would say when he answered. She'd simply wanted to hear his voice.

"Hi, Tyrone."

"Hello, Ella."

His voice lowered, and heat blanketed her skin. She bit into her lip, mind racing to find a reason for the call, because this man had scrambled her brain with a simple greeting.

"I didn't happen to leave my…comb over there, did I?"

There was a slight pause. "No, you didn't. I haven't seen it since you left, anyway."

"Oh, good. I was wondering."

"I'm glad I could put your mind at ease. You must have left it somewhere else."

"I can't imagine where. Maybe it fell out of my purse in the car." She grimaced. She sounded like a fool.

"Maybe."

Silence.

Ella tapped her foot on the floor. "Um, you know, since I have you on the phone, are you busy this weekend? I thought if you weren't busy, and I'm not busy, either. If you wanted to go out again, I thought…" Oh goodness, she sounded foolish. So out of practice.

"Are you asking me out?" Tyrone's voice sounded amused, and she became even more embarrassed.

"Yes, I guess I am." She dropped her forehead into her palm.

"Hmmm, this is new. I kinda like it."

Her head popped up, and she exhaled. She waited.

"So, what did you have in mind?" Tyrone asked.

She didn't have anything in mind. She just wanted to see him. "Since we did what I wanted to do last time, we could do something you like this week."

"Okay." He was silent for a moment. "You like Jamaican food?"

"I haven't had it in a while, but I do."

"There's a really nice place near downtown. Food's terrific, and there's a lounge upstairs where we can sit and listen to music or dance afterward. Sound good to you?"

"Sounds excellent."

"How about Friday night?"

"Okay."

"What time are you picking me up?"

She grinned. "Oh, I'm picking you up this time?"

"Well, you did ask me out."

She imagined him wearing a grin as large as hers on his sexy lips, and his eyes filled with amusement. "You modern men, I swear."

"Gotta keep up with the times, Miss Brooks."

She laughed. "All right, I'll pick you up. How about eight?"

"Don't be late. I'll see you then."

After they hung up, Ella stood with the phone pressed to her chest. Her heart beat at a fast, out-of-control tempo.

She walked over to the window and watched the people and cars go by below her. She hadn't anticipated this type of giddiness where Tyrone was concerned. Even though she told herself this was casual, it didn't *feel* casual. And she was changing. Tyrone was making her softer. Funny instead of glacial. Perhaps that personality had been there all along, but with him she could unlock that small compartment and set that side of herself free.

Her father had that effect on her mother. No one ruffled Sylvie Johnson, yet Oscar Brooks could make her blush. No one could calm her spirit, but he did, simply by entering the room. Perhaps because he allowed her to be herself, and loved her the way she was, and for him, she became a little softer, a little gentler because his unconditional love and affection was what she needed.

Tyrone seemed to be having the same effect on Ella, and her brow wrinkled in consternation. That could be good or bad. For now, she'd assume his effect on her was good.

She glided over to her desk. Now to get some work done.

CHAPTER 21

*S*uspended.

Tyrone left work without a word to anyone and drove around, fuming. That piece-of-shit thief had filed a formal complaint against him, and after an investigation, the sergeant had seen fit to give him a ten-day suspension. For the first time in a long time, Tyrone left work early. He drove around for a while, not knowing what to do with himself, and wound up over at the boys' club.

He spent the afternoon shooting hoops with the middle school kids and pulled aside a new boy sitting alone on the bleachers. After five minutes of prodding, the boy shared that some older kids had been pressuring him to cruise the neighborhood at night and participate in underage drinking. Tyrone spent the next hour talking to him, gave him advice on how to deal with peer pressure, and explained how acting rashly could affect his future. Something he needed to learn himself. Recognizing how loneliness and the desire to belong could lead to bad decision-making, Tyrone introduced him to some of the other boys and then took them all out for burgers and fries.

Afterward, he set off for his parents' house. The place was too large for only the two of them and his younger sister, currently in her sophomore year at Spelman, but there were eighteen holes of golf practically in the backyard and plenty of space for entertaining and acting as hosts for their grandchildren on the weekends.

He let himself inside and walked to the back where his father, a big, dark-skinned man with salt and pepper hair, worked in the kitchen. In this house, Clinton Evers did the cooking. Not that Tyrone's mother couldn't, but they'd come to a compromise early in their marriage, which worked for them. One of Clinton's favorite things to do was see what was in the fridge and the cabinets and create a meal. His dad was good like that, but Tyrone hadn't inherited the cooking gene.

"Hey, Pops." He gave him a fist bump.

"Hey, son."

"Hi, Ma," Tyrone called out, knowing his mother was somewhere close by. Except when they went to work, his parents were never far apart from each other.

"Hi, honey," she called back from the den. He couldn't see her, but he knew that's where she was, probably watching prerecorded episodes of *Family Feud*.

"What brings you here?" His father prepped a couple of ribeyes with a homemade marinade. He always prepped the meat the day before. A pot of gumbo simmered on the stove, suffusing the air with the tempting aroma of spices.

Tyrone folded his jacket, placed it on one of the stools in front of the bar, and sat on the stool next to it. "Just thinking about life."

"Oh boy, what happened?"

Tyrone took a deep breath and launched into the story of his suspension and how he earned the disciplinary action.

"The whole time you were telling me what happened, I didn't sense any regret in your voice." Clinton watched him closely.

"I know I messed up, but honestly, I don't have any regret." If his buddy and the other officer hadn't pulled him off Boston Accent, he would have beat the shit out of that guy, which would have resulted in much worse consequences than a suspension. A lawsuit and additional fallout might have been the outcome. "My only concern is how it makes me look to a certain person, and whether or not I should say anything."

His father's brows pinched together. "Who are we talking about?"

Tyrone heaved a heavy sigh. He might as well tell his father everything. His father was one of his best friends and gave really good advice. He was the one who'd convinced Tyrone to go into law enforcement since that's where his passion lay, even though there wasn't as much money in the profession as law.

"The victim in a closed case. I like her a lot. She's unlike any woman I've ever been involved with before. And she's extremely wealthy."

Clinton stopped working and rested his hands on the counter. "Wait a minute, are you talking about Ella Brooks, Sylvie Johnson's daughter?"

"One and the same."

"How serious are you two? I'm trying to figure out if I can get free beer out of this." His father chuckled at his own joke.

"Come on, Pops. I can't get you free beer. And if I could get free beer, I'd be trying to get it for myself."

"Well whatever you don't want, send my way." Clinton grinned. "But enough of that, what's going on with you and this young lady, Ella? And how soon can we have a billionaire in our family?"

His mother's voice came from the other room. "Would you stop making jokes and listen to what your son has to say? He's asking for your advice, and you're acting like you're doing standup at a comedy club."

"Woman, I need you to mind ya business and let me and my son have our conversation in peace."

"Who you think you talking to, Clinton?"

"You. You run your courtroom, and I run this house. Mind ya business and let the men talk." He grinned at Tyrone. "Continue."

Tyrone laughed and shook his head. His pops talked so much shit. Meanwhile, the white shirt and blue pants he wore probably matched what his mother was wearing in the den because she picked them out. Seeing his parents together was what had made him think he could have the perfect marriage. They were obviously still crazy in love and expressed affection by picking at each other. He'd seen them behave the same way all his life and had hoped to have the same type of relationship with his wife.

For a while they did, but along the way, the marriage changed. He couldn't deny that he worked hard, but his running late and missing a few engagements didn't justify Nyla stepping out on him, and certainly not with his best friend. Knowing his friend had smiled in his face while boning his wife still enraged him. It was the ultimate betrayal, by both of them.

"We're not serious yet," Tyrone said, finally answering the question.

"Still in the getting-to-know-you stage, huh?" Clinton shifted the meat into a plastic container.

"Yeah." Truth be told, he didn't want to screw this up. He anticipated their date on Friday night, but he wanted to be upfront with Ella about the suspension and worried his behavior might taint her perception of him. She was cultured and classy. She might not look too kindly on a cop flying off the handle in a fit of rage.

His father washed his hands and put the meat in the refrigerator. He removed two beers, opened them, and handed one to Tyrone. "What are you really concerned about?"

Tyrone stared at the bottle, examining his feelings. "Hypothetically speaking…"

"Of course."

"What if Ella and I were to get serious and marriage comes up? I'm not so sure I'm interested in getting married again. It's only been a year since the divorce."

"Hypothetically speaking…"

"Of course."

"The fact that you're thinking about getting married again means you're probably ready."

Tyrone laughed. "Come on, Pops. It's way too early for that. We hardly know each other."

"Uh-huh. Listen to your old man. I been alive a lot longer than you. You like this woman a lot more than you're letting on." He took a swig from the bottle. "Look, I know you're worried, and rightly so. When a marriage fails, it's normal to wonder what you could have done differently and if history will repeat itself. You're going down a different path. Gotta get a different map. Remember, Nyla made the choice to break your marriage vows. Instead of talking to you, instead of going to counseling, instead of yelling at you or whatever it would've taken to get through to you, she chose to step out. Ella is a completely different woman, and you can't walk into this relationship with the same baggage."

"Which means being honest and upfront."

"About everything. You can't dictate other people's actions. All you can do is control your own, and from what I can tell, I raised a very good son. Everybody wants to feel affection—men, women, children—hell, even our pets. Ain't too much you can do to impress Ella with material things, but I bet you can impress her in other ways. Show her that you care about her and are paying attention. She likes a certain flower, get her that flower. Rub her feet. Cook her breakfast. Whatever it is, do it. You make a woman feel cared for, and you'll have her devotion. She'll do anything for you, and you'll never get rid of her. Hell, look at your momma. She ain't going nowhere."

"Clinton, why you gotta tarnish my character in all the conversations where you give him advice?"

"You make such a good example, baby." His father snickered.

Tyrone sipped his beer, pondering his father's words.

"Final thoughts," Clinton said.

"Shoot."

"You're the marrying kind."

"Excuse me?"

"When it comes to marriage, there are two sets of people. The ones who get married because it's expected of them, but they could do without being tied down in that way. Then, there are the ones who want to make their commitment to another person permanent and public. You fall into the latter category."

"I'm not so sure."

"Oh, I'm sure. You're the marrying kind. The question you need to ask yourself is whether Ella is the marrying kind, too."

The marrying kind. His father wasn't so far off, but after the divorce, his trust had been shattered, and he considered staying single for an indefinite period. He was not in a hurry to get serious with anyone. Ella Brooks could definitely make him change his mind. And for that reason, he needed to tread carefully.

CHAPTER 22

*W*hen they touched base during the week, Tyrone told Ella to dress casually, so that's what she did. She wore a long, shimmery old-gold skirt and paired it with a fitted white top that clung to her torso. She threw a denim jacket over the outfit and let her long hair loose in a body wave style. Nude lips and large silver earrings peeking between her hair strands completed the outfit.

She buzzed with energy at the thought of going out with him again, like someone hopped up on caffeine after five cups of espresso. When she picked up Tyrone outside his apartment and he entered the limo, she right away wanted to crawl over the seat and sit on his lap and give him a big kiss. He smelled so good and looked even better. It didn't seem right that she should have him all to herself for the evening. But yet, she was the lucky woman who would be on his arm.

"Hi," she said.

"Hi." He scooted over and promptly gave her a kiss on the lips, which she immediately leaned into and savored, flicking her tongue against his and moaning softly before he pulled her into the crook of his arm and the driver took off.

The restaurant was small, comprised only of booths, with a small band playing reggae in a corner by the bar. As they walked toward the table, Tyrone leading the way and holding her hand behind him, Ella didn't miss the looks women cast in their direction, or rather, cast at him. She couldn't blame them. He was a beautiful man with golden skin, who moved in a way that suggested he was very self-aware. The jeans hugged his ass without being tight, and the long-sleeved shirt only highlighted his chest and biceps.

They sat down across from each other, and the night advanced quickly as they chatted and sipped on drinks. He told her about his current cases, one of which resulted in an owner getting shot when he unexpectedly came downstairs and caught the thieves in the act. Based on evidence, they thought the case was related to other burglaries within a thirty-mile radius.

Over a delicious plate of braised oxtails, red peas and rice, and fried plantains so delicious she almost licked her fingers, she told him about her work week and the fact that she was getting back into the groove faster than expected.

"Your mother must be happy."

"She is."

"And you?"

"Happy and feeling, I don't know, relieved that it's all coming back to me."

"I can't believe you ever doubted yourself. You're pretty badass."

"No one's ever called me that before. I kind of like it." They smiled across the table at each other. "My next task is to find a new house." Tyrone was the first person she'd mentioned the idea to. He was so easy to talk to, and she was happy to see that didn't change because they had slept with each other.

He frowned at her. "Why?"

"Not because of the break-in. I feel restless. I moved into the penthouse because Wayne wanted us to, but I want the girls to have more space, like my siblings and I did growing up. Hannah and Sophia have asked about getting a puppy a few times, but I've always hedged against getting one because of the penthouse. If we had a yard, I'd be more inclined to grant that wish. I'm going to start looking right away." She'd put it off for long enough, but now with a new spark, she wanted to move forward and purchase the real estate.

"You're going to be a very busy woman in the coming weeks."

"A little. Not too busy."

"I hope not." Tyrone offered a curried shrimp on his fork. "Here, try this."

Their eyes locked across the table, and the intimate gesture of eating off the same utensil sparked a fire in her chest.

"Delicious." She chewed. "Everything's been good."

"Wait 'til we get upstairs."

After dinner, they went upstairs to the lounge, a dimly lit location filled with strategically placed seats. Unlike downstairs, there wasn't a band, but a DJ played reggae music and dancehall, while guests gyrated on their chairs or on the small dance floor at one end of the room.

While Ella settled on a loveseat, Tyrone went to the bar and ordered drinks. He came back carrying a piña colada for her and a beer for him.

Crossing her legs, she leaned into his solid body, and he placed a hand on her thigh. Their touching felt so completely natural, as if they had been doing it for years.

"You're not going to arrest anyone, are you?" she asked. The scent of smoke, not the nicotine kind, wafted on the air.

He chuckled. "No. I don't waste my time or energy on this type of thing. You like the music?"

Ella nodded, although this was more the kind of place her brothers would visit. She'd have to tell them about it, but knowing Reese and Stephan, they were probably already aware of this spot. What she liked even more was being here with him. She shifted restlessly. Horny for more of that good loving he delivered last week. When did she turn into this type of woman?

"So, how is work in general?" she asked.

Tyrone shrugged. "Work is work."

With such a vague answer, she sensed there was something wrong. "Is everything okay at the precinct?"

"Sure. Why do you ask?"

"I've gotten to know you well enough to know something's wrong. Tell me about it." She wanted to be the solid presence and listening ear to him that he was to her.

He sighed and placed an arm around her shoulders, running his hand gently up and down her arm. "There's a bit of an issue at work. Nothing I can't handle."

"What is it?" If she could help him, she would. "Do I need to put in a good word for you or something?"

He chuckled. "No, nothing like that." He squeezed her. "That won't help anyway. I received a temporary suspension."

Ella gasped. "When? And for what?"

He studied her for a moment, like someone debating with himself about how much they should share. "I'm about to tell you something, and it's kinda bad."

"How bad?"

She felt his fingers playing in her hair. "I got suspended because the night we busted the guys who robbed you, I got a little carried away. I roughed up one of the men."

Her eyes opened wide. "Tyrone."

"I know, it was dumb. But I...lost it."

"And you got into trouble."

"You could say that."

"Why didn't you say something to me?"

Color tinged his cheeks. "Because it wasn't important."

"This is important. This is your livelihood, and I know how much you love your job. How long is the suspension?"

"Ten days. I'll be back at work next week."

"I wish you would've told me."

The hand around her shoulders shifted, and he wound a strand of hair around his finger. "There was nothing to tell. Besides, I'm not sorry."

"Why not?" she asked quietly.

"Because the guy I roughed up is the one who touched you. I thought he should get a taste of what it felt like to have his hands bound and have somebody fucking with him. I barely touched the bastard, but I wish I could've done more."

She was so turned on by the reined violence she sensed in him. His dark brown eyes held no regret, and their intensity drew her in. The fact that he had not only risked his job, but had been willing to do bodily harm to another man on her behalf, was downright sexy. Most of the men she came into contact with were reserved and mannerly. Tyrone, on the other hand, was outspoken and didn't care about being improper. He was not reserved, he was not polite, and he wasn't afraid to express anger. She only wished she could have been there to see him in action.

"You shouldn't have done that, but thank you." She glanced away before he saw what was in her eyes. She knew she couldn't hide the deep lust she felt for him in that moment.

Something must've tipped him off, though. He squeezed her shoulder, and that innocuous touch in her present heightened sexual state felt erotic.

"Let's get some air," he whispered in her ear.

He stood first and held out his hand. She took it and followed him out onto the rooftop deck, where the cool fall air wafted over them. He pulled her behind a large outdoor fan.

"You're not drunk, are you, Ella?" Tyrone asked, lifting her skirt and pressing her back against the wall.

Drunk with anticipation. Drunk with wanting him. "No. I'm very sober." Her voice trembled. What did he have planned? Whatever he wanted, she was all-in.

"Good." Tyrone kissed her, plucking her lips between his and sucking gently.

His mouth fully covered hers, and his tongue traced the inside of her lower lip. She fastened her arms around his waist, pressing her tingling breasts into his chest.

He pressed his face into her neck. "Damn, Ella, you taste so good."

This man, this man, this man. Just the way he said her name all deep and throaty, whispered into her neck, was so sexy, she wanted to give him anything he asked for. Anything. Everything. And much as she tried to bury the truth as quickly as it came, she couldn't. The truth couldn't be denied and burned the back of her throat.

She was falling in love with him.

He took her mouth again, and her fingers bunched into his T-shirt, holding on tight as her knees weakened. She wanted him so much, her entire body ached. She barely noticed the cool air when pressed against his warm body like this and allowed to revel in his heated kisses.

Tyrone unzipped his jeans and pulled out an impressive boner. Her pulse thudded faster as he gathered her skirt and the fabric pooled over his forearms. He dragged her panties to the side and looked directly at her as he moved, the heat in his eyes chasing away the chill in the air.

He lifted one leg to his hip and pressed his hard length against the apex of her thighs.

Trembling with anticipation, Ella wrapping her arms around his neck. They were going to do it. Right here, out in the open. This was crazy. Reckless. Incredibly thrilling. As if her heart were attached to a hot air balloon let loose to float upward into the sky.

Tyrone kept his gaze pinned to hers. "You still good, Ella?" he whispered.

"Yes." The word struggled to come out, but she managed.

His fingers stroked the wetness between her legs. "You sure you good, baby?" He struggled to speak now. His voice was a hoarse rendering of its former self.

"Yes," she gasped, clinging to him, pressing her face into his chest. *Please hurry*, she almost begged.

Tyrone entered her, sliding up into the slick heat between her legs.

"Lift those pretty legs around me, baby," he murmured.

He hoisted her in his arms, and her legs wrapped around him. Up against the wall, his mouth on her neck, he pumped his hips.

Ella moaned, joining him in the erotic dance, her fingers curling into fists at the back of his neck as pleasure spiraled through her loins.

"That's it, sweetheart. Just like that." Tyrone grunted, his coaxing words making her ache and her body wetter for him.

A couple stumbled out onto the rooftop. The laughter and sounds of music from the inside temporarily stilled her. But Tyrone didn't care. He didn't miss a stroke, and when the other people saw them, they gasped and hurried back inside.

Ella jumped right back into the rhythmic thrusting with him.

The old Ella would never do such a thing. The old Ella would not be on a rooftop outside a weed-filled lounge, getting screwed.

The new Ella, however, reveled in the pleasure of it all. The new Ella was falling for a man who made her feel alive again. The new Ella orgasmed, buried her face in the neck of this sexy, sexy man, and let out a cry that was new, and wild, and free.

CHAPTER 23

*T*yrone jogged up the stairs. Damn elevator was taking too long. He would call Ella and tell her his plans had changed. He could see her tonight after all. He'd told her he couldn't attend an event or see her later because he had to work, but one of the other detectives wanted to switch weekends, so he had the night free.

He reached the fourth floor and whistled on the way to his apartment. When he realized what he was doing, he shook his head and laughed at himself. This woman had him whistling down the hall like a damn fool.

When his apartment came into view, he skidded to a halt. His ex-wife was in the process of leaving him a note but stopped when she saw him. She tucked the paper into the back pocket of a pair of snug-fitting jeans.

Just his luck, when everything seemed to be going right in his life, his ex-wife shows up to start some bullshit. He knew there would be bullshit because Nyla was a master bullshitter.

He moved slowly toward her. "What are you doing here?"

"Hi, Ty." She smiled. "I was in the neighborhood and thought I'd stop by to say hello." She was cute, petite, with bronze-toned

153

skin and large, doll-like eyes that fooled a man into thinking she was innocent.

"How'd you get this address?" Tyrone's eyes narrowed to slits.

"You can find anyone online nowadays."

Wonderful.

"Look, I have plans to go out. What do you want?"

"Can we go inside and talk for a minute?"

Tyrone hesitated. He hadn't seen his ex-wife but one other time since their marriage officially ended over a year ago, and that had been at a baseball game this past summer. The conversation didn't end well, and he didn't expect this one to end any better.

"You have two minutes," he said gruffly.

He opened the door, flicked on the light, and let her in. Her eyes followed his movements as he removed his jacket and tossed it on the sofa.

"This is a cute apartment," she said, looking around.

Right then, his cell phone rang. Ella, but he sent the call to voicemail.

"Thirty seconds," he warned Nyla.

"Do you have to be so cold?" she asked.

He would have preferred not to have to speak to her, ever. The last thing he wanted was an argument and suspected that's exactly what she wanted. There was no reason for them to talk to each other. This past summer he'd wanted to avoid her, too, when he'd seen her with his former best friend, Jeremy. The minute she saw him, she dropped Jeremy's hand, but not before he saw. They came over to say hi, and within seconds, the three of them were involved in a shouting match that eventually had to be broken up by a security guard.

"One minute."

"Ty." She touched his arm and he jerked away. Then she gave him that look, a wide-eyed look of innocence. He'd fallen for it from the beginning, but Nyla was not innocent.

"So this is how it's going to be? We have to pretend we don't know each other? We can never talk?" she asked.

"What do you want me to say? We're divorced."

The phone rang again. Ella calling back.

"Are you going to get it?" Nyla asked.

He almost sent the call to voicemail again, but answered, turning his back to Nyla. "Hello?" he said in a low voice.

"Hi, did you put me through to voicemail just now? I wasn't sure…"

"I'm kind of in the middle of something."

"Oh. Are you in a meeting?"

"If you want me to leave, I can leave," Nyla said from behind him.

Tyrone swung around and glared at her.

"Who was that? Are you still at work?" Ella asked.

"I'm at home, and it's nothing. Nobody."

"It didn't sound like nobody."

"Let me call you back."

"Why? What's going on?" Ella's voice got louder.

"Give me a few minutes and I'll call you back." He hung up without waiting for a reply. "Make it snappy. Say what you came to say," he told Nyla.

"I thought we could be friends."

"Friends? That's why you tracked me down and showed up at my apartment?" He chuckled and shook his head. "We were married for eight years, and now you want to be friends? I'm betting that being friends with you is no better than being married to you, so that's a hard pass from me. I don't want to be friends with you. Get that through your head. Me and you, we're done."

"Why are you so cruel to me all the time?" Tears shimmered in her eyes.

With so much hostility between them, it was hard to believe he'd once loved Nyla and thought they'd spend the rest of their lives together. So much for growing old together.

"You're so good at playing the victim."

Her eyes cleared and lips firmed. The claws were about to come out. "And you're perfect, aren't you, Ty?"

155

"Never said I was perfect."

"Good, because you aren't. You were a lousy husband."

"And you were a lousy wife. You fucked my best friend."

She flinched but came back at him. "You ignored me, so busy trying to be the big hero."

"You *fucked* my best friend. Me doing my job and helping people justified you fucking my best friend behind my back for almost a year?"

He had seen them at a sports bar, hugged up in a booth out in the open, like a couple. The way she gazed up at Jeremy, smiling, touching his face, showed how familiar they'd become with each other. Right under his nose. This man had been at his house, eaten his food, and he'd taken him along on fishing trips with his brother and father.

"I can't talk to you." But she didn't leave. She stood right there because she wanted absolution for her guilty conscience.

"Nah, you can't. Ain't shit you can say to excuse what you did."

"You're such an asshole."

"Yeah, *I'm* the asshole." He snorted.

"You refuse to take any responsibility for your part in ending our marriage. You were always gone, working or mentoring or whatever. You cancelled dinners and special events. One year it was obvious you forgot our anniversary, but you came up with some lame excuse for why you hadn't bought a gift yet. Busy, busy, busy. You were never there for me."

"Oh, right, it's my fault you couldn't keep your goddamn legs closed."

Whack! The slap landed so hard, it twisted his head to the right.

Nyla slammed a hand over her mouth in shock and stepped backward.

"You fucking—" Tyrone grabbed her by the arms and squeezed. He yanked her up on her toes, intending to shake her until her teeth rattled. But something held him back. Some innate sense of decency and a modicum of control, hanging on by a thread. "You ever put your hands on me again…" He gritted his teeth.

"You'll what? Show some emotion? React?" Her voice trembled.

"Is that what you want? You want me to hit you? There's something wrong with you."

"At least I'd know you cared. You didn't even—"

He let her go abruptly and stepped away, shaking. He placed a steadying hand on the back of the sofa. The energy it took to resist hurting her back siphoned all the strength from his body.

He knew what she was about to say, because she'd said it before. Much as he'd wanted to, Tyrone didn't beat Jeremy's ass or curse her out when he found out about the affair. He quietly left the sports bar, moved out all his shit, and left her in the house.

"Did you even care? Just a little bit?" She had the softest voice, and with her petite frame, she reminded him of a tiny bird. Delicate and needing protection.

"I plotted ten different ways to murder the two of you and get rid of the bodies without getting caught. But I knew I'd be the first person they looked at, and if I made one mistake, I could end up in prison. I ain't risking going to jail for you or anybody else. I loved you, Nyla, but lucky for you, I love myself a helluva lot more."

Tears filled his ex-wife's eyes. She bit down on her trembling lip. "I'm sorry. I wish we didn't have to hurt each other," she whispered, rubbing the spot on her arms where his fingers had pressed into her skin.

"We wouldn't if you'd stay the hell away from me."

"I want us to get along."

He had to get away from this woman. "You want us to get along? I couldn't tell."

"I do want us to get along. Even if it's not obvious," Nyla said quietly. She sniffed and rubbed a hand across her eye.

He didn't see how that would ever be possible. Over a year later, and he still held so much anger inside over the demise of their marriage. He, a seasoned detective on the police force, saw the subtle changes in her and never figured out she was cheating on him. She bought new clothes, but that was because she lost weight after starting a rigorous exercise routine. The make-up, the new haircut. But most of all, he should have known because she stopped nagging him about work and volunteering at the boys' club.

All the clues he missed coalesced in a rush when he saw them in that sports bar.

After moving into this one-bedroom apartment that felt more like a prison than a home, he spent even more time volunteering and at the office because he didn't want to face coming home to an empty place. No one was there to greet him or keep dinner warm in the oven after a long day. Dinner became takeout on the way home or a frozen meal heated in the microwave. Wasn't it in the Bible somewhere that man was not meant to be alone? He believed it. He was a shining example of that.

Her relationship with Jeremy didn't even last. Not long after he saw them at the stadium, his ex-friend had the audacity to reach out and ask his forgiveness and inquire whether or not they could be friends again. He said he and Nyla had split.

Tyrone never dropped the F bomb that many times in one conversation as he did that day and then immediately hung up the telephone. As far as he was concerned, there was nothing his former friend could say to make them friends again. He couldn't be trusted, and neither could she.

The phone rang. Ella again. *Dammit.* He sent the call to voicemail.

"It's her, isn't it?"

"What?"

"That rich bitch." Now he knew why she was really here. She'd come to get information about Ella.

"Don't call her that."

She sniffed. "A friend showed me a picture online of the two of you at Pancake Shack. She's your latest project, isn't she? You have to save the world, don't you, at the expense of everything and everyone, including your own wife. Is she going to be okay with your late nights? And what happens when you get tired of her and move on to the next project? What happens when you don't have time to spend with her because you're off saving the world? You and your damn savior complex."

"Get out."

"You know I'm right. You're going to disappoint her the same way you disappointed me."

Tyrone marched to the door and yanked it open. The phone rang. Ella again. He sent the call to voicemail and glared at Nyla. "Get. Out. In the future, when you see me, pretend you don't know me."

She swallowed, but he ignored the wounded expression in her eyes. "If you ever change your mind—"

"I won't."

She came slowly toward him and paused before stepping outside. He refused to look at her.

"I *am* sorry, Ty. I wish you would believe me."

She waited for him to speak, but he remained silent. When she walked out, he slammed the door shut. Hard.

CHAPTER 24

$\mathcal{T}$yrone needed to call Ella, but he needed a few minutes. Fuming, he dropped onto the sofa and buried his head in his hands. Nyla's words ran around in his head like an athlete around a track. Over and over. He shouldn't let her get to him. He knew she played mind games, but still...

What happens when you don't have time to spend with her because you're off saving the world? You and your damn savior complex.

You're going to disappoint her the same way you disappointed me.

She was good at making him second-guess himself. *She* cheated but twisted her actions into victimhood and made *him* sound like the bad guy. Yet, a little bit of doubt nicked his conscience. She was wrong about their anniversary. He didn't forget that year, but there had been times when he cancelled plans with her, and there had been times when she'd wanted him to attend a birthday party or something else with friends, when he couldn't make it because of work.

He didn't know how long he sat there, brooding over their confrontation, but at the sound of loud pounding on the door, his head snapped up.

What the...?

Tyrone yanked open the door. Ella stood on the other side in a fur-trimmed coat. He would be happy to see her if fire didn't light her topaz-colored eyes and lines of anger crease her forehead.

"Where is she?" She pushed past him, storming into the apartment.

"What the hell do you think you're doing, coming in here like a madwoman?" Tyrone shut the door. He wasn't in the mood for this.

She swung around, eyes wide. "A madwoman? You haven't seen a madwoman. Where is she? I heard a woman's voice on the phone." She shoved open the bedroom door and stood in the middle of the room.

He followed. "Ella."

She hauled open the closet and shoved aside his clothes, knocking a pair of pants and two shirts onto the shoes below. "I'm not an idiot, Tyrone. I heard a woman's voice, and you told me you were working tonight. That's why you couldn't attend the dinner with me."

She elbowed past him toward the bathroom.

"My plans changed. One of the other detectives wanted to swap, so he took this weekend and I'm taking next."

"Oh right, and then what, you called up your girlfriend?" The bathroom door slammed against the interior wall when she shoved it open.

Tyrone watched her drag across the shower curtain with such force, he couldn't believe she didn't wrench down the rod.

She marched toward him. "Who is she?"

Behind the anger, he saw the hurt. He knew that feeling all too well, caused when someone you trusted had mishandled your heart and left you wounded and open.

Before he could speak, she pounded her fists against his chest. "Who is she?"

He took the blows, tightening his body into a solid mass of acceptance. "My ex-wife came by. I had no idea she was coming. I didn't invite her, and I made her leave when she said what she'd come to say. Which was nothing I wanted to hear."

She shook her head vigorously, biting into her lip in an effort to fight the burgeoning tears in her eyes.

"I'm not lying to you, Ella. There's no one else," he said gently.

She stepped away from him. "Why didn't you say that over the phone?" A teardrop hovered on the edge of a bottom lash before spilling onto her cheek, and she angrily swiped it away.

"Because she and I were in the middle of an argument and I wanted to get her out of here."

He prowled forward, and she backed up to the wall, her brow wrinkled as doubt and mistrust fought for dominance against certainty and faith in him. In them.

She grabbed his shirt, bunching the material in her fists. "Ty…" Her voice fluttered low, disappearing like smoke into the air. The pain in her face ripped through him. It made him sick that he was the cause of her insecurity.

"Baby. Sweetheart. Trust me."

Puffs of air left her lips, and her head fell forward. Her hair shifted forward, too, hiding her features. "I want to."

He gently grasped her wrists and lifted her fists to his mouth, brushing her knuckles with tender kisses. "You're the only one. You've been the only one since the day we met."

She lifted her head. "Really?"

"Yeah."

"I didn't know."

"Now you do."

"You never said."

"I didn't have to say."

"So, you're saying—"

"Yes."

She held her breath.

In the midst of their conversation, he'd swollen and needed relief. "No one else, Ella Brooks. No one else but you, and no one else but me." He crowded her against the wall.

She flung her arms around his neck and seared her lips to his. He shoved a hand into the bountiful thickness of her hair and pushed into her mouth, lashing at her teeth and tangling his tongue with hers.

When he lifted his head, her lips had plumped from their rough kisses.

"So why'd you come over here all worked up, hm?" He worked on the buttons of her coat. "You came over here to beat my ass?"

"No."

She shook her head, letting the coat slide down her arms to the floor. She wore a body-hugging taupe dress the same shade as her taupe heels. The sleeves were tight around her arms and wrists, but the scalloped neckline was made of black lace in an off-the-shoulder design that showed off her sexy shoulders. Her shoulders, her damn shoulders turned him on.

He wished more than ever he'd been able to attend that dinner with her. To walk into the room with this vision on his arm, he would have been the envy of every man present.

"Yeah, you did. You wanted to do to me what you didn't do to your ex. Say to me what you didn't have the guts to say to him." He pushed her so her back hit the wall.

Her lips trembled. "I thought you were with someone."

"And what would you have done if you found someone here?"

"I don't know." She glanced away.

Catching her chin, he forced her to look him in the eye. "You know. What would you have done if you found someone here?" While he talked, he undid the buckle on his pants and unzipped.

"I…I would have scratched her eyes out."

"Why is that?" He unzipped the dress and pulled down her panties. She stepped out of them and then tugged the dress off her arms, revealing a strapless bra.

"Because you're mine." She grabbed his ears, her voice growing fierce.

Tyrone grabbed her bare ass and squeezed. "Damn straight."

She kissed him again, hard enough to make him fully aware of how much he belonged to her.

He lowered to the floor and pressed his face against her waxed privates. A soft gasp escaped her lips. From below, he saw her head tilt backward and her mouth fall open in anticipation. He loved going down on her. Smelling and tasting her desire for him only made him harder. Spreading the petals between her legs with his thumbs, he sucked her moist, swollen clit into his mouth.

A jagged cry left her throat, a sound that spurred him on. A sound that made him lift her leg over his shoulder so he could get even more. No matter how many times they made love, he could never get enough. Every moan, every gasp, every sweet-breathed pant belonged to him now.

Her fingers clutched at the short hairs on his head as he held her against the wall. Her undulating hips smeared her sweet honey over his lips and beard. When she came, he felt the tremors on the tip of his tongue.

She collapsed against the wall with a whimper, but Tyrone wasn't done.

He lifted her onto the bed and followed her down, making short order of her bra, which he tossed to the floor. She used her toes to push his pants past his bottom to his thighs. Only after he had played a particularly rousing game of suck and lick with her breasts did he withdraw and take the pants completely off.

He entered her with one smooth thrust, and she moaned. Their lovemaking became wilder, rougher, more passionate than usual. He took her with a savagery that she clearly welcomed, clawing his back, clamping her legs around his waist and holding him hostage as he filled her body.

Ella arched her hips into his and countered each thrust with an energetic one of her own. She lovingly ran her hands over the curls on his head while sinking her teeth into his neck and marking him.

When she climaxed this time, all her limbs enclosed him in a tight embrace. Her hips hit his in frenzied thrusts while panting breaths beat against his skin when she pressed her nose to his neck.

"You're mine, too, Ella. You feel me?"

She moaned an incoherent answer as she kissed his sweat-damp shoulder, and Tyrone dragged her knees high against her chest and drilled deeper. He couldn't get enough and wanted to remove all doubt. From her. From himself, that he could hold on to this woman. That they belonged together.

He licked the elegant slope of her neck right before an orgasmic current tore up his spine, and the sound that tore from his chest was at once unfamiliar but understandable. It was a sound of satiation and total surrender to a woman unlike any he'd known before. He collapsed onto his elbows, holding his weight off her but burying his face into her neck. He inhaled the scent of Ella, her hair, the dampness of sex.

Her hands smoothed over the lower part of his spine and came to rest on his ass. He could lay here all night, face buried in her neck, holding her and being held by her.

* * *

"WHY WERE YOU CALLING ME EARLIER?" Tyrone asked. She was draped half on top of him like an elegant piece of dark cloth. He lifted her hand and kissed her palm. Every part of her was soft. He placed her hand flat on his chest and covered it with his own.

"I had a surprise for you."

Ella shifted tighter against him, as if their current position, laying naked in a tangle of arms and legs on top of the sheets, was not intimate enough.

"For me?"

She nodded.

"What was the surprise?"

She pulled back so he could see her face. "My mother knows the owner of the Atlanta Falcons, and she arranged for you and your father to get into the locker room to talk to some of the players."

Tyrone bolted upright, tossing her off him onto the mattress. "What! What! Tell me you're kidding. Tell me this is a joke."

She giggled. "I'm not kidding. It's true."

He showered her face with kisses as she laughed and begged him to stop. Rolling onto his back, he pulled her on top of him and kissed her thoroughly and deeply.

"Why?" he finally asked.

She shrugged. "Just because."

"Thank you, sweetheart."

Her eyes softened on him, and she traced the head of the snake on his biceps.

"You surprised me tonight," he said.

Her eyes flicked to his. "How?"

"I didn't know girls like you fight."

"We don't."

"So I got the one who does, huh?"

"I didn't know I had it in me."

He pushed his fingers into her thick, soft hair. Unexpectedly, they brought out sides to each other's personality they preferred to stay hidden.

"I know you work a lot, but I want you to come to my parents' wedding with me. Do you think you can get off?" She'd told him the date, but he hadn't asked off yet.

"I will," he said.

"I promise you'll have a good time."

"I'm sure I will." He rolled her onto her back. "I want you to stay the night, cause I want more of this." Sliding his hand between her legs, he stroked her clit. "And this." He licked a dark nipple.

She moaned his name, arching her back. They made love again, slower but no less intense. Palms pressing into his chest, Ella rode his hips, eyes closed as he buried deep inside her with each thrust. Their bodies moved perfectly in synch, and in the final iteration, she collapsed atop him, panting, unable to move. She just lay there, energy depleted.

Tyrone gently brushed back the cascade of hair, uncovered her face, and kissed her nose. She was generous with her body and let him lay claim to every entrance tonight, welcoming him into all parts. Her mouth. Between her legs. And then he tested her boundaries. With his coaxing words, she let him slide into that sweet, tight ass he couldn't stop grabbing. The one virgin spot where no other man had ventured before. She'd trembled and whimpered, biting her lip and lifting her soft bottom against his pelvis. He could still hear her little cries.

Tyrone smoothed a hand down her back and squeezed her left butt cheek. She moaned and shifted on top of him.

I love you.

His chest hurt, like someone had tightened a fist around his lungs. He never thought he'd say those words again. Technically, he hadn't said them, and thinking them made him concentrate on the moment.

He closed his arms around her, as if to stop her from floating up and away. Could they make their relationship work, or would she grow tired like Nyla did? Tired of the long hours and feeling neglected in favor of his job. Ella hadn't complained yet, not outright anyway. She'd hinted that he could come work for her family, but in what capacity? And did he really want to be like her ex-husband, taking a job with the company because he was married to a family member? His pride wouldn't let him.

For now, everything was fine, but he needed Ella to understand how much she meant to him.

He tilted up her chin and forced her to look into his eyes. This woman was his present and his future. No doubt in his mind. Her poise, beauty, and sense of humor got him through the roughest of days. He had to tell her now, using words that he used to think he'd never say again.

"I love you," he said, not breaking eye contact. He was crazy. It was too soon, but verbalizing his feelings relieved the tightness in his chest, and his lungs expanded like a tire filling with air.

"You don't mean that. Our emotions are heightened from our fight." She searched his face, seeking the truth.

"So you're telling me how I feel now?"

"No," she said softly.

"I do mean it, and I'll say it again. I love you." He brushed the hair at her temple.

"Tyrone," she breathed, caressing his face. Her soft touch sprinkled affection across his skin. "I love you, too. I've wanted to tell you for a while now."

"Yeah?"

"Yeah."

Bright smiles lit up their faces, and he rolled her over for another kiss.

CHAPTER 25

"*M*ama. Mama."

At the sound of her daughter's soft voice, Ella lifted the sleep mask off her eyes. Sophia had climbed up on the bed and lay with her head on the pillow next to Ella's, so close she wondered how she didn't feel her daughter's breath on her face. A satin bonnet on her head protected the little girl's newly done twists.

Ella smiled and cupped her daughter's cheek. "Good morning."

"Good morning."

"Did you sleep okay?"

Sophia nodded. Then she raised her head to look over Ella's shoulder. "Mama, there's a man in your bed," she whispered.

Ella sat up so suddenly, Sophia squeaked and bounced backward. Ella caught the little girl by her pajama top and kept her from falling off the side of the bed.

Dammit!

Tyrone groaned behind her. "Hey, what's—"

"Shh!" She swung around to look at him, bare chested and rubbing sleep out of his eyes. "My daughter's in here."

He stared at the little girl who stared curiously back at him.

"Hi," Sophia said.

Tyrone glanced at Ella and then back at her daughter. He smiled. "Hi."

"Tracy! Tracy, get in here!" Ella hollered. Was the nanny even here yet?

Tracy came running through the open door, and when she saw the scene before her, she gasped. "Oh no! Miss Brooks, I'm so sorry. I turned my back for a second while I took Hannah to the potty."

"I understand. Could you please just…"

"Yes, ma'am. Right away, ma'am." Tracy raced across the carpet, eyes averted, and lifted Sophia from the bed.

Still curious, the four-year-old peered over the nanny's shoulder as she was carried from the room. She waved at them. "Bye, Mister. Bye, Mama."

"Bye. See you in a little bit," Ella said.

The door closed, and she dropped her face into the pillow, but at Tyrone's hearty chuckling, she swung around to glower at him.

"It's not funny."

"Oh come on, it's a little funny." The sun coming in through the window illuminated his dark-gold skin and that sleepy, sexy look. She wanted to kiss him at the same time she wanted to shove him off the bed.

The night she stormed over to his apartment had been weeks ago, but every time she thought about it, she couldn't believe her behavior. She'd never fought a day in her life, but she'd been ready to fight that night, turning into one of *those* women. Possessive, out of control, and verging on violence.

She hadn't reacted the same way when her ex cheated. She'd been hurt and angry, yes, but didn't come close to the rage that propelled her to Tyrone's doorstep. She climbed three flights of stairs because of the damn elevator, without getting winded, in high heels, to force a confrontation. She couldn't believe she'd behaved that way.

But who could blame her? She wanted him all to herself, and

that night had established they were in a monogamous relationship. So, something good had come out of it.

"No, it's not funny. I should have locked the door last night," Ella said.

Last night, she and Tyrone joined Simone and her husband, Cameron Bennett, for dinner. Cameron owned and managed Club Masquerade, the hottest nightclub in Atlanta, with his siblings. He loved to cook and prepared a delicious chicken dish at their loft apartment where Simone had moved while they decided where they wanted to live next. She and Tyrone stayed after dinner, listening to Cameron's old blues records collection. By the time Tyrone brought her home, it was well after three in the morning, so she invited him up to spend the night. They snuck into her bedroom, so as not to wake the sleeping occupants of the house. Tyrone stripped down to his boxers, and she donned a nightshirt before they fell into bed together. But she forgot to lock the door.

Ella groaned and covered her face.

"Come on, it's not that bad." Tyrone pulled her down onto his chest.

"She's four years old." Ella settled onto his warm body, sliding a leg between his hair-roughened thighs and smoothing a hand across his chest. Waking up with him in her bed was such a nice treat.

"She doesn't have a clue about what's going on between us."

"She didn't need to see us in bed together."

"Tell her it was a grown-up sleepover. She doesn't know any different and will probably forget all about what she saw in a day or two."

"Not my daughter."

Tyrone stroked her hair. "Well, you did say you wanted me to meet your kids at some point. Not the best way to go about it, but it's done. One down, one to go."

Ella's head popped up and she glared at him.

"What?" he asked innocently.

171

"Not another word out of you." She returned her head to his chest.

"Yes, ma'am." He didn't speak again, but she felt his body trembling from silent laughter.

They lounged in the bed a little bit longer, both of them loathed to get up and face the morning. They finally dragged themselves from the bed and took turns washing up in the bathroom before getting dressed.

"Want to make sure the coast is clear?" Tyrone asked, standing by the door.

That's when she knew she couldn't sneak him out. They'd only been officially dating six weeks but had known each other longer because of the case, and she wanted him to meet her daughters. "Why don't you have breakfast with us?"

He raised his eyebrows. "You sure?"

"Yes. Then I can properly introduce you to the girls. If you want that."

"I would like that," he said quietly.

They both knew this was a big deal. They were about to cross a line of intimacy that would deepen their connection.

Ella exited first, and he followed her into the kitchen, where she introduced him to the weekend chef, Elsie, and told her what they wanted for breakfast. While they sipped coffee in the sitting room and waited for Elsie to finish cooking, Tracy brought in Hannah and Sophia. They looked almost like twins with their hair twisted into an identical design. Both gazed up at Tyrone with childish curiosity.

Ella crouched in front of them. "Girls, I want to introduce you to someone. His name is Tyrone Evers, and he's my friend."

"Hi," Hannah said.

"Hi," Tyrone said back. He crouched before the girls, too. "Nice to meet you. I've heard so much about you."

"I saw you in Mama's bed," Sophia announced.

Tyrone snorted, and Tracy covered a smile with her hand.

"Sweetie, please stop saying that," Ella said.

"But I did!"

"I know you did. We were…having a sleepover, but the sleepover is finished, okay?"

"Like when we sleep over at Nana and Poppa's house?"

"Yes, exactly like that."

Sophia frowned as she absorbed this information. Then her eyes brightened. "Mama, we need a bigger house, and you can buy a bed so he has his own room and bed, like we do when we sleep over at Nana and Poppa's house. Then you can have your bed for yourself, and there'll be lots of room when me and Hannah come in, in the morning." Sophia grinned, pleased with her suggestion.

"That is, um, a good idea. I'll think about that, sweetie. Thank you for that suggestion." Ella rose to her feet as Tyrone rose, too, coughing to cover his laugh. Ella glared at him before turning to the nanny. "Will you be joining us for breakfast?"

"Yes, ma'am."

"All right, everybody, let's get seated. Breakfast should be ready soon."

The girls skipped toward the dining room with Tracy behind, and Ella and Tyrone pulled up the rear.

His hand brushed hers. Such a simple touch set her skin on fire. *Thanks*, he mouthed.

She reached for his hand because she couldn't help herself. She had to touch him back and briefly squeezed his fingers between hers. She'd grown so comfortable with him in a short time. Fearless, really. Their connection had been swift and strong, only growing stronger as time passed.

She and Tracy helped the girls into their booster seats, and then the adults sat around the table. Minutes later, breakfast was served, and as Ella ate and listened to her daughters chatting away and giggling as Tyrone teased them, a deep affection for him stirred inside her and filled her chest with warmth. Sipping orange juice, she watched as he pretended he'd steal bacon off Sophia's plate and she squealed, shoving the last piece in her mouth so he couldn't have it.

No surprise, he'd charmed her daughters the same way he'd charmed her.

* * *

TYRONE GAVE her a quick kiss at the front door. "I'll call you later. Have fun house-hunting."

Ella pouted. "Wish you could come with me."

"I'll try to make it next time. Who knows, maybe this will be the weekend you find your dream house."

"I don't know, the whole process has been draining, and nothing quite fits and makes me go, 'This is it.'"

"When you find the one, you'll know."

Wasn't that the truth.

He grabbed her around the waist and pulled her in for another kiss. Ella rested a hand against his chest and opened her mouth for the tip of his tongue. Despite needing him to leave so she and the girls could get ready to go, she couldn't help melting into his hard frame and enjoying the feel of his mouth against hers. Gosh, this man was addictive.

"Bye." He patted her bottom and left.

Ella leaned back against the door and bit into her bottom lip. She considered what had happened this morning and finally indulged in a giggle. It really was funny, come to think of it.

Slowly, the smile eased from her face.

Both having been hurt in their marriages, she knew he more or less felt the same way she did. He didn't want to rush, and for the past two years, she was certain that a second marriage was off the table. It wasn't worth the trouble.

But she wanted what she'd had this morning. A new family with Tyrone and her daughters. Her kids waking them up too early, all of them eating breakfast around the table. Laughing with and at each other. Teasing. Giggling. She ached for more and for the first time in a long time thought she could get a second chance at a successful marriage and happy home.

CHAPTER 26

$\mathcal{A}$fter the housekeeper let them into the house, Ella found Stephan in the kitchen, leaning against the island, texting. As soon as he saw his sister and nieces, he grinned and crouched before the girls so they could run into his arms.

"Well, if it isn't Rugrat One and Rugrat Two," he said, picking them up, one in each arm.

The girls giggled. "I'm not a rugwat," Hannah said.

Stephan set the girls on the giant island in the middle, a massive half-moon shaped object that accommodated six on the rounded side. The entire kitchen was surrounded by glass walls so that tons of sunlight came through, and it was almost as if the outdoors were brought in to the home.

"What are you doing in my neck of the woods?" he asked Ella.

"Looking at two houses not too far from here. Instead of riding with the agent, I drove so we could stop in and say hi."

"How's the house hunting going?"

She wrinkled her nose. "Not too good. I don't think the real estate agent is clear on what my needs are, but he promised that these homes are closer to what I'm looking for. I also like that they're close to the school I want the girls to attend."

They were already guaranteed a slot at the Thomaston Academy, a prestigious school that boasted the children of dignitaries on its roll. They didn't have to interview and audition the way the less fortune children of millionaires did. Their slots were guaranteed by the hefty donations her family made to build a state-of-the-art technologically advanced library and a sports center that rivaled a complex for professional athletes.

The back door opened, and in came their cousin Malik. Big, strapping, and bearded, he lumbered over when he saw the girls.

"Cousin Malik!" The girls squealed at one time.

"What are you guys doing here?" He gave them each a hug and then gave one to Ella.

"Shouldn't I be asking *you* that?" she said.

Normally, he didn't spend much time inside The Perimeter, the highway that looped around Atlanta and connected the major interstates. He lived on a piece of property his mother left for him after she passed away. He was pretty much a country boy, preferring the peace and quiet of his secluded home.

"I just came to hang out for a little bit."

"Uncle Stephan, can we go look at the fishes?" Hannah asked.

"Fish," Ella corrected.

"Yes, we want to look at the fishes," Hannah said.

Stephan chuckled. "Yes, you may." He took them both down, one by one, and they scampered off. Stephan's huge fish tank contained a multitude of tropical fish, and they loved to stand in front of it and stare at them.

"Don't touch anything," Ella called out after her daughters. She wasn't sure they would pay her any attention, but her brother's home wasn't exactly children friendly. "And don't lose anything." Hannah would probably lose her scarf. Every time they came over, she left a toy or article of clothing behind.

"What features are you looking for in a house that you haven't found yet?" Stephan asked.

Ella thought for a minute. "Well, I definitely don't want anything with a large yard, which is what the agent continues to show me. I would love to have a gazebo, or at least enough space to build one. I also want columns and at least six bedrooms."

Stephan rubbed his chin. "I might have something for you."

"Oh really?"

"I was at the country club the other day, and you know the Anands' daughter? A friend of hers put a house on the market, not too far from here, but she's having a hard time selling it. The woman who owns it hit big in the music industry a few years back, but her career fell off. She needs to sell fast, but the house hasn't been staged and needs some work. Interested?"

"I'll take a look. Can you get the address and some more information? Maybe the real estate agent can take us by there today."

"Hang on." He lifted his phone from the counter and started texting.

"So, what have you been up to, Malik?" Ella asked, as they waited for Stephan to get the information.

"Not a doggone thing," Stephan answered for him.

Malik retrieved a bottle of orange juice from the refrigerator. "I can speak for myself. Mostly working on my sculptures in my free time."

"And he has a ton of free time." Stephan continued texting.

"Man, don't start with me." Malik shook his head and poured a glass of juice.

Stephan kept his head bent over the phone as the person on the other end responded to his text and the phone beeped. He laughed at the message, and then his thumbs moved swiftly over the interface again. "He's still doing that celibacy thing." He kept his attention on the phone while talking to Ella.

"He's still celibate?" Ella said.

"Um, I don't know if you guys know this, but I can hear you."

Ella smiled. "Sorry, but I'm surprised you held out this long. What's it been, two years or something?"

"A while," was Malik's response.

"How much longer are you going to go without having sex?"

He shrugged. "I'm actually kind of enjoying it. I feel like my head is clear and I have new focus."

"Good for you," Ella said sincerely.

Stephan snorted and looked up from the phone. "Whatever. But if you've managed to convince yourself you're happier this way, good for you." He narrowed his eyes on his sister. "You, on the other hand, have that I've-had-sex-recently glow about you."

"I'm not going to talk to you about my sex life, Stephan."

"Good, because I don't want to hear it. I was just pointing out that it's obvious you're having sex now." The phone beeped, and he looked down at the screen. "Okay, she sent me the address and a few pictures." He walked over and showed her the phone.

"Oh, my goodness, I love it. At least the outside looks nice. And those two pics of the great room are nice." Her mind already raced with the possibilities. "Ask her if it has a lockbox, because I want to get inside with my agent."

Stephan did just that, and the response came back confirming there was a lockbox.

"Perfect," Ella said. "We could head over there after we look at the other two. Thank you so much."

"Well, we don't know if this is the one, but maybe it is."

"I have a good feeling about this." Ella turned toward the door. "Girls, come along. We're leaving. Come say goodbye to Cousin Malik and Uncle Stephan."

The girls came racing in and said their goodbyes with plenty of hugs and kisses before they left to meet the agent at the first house.

* * *

ELLA DIDN'T like the last two houses. One had too much acreage, and she didn't like the floor plan of the other. As they pulled up to the one Stephan recommended, she could tell the girls were getting restless. They fidgeted and bickered in the backseat.

"Girls, I need you to be quiet. We're going to look at one more house, and then we'll be finished for the day. Okay?"

"Okay," they said glumly.

This was the first time she'd brought them with her. Maybe it was a bad idea, but she wanted the house she picked to be something they liked, as well.

The real estate agent, an older, portly gentleman named Charles, had driven ahead of them and was already there, standing in the open doorway. At first glance, the house didn't have a sprawling yard, and she appreciated that it was in a gated community. The best part, it was several million below her budget.

Holding her daughters' hands, Ella climbed the stone steps that led to stone columns at the front of the home, and the agent let them into the house. He showed them all around, through the six bedrooms and eight baths. There was an in-law suite, accessible from the inside and outside of the house, which contained an extra bedroom and bath and would be perfect for Mrs. Newcomb. The lack of maintenance Stephan talked about wasn't too bad. The wood floors needed to be redone, holes had been knocked in some of the walls, paint peeled in some of the rooms, the indoor pool would have to be drained and repaired, and there was a water stain on the ceiling in the master bedroom. None of which was a deterrent.

Back downstairs, the girls ran ahead and flattened their hands against the floor to ceiling windows that led out to the backyard, letting their warm breaths fog up the cool glass. Ella envisioned creating a backyard oasis with a gazebo and a landscaping redesign.

Her favorite room, however, was the solarium, currently empty, but she imagined with a table and soft-cushioned chairs for relaxing.

"I like this. What do you think, girls?"

They nodded vigorously. "I like it," Sophia said.

"Me too," her sister chimed in.

Charles led them into the yard and pointed out a cordoned off area. "Looks like they tried to have a garden there," he said.

Ella liked the idea of fresh vegetables and herbs that the chefs could use in the kitchen. Heck, maybe she would learn to cook and use some of them herself. And how wonderful would it be for her daughters to learn about gardening and growing their own food. The more she thought about it, the more she liked the idea.

"Mama, what's that?" Hannah pointed all the way to the end of the property line, beyond the wrought iron fence and a line of trees that acted as a natural boundary.

"That's a pond," Ella answered.

"Is it ours?" Sophia asked.

"No, it belongs to someone else," Ella answered.

"Can we have a pond, too?" Sophia asked, looking up at her mother expectantly.

"Yes! Can we, Mama? Can we?" her other little one chimed in, bouncing up and down.

She'd promised herself she'd be a different kind of mother, but looking down into their little faces, sweet and expectant and waiting for her answer, she couldn't deny them. In her opinion, to deny them would be worse than to indulge. And why shouldn't she? After all, she could afford it, and there was no one around to make her feel guilty. They could learn about sacrifice later.

"Maybe. We'll see."

The girls squealed and started running around the yard, skipping and jumping in their excitement.

"The pond looks like it's on a piece of land by itself," Ella said. "Any chance it's for sale?" Purchasing the piece of land would extend the acreage more than she liked, but she'd make an exception for the girls.

"It is by itself, but it's owned by the people in that house." The agent pointed. "I know this community, and they're not going to sell because he doesn't want anyone building behind his home."

Ella watched her daughters happily prancing around the yard. "I'd like to make an offer." She was just as concerned about privacy as the neighbor and had no intention of building on the land. "My children want a pond. I'm going to give them a pond."

Charles cleared his throat and spoke carefully. "I'm not sure you heard me. It's not for sale."

Ella lifted her head to an imperial angle, feeling more like herself than she'd felt in a long time. "It's not for sale *now*. But anything, Charles, can be bought for the right price. I'll take this house, and we'll make the neighbor an offer. I'm willing to pay a premium."

"Yes, ma'am."

"Girls, come on," Ella called.

The two of them scampered over. Ella lifted Hannah onto her hip and took Sophia by the hand.

"Is this our new house, Mama?" Hannah asked. She'd asked the same question after the first two homes, and both times Ella answered in the negative.

She stopped in the middle of the spacious family room and looked up at the two-story ceiling, imagining the types of events and parties she could throw in this space. She imagined the girls running around in the yard and watching them play near the pond, and she imagined sitting at the breakfast table with Tyrone, sipping his world-famous coffee and catching up before they both left for work.

She wanted the house, and she didn't care that her ex-husband would be displeased and probably accuse her of being ostentatious. She liked the property and her daughters did, too. More than anything, a new home signified a new beginning for the three of them.

"Yes, sweetie. This is our new house."

CHAPTER 27

"What does he want?" A frown lined Sylvie's brow.

"I don't know, Mother." Ella sighed. "Well, that's not true. I have an idea. I'm sure the request for a meeting has something to do with Tyrone."

They were sitting on a sofa next to each other in her mother's office in the middle of the afternoon. Wayne had called to say he was stopping by, which was very unusual. His planned visit had unnerved her, and she'd come to discuss it with her mother.

By the sour note in his voice when he said he wanted to discuss the type of people the girls were exposed to, she suspected her daughters had mentioned Tyrone. They were spending more time together. She, Tyrone, and the girls had gone back to take a look at the house, went to dinner, and on the way back home stopped for frozen custards, which they ate with the heat cranked up in the limo. Then, one Sunday, they went over to the Evers' house to watch football, everyone dressed in Falcons' gear, per Tyrone and his father's insistence.

Sylvie huffed, crossing her arms, and arched a perfectly shaped brow. "As long as the children are fine, he has no say in how you live your life as a single woman. He thinks he can keep you under his thumb, but never again." Sylvie wagged a finger in the air. "He should count himself lucky I had no idea the extent to which he stifled you during your marriage. I would have put a stop to his behavior if I did."

"Mother, I'm an adult and that's not your job."

Sylvie's eyes narrowed. "Did he ever hit you?"

"Never." Ella answered swiftly.

Wayne may be a jerk, but he wasn't an abusive jerk. Because he grew up in a traditional household where the man was the head and the breadwinner, she'd stopped working, dressed the way he wanted, and gave him final say on where they lived, all to make him feel like the *man*. All those concessions to make him happy, and he still cheated. He never put his hands on her, but he beat her down just the same. Her spirit and personality had been crushed under the weight of his insecurity.

"Well, I wish you'd told me much of the changes I saw in you were because of him. The nerve of him, telling you to leave your job."

Coincidentally, today at lunch, she and her mother had a long talk, and Ella confessed, in depth, the problems she'd had in the marriage. The heart to heart had been soul-cleansing but only fed the flames of her mother's ire toward her ex.

"I didn't mind at the time. He wanted to lead, and I wanted him to, but that was a bad idea."

"Nothing wrong with letting a man lead. You do what's best for *your* relationship, and don't let anyone tell you different. But not all men are leaders, my dear, and that's where the trouble lies. I'm going to tell your father. He won't be pleased."

"Do you have to tell Father?"

"Of course I'm telling your father. We don't have secrets."

Oscar hadn't liked Wayne from the beginning, and she didn't want any more animosity between them. In his words, her ex gave off a 'bad vibe.' But unlike Sylvie, after Oscar had spoken, he accepted her decision to marry Wayne. Her mother never accepted the decision and never believed Wayne was good enough. On the day of their wedding ceremony, she told Ella she could still change her mind—minutes before she walked down the aisle!

"I knew something was wrong." Sylvie squeezed her hands.

"I didn't want anyone to know. I was embarrassed."

"I can still—"

"Mother." She observed the obstinate set to Sylvie's mouth. "Do not go on one of your rampages."

Sylvie remained silent, focusing her attention on the furniture magazine on the table that featured her designs on the cover.

"If you meddle, I'll tell Father."

Sylvie stared at her. "Why would you get your father involved?"

"Because you never listen. Do I need to call him?"

"Oh, for heaven's sake," Sylvie huffed.

"Mother." She knew her mother well enough to know that if she didn't get a firm answer, she'd use that as a loophole.

Sylvie pursed her lips and looked heavenward. "I won't interfere."

"Thank you."

She hugged Sylvie and laid her head on her shoulder. "I know you mean well, but let me deal with him. Let me fight my own battle. Trust that you raised me well and I can handle anything that comes my way."

"Of course you can. You're perfect."

"You would say that. You're my mother."

"Even if I wasn't your mother, I'd think you were perfect." Sylvie rested her head against hers and patted Ella's cheek. "You're more like me than the other three, you know. Stephan is always off doing God knows what, Reese adores his father, though I think he still carries some anger because of the divorce. Simone's heart is so big, she won't touch the business. She wants to save the world. But you, you're my twin." Sylvie held her hands and looked her in the eyes. "Don't you ever let any man make you feel like you're not good enough ever again. You're better than good enough. And whenever you need me, I am here. Always. I. Am. Here."

Grateful tears filled Ella's eyes. "I know, and I'm sorry I didn't—"

"Sh." Sylvie shook her head and patted Ella's hands. "Don't apologize. Just remember who you are. You are Ella Brooks, my darling, Sylvie Johnson's daughter. *My* daughter." A spark of fire flared in her eyes. "Give him hell."

* * *

"Miss Brooks, your ex-husband is here." Ella's assistant sounded reserved. Her ex was probably standing right over the desk being his usual obnoxious self.

"Give me a few minutes and then show him in."

She took a deep breath. After her mother's pep talk, she felt better prepared for whatever Wayne's visit would entail. A few minutes later, he came through the office door, and she stood and moved in front of the desk.

"Hi, Wayne."

Critical eyes assessed his appearance in a dark suit and dark tie. A couple of weeks ago, he'd been promoted to general manager of the restaurant where he worked after an unexpected resignation by the previous manager. He walked with more confidence, head held higher. His curly hair was tamed with gel, and he looked refreshed. The new position must have done wonders for his self-esteem.

He looked around. "You made some changes. Looks nice."

"Thanks." She'd redecorated, painted the walls a neutral palette, and incorporated bright pieces from the company's furniture collection.

Wayne stuck one hand in his pocket. "This isn't easy for me. As a matter of fact, I'm a little uncomfortable having to address this with you because I didn't think I would have to."

Just spit it out, Ella thought.

"This weekend, when I had the girls, they wouldn't stop

talking about your new boyfriend. Not only that, Sophia told me about your sleepover."

Crossing her arms over her chest, Ella asked, "Do you have a question?"

"We had an agreement, that we would keep our partners away from the girls. It seems that the rules we agreed to don't apply to you."

"We agreed to introduce the kids to our partners when we felt comfortable, but both agreed it would be a bad idea to have a revolving door of people coming in and out of their lives. Sophia seeing Tyrone—"

"Is that really his name?"

"Yes." She frowned.

He laughed a little and smoothed a hand down his tie. "That's quite a step down for you, isn't it? I mean, a name like Tyrone can only mean one thing. Is he some kind of bad boy thug or something?"

Ella cocked her head to the side. "Don't do that. It makes you look ignorant."

His head jerked back and he straightened his shoulders, probably because he wasn't used to her talking to him like that.

"I'm concerned about the type of man you're exposing my children to, especially since you seem to have no qualms about him spending the night and letting our daughter see him in your bed."

"First of all," Ella said, placing a hand on her hip, "Sophia thinks it was a sleepover. She's a child and doesn't know any better."

"But she's curious and confused."

"Confused about what, Wayne?" Ella asked, already tired of the conversation.

"The last time she saw you in bed with someone, that person was me."

"Over two years ago, before we divorced. I don't think there's any confusion on the part of Sophia about seeing a man in my bed.

I forgot to lock the bedroom door. That's all. It won't happen again. Anything else?"

"I would like to know more about this mystery man, if that's not too much to ask. Or are you worried because you know he's probably not up to, shall we say, the appropriate standards?"

The gall! She held back a laugh, because she knew he considered himself not up to the appropriate standards. He didn't have the right background or go to the right schools. He didn't come from money. Yet here he was, having the audacity to thumb his nose at someone else.

Ella couldn't think of a single member of her family who liked Wayne. They'd simply tolerated him, first because he was her husband, and second because he was the girls' father. In retrospect, there were times in their marriage when he bowed out of attending family events, which didn't endear him to them any more.

"He's not a mystery man, and the only standards that matter are my own. I don't need your approval to see Tyrone." She wanted to shove him out the door, but he was the girls' father and should know about the man she allowed around them, the same way she'd want to know about any women they spent time with. "For the record, he's a police officer with the city. In fact, he was the detective that worked on my case."

"Oh no, Ella, please tell me you don't have some kind of hero worship crush on this man. He may very well be using you."

His false concern grated. "He's not."

"And you know this how?"

"I realize I'm not a very good judge of character, or so it may seem from my previous relationship." She went silent and let the words sink in. When he realized the jab was directed at him, Wayne's lips firmed into a thin line of displeasure. "But he's a good man."

"A man you're sleeping with."

"We're divorced. Did you think I'd spend the rest of my life alone? Do us both a favor, mind your own business, and don't worry about my sex life. I'm sure yours is going very well, and I'm happy to say, mine is going very well, also."

"You? Come on, Ella. We both know you're not exactly the energetic type. I could barely get you to do anything adventurous. You behaved as if having sex with me was a chore. Why do you think I stepped out on you? I had to get satisfaction somewhere."

Ella swallowed the stab of pain. Low blow. Every insult or rebuttal she'd never said over the years swelled on her tongue. If he managed to make it out of the office without her scratching his eyes out, she'd nominate herself for sainthood.

She could go off but wouldn't give him the satisfaction. Instead, she channeled her mother's cool poise. Studying her nails, she said, "My lack of interest in sex had nothing to do with me. The right man can make a woman do all sorts of things. The right man can open up a whole new world and change your life." She flicked her gaze up to him. "You weren't that man. But don't worry, I've found him."

His jaw tightened, and he flicked his gaze over her pencil skirt and blouse. "You've changed, and not for the better."

"You would say that now that I'm no longer an extension of you."

"What the hell has gotten into you?"

Ella angled her chin higher. "I don't know. A good man. Good dick."

His face reddened. "That's how you talk now?"

"Like you said, I've changed. If there's nothing else…" She dismissed him with the flash of a smile and marched behind her desk. She didn't care about his feelings anymore, and why should she? He'd didn't care about hers.

One hand on her hip, she studied him. Wayne stood in the same spot, mouth hanging open.

"*Bye.*"

The one word woke him up. Straightening his shoulders, he said, "We need to talk about this guy, Tyrel or whatever."

He'd purposely messed up Tyrone's name, but she pretended

not to notice. "The girls are fine. They adore him and he adores them, which I'm sure you know, because they were talking about him. As a matter of fact, everyone who's met Tyrone adores him, and one day I'll let you meet him. I'm sure you'll adore him, too. Though, I can't say the feeling will be mutual." She smirked and watched his eyes narrow. "Anything else?"

"Don't lose sight of the fact that you're a mother first. Whatever you're doing with this man comes second, way second, to the welfare of my children."

"I don't need you to tell me how to be a mother. I always put *our* children first." She refused to give him the last word.

Wayne shook his head, as if he still couldn't believe how much she'd changed. With a hardened jaw, he swept out of the room.

When the door closed behind him, Ella burst out laughing.

CHAPTER 28

So this was how the other half lived.

The view from one of the seaside suites at the Four Seasons Cap Ferrat on the Cote d'Azur in the south of France was spectacular. Sylvie and Oscar had flown the entire wedding party and guests to the little village of Saint-Jean-Cap-Ferrat, increasing their population by a couple hundred. Sylvie's favorite color was white, and a caravan of white classic Rolls-Royces had transported everyone from the airport in Nice.

The iconic hotel sat on a hill, surrounded by a fourteen-acre park and boasted an Olympic-size pool and a chic design in light colors of beige, white, and gray. Outside the sliding glass doors, sailboats dotted the Mediterranean Sea sparkling below.

This trip was Tyrone's first time in Europe, and only the second time he'd used his passport. The first time had been during an eastern Caribbean cruise with his ex-wife several years ago, an idea he'd had to add a little spark to their marriage and see if they could get back on the right track. Epic fail.

"Hey." Ella came up behind him and rubbed his back. "I'm about to leave."

As one of her mother's bridesmaids, she wore a sleeveless

champagne-colored dress that cinched her middle with a wide waistband and brushed the floor in a loose skirt. Her hair was swept up into large curls, with several tendrils framing her face.

"How do I look?" She twirled in a circle, and he couldn't help but smile. She fit perfectly into the elegance and luxury of the place.

"Gorgeous, as always."

She grinned, and he pulled her in for a quick kiss on the cheek so he wouldn't ruin her makeup.

"You're excited about your parents getting married."

"Absolutely. They belong together."

Tyrone stroked his bearded chin. "Hmm, I know two other people who belong together, too."

"Oh really? Who?"

"You and me."

She leaned into him and ran a hand up and down the front of his chest. "I couldn't agree more." Her smile shifted into a sigh. "I'd better head over to the villa to spend time with Mother, help her get ready and protect the team from her perfectionism." Her mother brought an entourage of hairdressers, make-up artists, and other assistants to help her look her best. "You know where to go?"

"I'm not a kid."

"I know. You're a grown-ass man."

He chuckled. "I'll hang out at the bar while you're gone. Come on, I'll go down with you."

They exited the suite hand in hand and made their way downstairs to where a few other guests stood. Ella greeted them with hugs and air kisses and made introductions. Two of them were her cousins from Seattle. Cyrus Johnson, the head of the family's conglomerate, and his second in command, Xavier Johnson.

Cyrus had a serious, no-nonsense disposition and in some ways reminded Tyrone of Sylvie. Xavier had long dreadlocks and a casual, friendly air about him. Tyrone shook hands with the brothers.

"Take good care of him," Ella said to her cousins.

"We will." Xavier chuckled. "We were headed to the bar for a drink."

"Great minds think alike," Tyrone said.

"See you later." Ella waved goodbye.

Xavier, Cyrus, and Tyrone strolled into the bar, sat down, and ordered drinks.

Tyrone noted that Cyrus ordered a club soda. "Saving your alcohol consumption until later, huh?"

"I don't drink."

"Oh."

The way he said it suggested there was a profound reason behind the decision, and though he was curious, Tyrone didn't press the issue.

"How is Ella doing?" Xavier asked. "You know, since the incident."

"Really well. Ella's a tough, strong lady," Tyrone answered.

Xavier nodded. "She's definitely tough, but everyone needs someone to lean on every now and again."

"True." He remembered how she'd had trouble sleeping at first, but she didn't have that problem anymore. "The therapy sessions and knowing those guys are facing trial have helped."

"Good. Now we just have to look forward to this wedding and hope the weather holds fair, or there will be hell to pay." Xavier crossed his fingers.

"Can't do much about Mother Nature," Tyrone said.

"If Mother Nature knows what's good for her, she'll behave herself. She doesn't want to see the wrath of Aunt Sylvie," Cyrus said.

At that point, they all three laughed.

* * *

As THUNDER ROLLED OVERHEAD, Ella walked down the aisle on the arm of her cousin Malik and smiled at the assembled guests. She caught Tyrone's eye, who looked dashing in the light-colored suit required. He chose a cream-colored one with a vest and a cream and white tie. Constance Johnson, her deceased uncle's widow, sat on the front row with other family members from Seattle. Members of her father's family were also in attendance, some coming from her grandmother's side in Brazil, but most from her grandfather's side in the States.

She and Simone stood side by side with the other two bridesmaids and watched their mother come down the aisle. Sylvie wore a dress she designed herself, a masterpiece with a sweetheart neckline and long, sheer sleeves that hung six inches past her fingers and split on the inside of her arm up to the elbow. Both the neckline and the circumference of the waistline were decorated with white rhinestones. Her hair was smoothed back from her face and secured in thick twists at the nape. The only jewelry she wore were her engagement ring and a pair of diamond earrings. She didn't need any other embellishments. Not with her skin and brown eyes glowing with happiness.

Ella saw the tears in her mother's eyes as she approached and could barely contain the emotion that gathered in her chest.

The minute she arrived beside her father, he took Sylvie's hand and tucked it into his arm. She leaned on him, and they stood that way during the entire ceremony, reciting vows they'd written themselves. At the end, when the officiant said, 'You may kiss the bride' with a heavy French accent, Ella's breath caught at the way her father looked at her mother. It was so obvious to anyone present how much he adored her by the expression on his face. With a watery smile, he kissed his bride. It was official. Her parents were remarried.

Cameras flashed, and Ella didn't miss how so many in the audience teared up with emotion. She knew this time their love, their marriage, would last. More than anything, she wanted the same.

CHAPTER 29

A long, white carpet led the way to the yacht moored in the harbor where the wedding reception would take place. The wedding planner, carrying an iPad and wearing an earpiece, directed the foot traffic and kept an eye on the attendants helping people onto the boat. Earlier, a pending storm loomed above, but the sky had cleared. As if by sheer will, the joyful occasion forced nature to behave.

For the reception, Sylvie changed into a dramatic white cape dress, and the happy couple danced cheek to cheek on the yacht in the cool night air. Ella suspected they might have forgotten that anyone else was present. They seemed lost in their own world as Oscar kissed away a tear that scrolled down her mother's cheek. They were the center of attention, with violinists slowly circling them and wailing out an emotional rendition of "At Last" that lifted toward the starry sky.

Her parents were opposites in every way imaginable. Oscar was the calm to Sylvie's stormy. The flexible to her headstrong. But they worked. They complemented each other, and the truth was, she'd never seen them as happy as when they were together. Their reconciliation shaved years off their faces.

Watching them made Ella think about a future with Tyrone. She didn't want to wait until her fifties to launch a life with the man she loved. Love was rare and should be protected and appreciated when found. Nurtured so it could bloom like a rose and impart its sweet fragrance on the lives of those around it.

"They're married." Simone sighed.

Malik came up and flung an arm around each of their necks. "I can't believe Unc took the plunge again. Ever thought this day would come?"

"No."

"Me either. Much as Unc complained about her, I never expected a part two on their relationship. And I definitely never thought your mom would take him back."

"Neither did we." Simone laughed. She sipped her champagne.

The song ended, and Sylvie and Oscar seemed to finally remember that there were other people present and looked at friends and family in the midst of the applause that followed. The rest of the band joined the violinists and struck up a new, more uptempo beat, and guests crowded onto the makeshift dance floor.

Simone scanned the crowd. "Where's my husband?"

"You love saying that, don't you?" Malik said.

"I do. Where is my husband? Let me go find my husband. Where is the love of my life?"

Malik started gagging, and Ella groaned. Beside her, Tyrone chuckled and shook his head at their antics.

Wearing a cream suit that looked superb against his chocolate skin, Cameron sauntered over with Reese and Stephan. Standing behind his wife, Cameron placed a hand on Simone's hip. "Is there any chance this means we don't have to worry about your mother anymore?" he asked.

Malik and all of the Brooks siblings laughed.

"Good one." Simone reached back and patted his cheek.

Reese gave him a sympathetic pat on the shoulder.

"I thought it was at least worth asking," Cameron said.

"Should I be worried?" Tyrone asked.

DELANEY DIAMOND

"No." Ella looped an arm through his. "Mother can be a little meddlesome, but she's gotten much better. I promise."

"After all that laughing, I'm not convinced."

"You're a wise man. Stay on your toes, Tyrone," Cameron said.

Ella's gaze landed on Stephan's frowning face. "What's the matter with you?"

"He's upset Mother and Father are married again," Reese answered.

"I'm not upset," Stephan muttered, stuffing his hands into his pants pockets.

"Why would he be upset?" Simone asked.

"Because now that Father's officially back, he can't get away with the same nonsense he's been able to for years. Mother's already tightened the purse strings, and she's a lot less tolerant of his behavior. It's only going to get worse."

Stephan glared at Reese, and they all laughed. "I know how to handle Mother," he said.

"Oh you do, do you?" Ella said.

"Watch this." A devious smile came over his face, and Stephan danced between the other guests and made his way over to his father and mother, sliding in between them.

"He's such a momma's boy." Ella said, resting her head against Tyrone's shoulder.

"And would rather die than admit it." Simone shook her head.

Sylvie alternated between father and son, bliss permanently affixed to her lips and lighting up her eyes.

"Hold this." Reese handed his drink to Simone.

"Not you, too," she chided.

"Can't let them have all the fun." With a bobbing head, he shimmied over and formed a circle around Sylvie with his brother and father. Hands in the air, she danced in the middle of the most important men in her life.

Ella slipped her fingers between Tyrone's, and they tightened their hands around each other.

"Wanna dance?" he whispered in her ear. His voice was low

196

and husky and made her want to do more than dancing, but she nodded and let him lead her into the middle of the deck.

Before long, Simone and Cameron joined them, and their entire group mixed up partners. One minute she was dancing with her father, the next with Cameron, then her brother, and back to Tyrone. What thrilled her the most was how well Tyrone fit in. There was no awkwardness or stiffness. And that, more than anything, let her know she was on the right track with him.

* * *

"So, what did you think?" Ella asked. She stood at the mirror removing her jewelry, while Tyrone lounged on the bed with his fingers linked behind his head. He'd removed his shoes and socks and tossed his jacket.

They partied until late, which wasn't easy considering the time difference. Everyone started winding down after midnight, which was when the Rolls-Royces made an appearance and started the procession back to the hotel with guests. Oscar and Sylvie said goodbye to everyone and took off for the airport, where a private plane would take them to the next destination, Monaco.

"I had a great time. Good food, dancing, and I rubbed elbows with a bunch of rich people. It's nice to see how you guys party."

Ella glanced over her shoulder at him. "That's not sarcasm, is it?"

He chuckled. "Absolutely not. I really did have a good time." He smiled at her.

"Good to hear."

"So how long will your parents be on their honeymoon?"

"Ten days. I'm actually surprised my father was able to convince Mother to take that much time off, but I think she really needed the break. She seldom takes a vacation, and when she does, she's still in touch with her businesses."

"So having you on board probably puts her mind at ease, I take it."

"Yes." She walked over. "Could you unhook this for me?"

She held out her hand, and he removed the tennis bracelet from her wrist. She went back over to the dresser.

"If something really goes wrong that needs her attention, I'll get in touch with her. But she knows I can handle almost any problem that arises. Besides, she needs this break and time alone with my father, just the two of them."

"Too bad we have to go back in the morning. I would have liked to see more of the area."

"It would have been nice to take a few extra days here."

He couldn't tell if she were simply making conversation or if definite disappointment filled her voice. The reason they were going right back was because he could only take half a week off, all of which had been spent in wedding activities. Sgt. Cross had made a fuss already, and Tyrone felt obligated to keep the peace after his suspension.

"Sorry about that, sweetheart. Next time." He held out a hand, and she walked over and took it.

She sat on the side of the bed and rested an arm next to his shoulder, leaning into him. "Would you really like to come back another time?"

"I would. You could be my tour guide."

"I don't speak a lick of French. I chose to learn Spanish and can manage in Portuguese because of my father's side of the family. Stephan is the French speaker in the family. Reese speaks a little bit, too, but Stephan has a natural tendency toward languages. He speaks several fluently."

Ella slipped off her shoes and lay down on the bed next to Tyrone. She ran a hand over his torso. "Glad you came."

"Me, too. I danced on a yacht in the Mediterranean with the most beautiful woman I've ever met. What could be better?"

"You, sir, are definitely getting laid tonight."

He laughed and kissed her soft lips. "That's not why I said that."

"No matter the reason, you're still getting laid."

198

He bent his head to whisper in her ear. "In that case, I'm gonna fuck you so good tonight. Give you a European fucking." He nestled his hard length in the apex of her thighs. It didn't take much for him to get hard around her.

She flung her arms around his neck and wrapped those sexy long legs around his hips. He started on her neck, kissing and sucking.

"You ready?" he whispered. One hand cupped her breast and squeezed.

Ella moaned and arched into his hand. "Always. I'm always ready for you."

He kissed her again, rubbing his hips into her soft center. By the time they were naked, they'd worked themselves into such a frenzy that he swiftly joined their bodies, dragging her leg across his back.

Their heavy breaths mingled together. Under the bright lights, he got to see every emotion flicker across her face as she strived for release. When she came, her head tilted back, the way it always did, and she gave herself over to the tremors that took over her body.

Knowing he gave her so much pleasure, watching her release, always pushed him right to the brink. When he finally fell over into bliss, he rolled onto his side, dragging her with him.

Her bound hair had loosened, and he removed the clip and weaved his fingers into the black silk. She moaned softly, and he squeezed her tight, probably tighter than he should.

"I love you," he said, before his exhausted body drifted toward sleep.

At first, he didn't think she heard him. Her breathing didn't change. But then he felt her cheek, against his chest, curve into a smile.

Quietly, she whispered, "I know."

CHAPTER 30

*H*umming, Ella let herself into Tyrone's apartment and set the bags on the table. She took her overnight bag into the bedroom and hung her coat in the closet before going back to the kitchen, where she retrieved her phone and sent a text to Tyrone.

Where are you? I'm at your apartment. Brought Chinese.

While she waited for his response, she placed the wine in the refrigerator to chill and removed the containers of Chinese food from the sack. Her phone beeped when Tyrone texted back.

Be there in 30. I'm starving.

She smiled, glad she'd picked up dinner. One less thing for him to worry about when he left work.

Tomorrow she closed on the house, well, two houses. As it turned out, the neighbor next door had been willing to sell not only the land with the pond, but his house for the right price. She didn't need two houses and had no idea what she would do with the second, but she'd figure all that out later. She was able to keep her promise to her daughters, and that's all that mattered.

Ella took a shower and rubbed body butter all over her skin

and then changed into a pair of jeans and one of Tyrone's hoodies. His clothes were so much more comfortable than hers.

In the living room, she flipped on the television, poured a glass of wine, stole an egg roll from the container of Kung Pao chicken, and settled down to wait for Tyrone. Forty-five minutes later, he still hadn't arrived, and now she was hungry and the glass of wine completely gone. She flipped channels, restlessly alternating between a sitcom and a police drama.

Finally, she rose from the chair and retrieved her phone to make sure she hadn't missed any calls or messages from him. She hadn't. She sent another text, and he responded right away.

Sorry baby. Something came up. Another 45 minutes or less.

Okay.

She sighed, reminding herself that he did important work, and lay down on the sofa to wait. At some point she fell asleep, because the next thing she knew, she was awakened by Tyrone coming through the front door. She lifted her head from the throw pillow and uncurled her legs.

"Hey, sorry I'm late," he said.

"What time is it?" Ella stretched her arms above her head.

He glanced at his watch. "Almost eleven."

"That was definitely more than 30 minutes."

Tyrone grimaced. "Sorry about that. We got a hit in the database on one of the cases we've been working. Chu and I wanted to follow up on the lead right away."

"I understand, but you could have called or told me not to wait," she said lightly, not wanting to make too big of a fuss.

He flipped open a styrofoam container. "Sorry about that, baby. Won't happen again."

Ella walked over to him. "No kiss for me?"

He grinned. "Where are my manners? I'm so hungry, all I'm thinking about is getting food in my belly." Sliding an arm around her waist, he pulled her close and kissed her softly. His hand slipped lower and grabbed her ass.

Ella cupped his jaw and pressed her lips firmly into his. "You work too hard."

He chuckled. "And still there's so much to do." He patted her bottom and released her.

She poured wine for them both and heated up the food while he went into the bedroom and changed clothes.

"Tell me about the closing," he called out.

"We're scheduled for ten o'clock in the morning. I'm so excited, and I don't know why. It's not as if I've never owned my own place before, but I feel like this house represents so much more than just a house for me and the girls. I feel like I'm emancipated." She laughed as she set the food on plates on the table.

Tyrone came out of the bedroom, tugging a black Henley over his head. "I can understand your excitement." He sat down and patted his thigh, indicating she should sit on his lap, which she gladly did. "We should do something to celebrate. You, me, and the girls."

"I like that idea." Ella stroked his jaw. "You're so good with them. I appreciate that so much."

Holding her hand, Tyrone kissed her palm. He was quiet for a while. "To be honest, I feel like, like they're my girls, too. Frankly, they make it easy, they're so lovable. I always wanted kids, but Nyla and I never got around to having any." He frowned, deep in thought as his eyes looked at some point past her shoulder.

Ella locked her arms around his neck. "Now you have a four-year-old and two-year-old at your disposal."

He grinned. "They're great. I'm lucky to have them in my life. And their momma, too."

She couldn't ask for a better response, to have the man she loved so accepting of her daughters, and knowing her daughters enjoyed him just as much.

She tapped his chest. "I know you're busy, but don't forget to ask off for New Year's Eve. As soon as you get the okay, let me know so I can tell Mother you'll be there."

Tyrone cursed softly. "I did forget. Sergeant Cross is out of town for a funeral until next week, but as soon as he gets back, I'll be sure to ask him."

"Don't forget again," she said.

"I won't, Miss Brooks."

"Thank you, Mr. Evers."

After dinner, they put away the leftovers and went to bed. As they lay there together, spooning with Tyrone's arm thrown over her waist, Tyrone said, "I'm sorry about tonight."

"It's okay. I know it couldn't be helped." He worked hard, and she didn't want to make a fuss over something so minor. It's not like she didn't know where he was. Unlike her ex, who avoided spending time with her and lied about his whereabouts, she knew Tyrone was working, and working to make their community safer. "Did you get the bad guy?"

"Not yet, but we're closing in."

"Good."

Before too long, they were asleep.

* * *

"Thank you so much." Ella shook hands with the closing attorney, Charles, her agent, and the previous owner of the house next door. Minutes later, she walked out of the closing with two sets of keys and a new attitude.

Her driver opened the door as she approached, and she slid into the back seat of the limousine. Right away, she sent a text to Tyrone.

I did it!!!!!

He probably shook his head when he saw all the exclamation points. Ten minutes later, a thumbs-up emoji came through with the words, *Proud of you.*

Ella grinned. New house and a wonderful man. Finally, her life was on the right track.

CHAPTER 31

"Call me. The girls and I are eating pizza tonight, and they wanted to know if you're coming over."

Ella hung up the phone and set it on the kitchen counter. That was the second message she'd left Tyrone in the past hour. Normally she didn't bother him while he was working, and if she did, he responded right away with a text or a phone call. But he hadn't so far, and she needed to know if he was stopping by. He ate almost as much as the three of them combined, so she wanted to be prepared.

With Christmas around the corner, his work schedule had become even more erratic and his hours longer because of the uptick in break-ins this time of year.

The phone rang, and she snatched it up but saw her sister's number on the screen. "Hi, Simone."

"Have you seen the news?"

"No. Why?"

Pause. "I don't want to worry you, but there was a hostage situation at the Country Club of Atlanta subdivision. A home invasion that went really wrong. Helicopters overhead and a shootout. I wouldn't mention it, except, well, except I recognized the sergeant from Tyrone's precinct. He was giving an update and said several officers had been shot."

Ella dashed into the living room and clicked on the television. She skipped over several channels until she came to the broadcast of the shoot-out. Could Tyrone be among the injured?

"Do you know if Tyrone was there?" Simone asked.

"I haven't been able to reach him." Ella swallowed, refusing to believe the worst.

"I'm sure he's fine. I just wondered, you know, since he's a police officer…"

Covering her mouth with her hand, Ella watched the newscaster report that there was one officer dead on the scene and two others in critical condition. She sank slowly onto the chair, searching for anything remotely familiar about the officers in the background. Dark-gold skin, an I-run-this-shit walk. None of them were Tyrone.

"He's fine. He has to be," she told her sister, glued to the TV.

"You're right. There's nothing to worry about," Simone said. But she wasn't very convincing.

* * *

When she heard the front door, Ella uncurled her feet from under her. After dinner and putting her daughters to bed, she'd stuck in front of the television the rest of the night, the phone beside her, waiting for word. Tugging the satin robe tighter around her body, she jumped up and went into the hall, catching Tyrone walking back to the bedroom. They had keys to each other's homes now, making "sleepovers" easier to schedule. Sometimes, instead of going straight home, Tyrone came to her place and spent the night.

"Tyrone."

He swung around, and she rushed over, hands running over him, inspecting his face, torso, and arms. "Are you all right?" He appeared to be unhurt.

"Yes, I'm fine."

"I was worried. I saw the news coverage of the shooting."

He shook his head. "It was a mess."

He looked tired, his face drawn and a frown marring his forehead. And yet, the next words out of her mouth were, "Did you get my texts? My messages?"

He shrugged out of his suit jacket, eyeing her in a way that indicated he did not miss the snippy tone. "I did when I got off, but since I was on my way here, I thought that instead of giving you a call, we'd talk when I got in."

He headed back to the bedroom, and she followed.

"I heard about the shoot-out and immediately thought of you. And when you didn't respond to my texts…"

"I wasn't at the location of the shooting initially. The officer-down call went out, and we all responded." Tyrone tossed the jacket on the bed.

She'd seen the convergence of police and emergency vehicles on television. Some people thought that level of response was overkill, but any shooting, especially when life was taken, was a serious matter. She'd lost her uncle Anthony, her mother's brother, to gun violence. He was a gentle soul, whose wife killed him and then turned the gun on herself.

Despite the "good cops" versus "bad cops" debate, anyone who killed a police officer, society's line of defense, was capable of killing almost anyone. The ripple effect of a death extended outward to family, friends, and the community as a whole, upsetting countless lives and potentially, generations.

Tyrone fell onto the bed and buried his head in his hands. "Here's what happened. They cornered him, he fired a bunch of rounds, a few officers were shot, and then the bastard did us all a favor and killed himself. The end."

"Are you all right, though? Mentally, I mean."

"Yeah, I'm all right." He rubbed a hand across the back of his neck.

Ella folded her arms over her chest. "I'm glad everything worked out, but I wish you'd called. I was worried. I couldn't find you, and no one could tell me where you were." Vestiges of fear remained knotted in her chest like a tight ball.

"You called the precinct?"

"After I kept getting your voicemail."

He ran a hand down his face. "You didn't have to do that," he said quietly.

"Of course I did." She didn't like the detached sound of his voice. Did he not understand the seriousness of her concern? If something had happened to him, what would she know? Nothing. She wasn't his wife or next of kin. They weren't obligated to share information with her.

"Not now, okay?"

"Not now? Then when?"

He snorted and muttered under his breath.

"What was that?"

"I said, not again." His gaze hardened. "I had to deal with the same crap with my ex-wife. You're basically telling me I have to go through the same thing with you?"

"You think it's crap that I care about you and that I'm worried about what happens to you?"

"You're questioning me and putting pressure on me after I've left a long and stressful day. I came here for an escape."

"I'm not trying to be difficult or make your life harder, but you could have taken a few minutes to put my mind at ease when the situation calmed down, and let me know you were okay. If this is how you treated your wife, then I understand..."

He glowered at her with tangible anger. "You understand what?" he asked in a harsh voice.

"Never mind." It was an ugly thing to say, and she already regretted the words.

Tyrone stood and walked over to her. "I need you to finish what you were about to say."

His dark brown eyes flashed angrily at her, and his jaw was set in a rigid line. She couldn't blame him for his fury, but she was furious, too. Because she was tired of being the amenable, considerate woman who constantly tried to keep the peace for her man to be happy, tiptoeing around his feelings. What about her? What about her needs and concerns? Was she supposed to act like nothing out of the ordinary happened tonight?

"You heard what I said."

"That's a shitty thing to say. For the record, Nyla's unhappiness had nothing to do with me not calling her. I did my job, and she didn't like it. This is my *job*, and that's not going to change. If you have a problem with it, that's your problem. I don't answer to anybody. I'm a grown-ass man."

"Well, excuse the hell out of me. God forbid anyone give a damn about you."

"There's a difference between giving a damn and being a nag."

"*A nag*? I'm not being a nag. You want me to pretend I don't care? Is that what you prefer?"

"I want you to ease up. That's what I want. You left me way too many messages."

That stung. "Ease up? I didn't know I was stifling you by inviting you to dinner and calling to check that you're okay. Forgive me."

He let out a heavy breath. "Ella."

He reached for her, but she dodged his hand and went through the door. She heard him behind her as she traipsed to the kitchen. Pizza boxes that contained partially eaten pies sat on the counter. She'd ordered enough for four, even though she hadn't been sure if he was alive or dead or wounded at the scene. She'd hoped he was fine and wanted him to have something to eat when he arrived.

"That was uncalled for," she said, her voice shaking. She stacked the pizza boxes on top of each other and tucked them in the fridge. No pizza for him.

"I didn't mean the words the way they came out."

Hands on her hips, she faced him. "Let me make one thing clear to you, Tyrone. I am done coddling grown-*ass* men. For years, I put aside my own wants and my own desires. For years, I stifled my sexuality and my adventurous spirit. For years, I allowed a man who I thought loved me to control almost all of my actions and turn me into a shell of myself. So forgive me if I'm not trying to appease you, because for years, I did that, and all I got was a broken heart, a broken marriage, and plenty of humiliation."

"I see. For years, you let another man run all over you, so I must be doing the exact same thing, right?"

"You're not even trying to understand."

"I understand perfectly. I've got my own battle scars, and they involve someone trying to take away something I love. Trying to force me to choose between her and my career. Lucky me, here I am again, in the same boat."

She turned away, unable to face him with her bottom lip trembling. She was all emotional and couldn't figure out how to reach him. All she knew was she didn't want him upset with her. She cared deeply about him, but cared deeply about herself, too. Should she have stayed quiet? Once he'd explained, should she have backed off? Did she have any right at all to speak up?

"I'm not asking you to choose."

"You sure? Because you're teetering awfully close to the edge. I know you already think I spend too much time at work."

"You want to work yourself to death, that's your choice." She folded her arms. "Are you coming to the New Year's Eve dinner? My mother needs to know so she can give a headcount to the caterers."

"I don't know. I could get another call or something could go wrong, and then she'll be pissed if I don't show up."

"Why don't you make a decision right now or don't bother?" she snapped. He knew how much she enjoyed the holiday season and wanted him to spend time with her and her family. He knew how important this dinner was but couldn't be bothered to make an effort to attend.

"Are you giving me an ultimatum?"

Was she? "I'm asking what's important to you."

He laughed softly and shook his head. "What's important to

me? You already know. My job is important to me. It's my life, and now you're asking me to change."

"That's not what I'm saying."

"Then what the fuck are you saying? Tell me."

"Not change. Compromise." He never even acknowledged her fears or worry when she couldn't find him.

"I'm a cop. This is what I do. I'm sorry I can't tell you for sure if I can attend your dinner party. I'm sorry I can't hang out in Europe, sightseeing for days or weeks or whatever you wanted after your parents' wedding. I have more important things to do."

"I get it. You're a hero. You help people solve puzzles. But don't you want to do anything else? I want to spend more time with you. I want to run barefoot in the backyard of my new home with my kids and sit on the patio watching them play, and I want you there with us. I want you eating dinners with us and reading the girls bedtime stories. I want more photos to put in my albums, and I want a man who wants the same things I do. I thought you were that person."

"I knew it was going to come to this. You're not angry about me not calling you. This is about my job, period."

"You're wrong."

"No, I'm not."

"Well, I say you are! I'm not settling again, Tyrone. I'm done settling. For almost five years I was in a relationship by myself. I can't, won't, do it again."

"I can't just walk away from my job, Ella. Maybe you have the privilege of doing that, but I don't."

"Yes, I know. I'm privileged. I can walk away from my job and still pay the bills and have a roof over my head because I come from a wealthy family and collect a hefty allowance. I choose to work, but I also choose how I spend my time. My family is my priority, no matter what. The people I love are my priority. What choice are you going to make? What's your priority?"

Pick me. Pick us.

"Didn't I have this job when we met? It's how we met, and

now, here you are, doing the same nonsense I had to put up with before. You're trying to force me to leave my job and turn my back on people who need me. You're trying to change me, doing the same thing, by the way, you said your husband did you."

"It's not the same, and you know it."

"Why can't you be satisfied with the way things are?"

"That's your answer?" Tears cut off her breathing and she tightened her arms across her belly, fighting back the hurt from his words. "See yourself out." She stalked out of the kitchen without another word.

CHAPTER 32

*E*lla found her mother supervising a team of decorators in the living room, setting up the tree and adding Christmas decorations and other knickknacks with a winter theme around the room.

"Oh hello, darling," Sylvie said over her shoulder. "Tom, Tom, dear. I think the flower arrangement should go over there, and that's way too much tinsel on the fireplace." She turned to Ella and rolled her eyes. "What do you think? Should I fill the silver vase with the white roses or with a combination of white and red? I can't decide."

"Whatever you choose will be fine, Mother."

Sylvie turned sharply in her direction. "What's wrong?"

"Nothing."

"I don't believe that for one minute. Care to talk about it?"

"Not if you're going to say I told you so," Ella said.

"I promise not to say I told you so. Come sit with me and tell me what happened."

Sighing heavily, Ella followed her mother into the second living room that had already been decorated. It smelled like the holidays, with the scent of cinnamon on the air. They sat down together, and Sylvie angled her body toward her daughter.

"What happened?"

She'd been going along as if nothing had happened, turned off her feelings so she wouldn't have to deal with the collapse of her latest relationship. She thought she was fine, but having someone to talk to and seeing the concern in her mother's eyes made her break down. With tears in her eyes, she told her mother about the argument and that she hadn't heard from Tyrone since. After she recounted what happened between them, she sat silently and waited for her mother's counsel.

"I'm going to be blunt," Sylvie said.

"I wouldn't expect anything less," Ella said.

"The two of you are being rather foolish. You love each other, you've professed your love for each other, yet you're allowing your past relationships to cloud your current one. If indeed this is a do-over, as you once told me, then it has to be a do-over in all aspects. You can't bring the baggage from your previous marriages into this new relationship. It's not fair, not realistic, and obviously a problem. You know how I feel about you getting involved with another man who doesn't have the same financial resources you do. I don't want you to wind up in another marriage like you did with Wayne. But Tyrone seems different. Based on everything I've seen, he seems like a decent man. I truly have no complaints about him and particularly appreciate the way he handled your case. I believe he's very much in love with you, like he said, and he'll be back soon."

Ella digested her mother's words. "I don't think he's going to call, but I'm glad I spoke up and said what I needed to."

"His loss if he doesn't call. Of course, you could always call him."

"I want to, but I don't want to be stuck in another relationship where I can't speak up." She'd always been able to talk to Tyrone and share her thoughts and feelings. His response to her speaking her mind surprised her but also hurt deeply because she never expected him to behave that way.

"Understood. And so you should stand your ground as far as that is concerned. Because I don't want to see you stifle your personality, either. But I don't think that's the problem. You've been allowed to be your true self with him, to have fun and show your true personality, haven't you?"

"Yes."

"Then the issue is not with you. It's with him and whether or not he's willing to let go of his past baggage and come into this relationship with an open mind. The last thing you want is for him to throw his previous problems in your face. That's not fair to you. And frankly, that's not going to be fair to your daughters, because then the girls will see the two of you fighting. As you well know, when the adults are fighting, it affects the children in a negative way."

Ella covered her mother's hands with hers. "Growing up with you and Father wasn't all bad. Once the two of you split, things did get better. You were happier apart for a while, but you've both grown. You realized your mistake, and now you're happy together again."

"I couldn't be happier. And that's what I want for you, too. Sometimes, you have to spend time apart from the person you love to truly appreciate them. Realize what's important. Just don't wait fifteen years like your father and I did."

Ella laughed without humor. "Assuming Tyrone does come back, I definitely won't."

* * *

CLINTON BENT over with his hands on his knees, panting. "I'm sixty-two, not twenty-two, you ass. What are you trying to do, kill me?"

Running in place, Tyrone chuckled. "Sorry, Pops."

They had stopped on the tree-lined street so his father could catch his breath. Clinton straightened and placed a hand against one of the tall oaks, still panting heavily. "What's gotten into you?"

"Nothing. Just anxious to keep going." Tyrone kept moving.

"Something's up, because you're acting like you're trying to kill your old man. Care to talk about it? And stop that damn jogging in place!"

Tyrone went still and allowed the adrenaline to drain from his body. He sighed heavily, swiping a hand across his sweaty face. "I didn't want to say anything, but Ella and I had a fight and haven't spoken since."

"When the hell did that happen? You just attended her parents' wedding a few weeks ago, for crying out loud."

He knew his father would be upset. He liked Ella and saw her daughters as additional grandchildren he could spoil.

"It wasn't working out." Hands on his hips, Tyrone marched away from his father, heaving deep breaths.

"Did this have anything to do with Officer Jones's death? You're not still stressed about that, are you?"

Tyrone shook his head. "I'm good. I'm more concerned about Gloria."

"How's she holding up?"

He shrugged. "As well as could be expected."

Tyrone didn't know Officer Jones well, but like everyone else in the precinct, he'd chipped in to help. That's what they did when they lost one of their own. They'd organized a fundraiser for his family to cover the cost of the funeral and anything else Gloria needed for the kids. He and some of the other officers planned to take the oldest, an eleven-year-old boy, to a Falcons game, and they'd set up a schedule whereby Gloria didn't have to worry about cooking dinner every night. Every week, officers and officers' wives and girlfriends brought by food. They'd even purchased an extra freezer for her to store all the meals she received. In every way imaginable, they provided support.

"So what happened between you and Ella? And why do I have the feeling you're regretting the break-up?"

Tyrone laughed. "We didn't break up, exactly. We took a break, I guess. Things were getting a bit too stressful between us. She started questioning me, and it felt like Nyla all over again. But I miss her. I'm not sure why I haven't called. Self-preservation or some BS reason like that." He paced in a circle.

"Oh, I see. So Ella's paying for what Nyla put you through. Is that it?"

"Come on, Pops. That's not it at all. I'm suffering, too."

"So, two people are miserable because your ex-wife wanted you to spend more time with her and cheated on you. Does that make sense to you?"

"No," Tyrone muttered.

He rested his butt against a car parked at the curb. "She's this incredible woman who I absolutely see myself married to. But even as I see marriage, I have concerns. I saw myself married for the rest of my life to Nyla, too. I don't want to screw this up with Ella, but at the same time, I don't want to fight over simple shit. Maybe...maybe we're not as compatible as I originally thought. Maybe we don't fit because our priorities are different. Her number one concern is spending time with family and hell, spending time with me."

She was considerate, always making sure he had food to eat and was comfortable. Except the night of the argument. He didn't miss how fast she put away that pizza.

"And you?" his father asked.

"I want to do meaningful work." Like his parents and brother, but in his own way and on his own terms.

"Listen, none of us can see into the future, but what I can say is if you love this woman and you believe she loves you, don't waste your time. Hell, life is short. Can you see yourself without her? Can you see yourself with someone else?"

"Honestly, no. I wake up in the morning thinking about her, and I go to bed with her on my mind. I worry about her, and I worry about her daughters as if they were mine. Maybe I'll give her a call, see how she's doing."

Clinton shook his head. "Don't do that. Don't play that game."

"What do you mean?"

"If you're not ready to be what she wants, don't play with her emotions, or yours, or her kids' emotions. It's not right."

"Are you saying I should walk away?"

"I'm saying do the right thing."

"I have no idea what you're talking about."

"I didn't raise no fool. You'll know soon enough."

"Easier said than done, if you ask me."

"Isn't everything?"

Tyrone watched a car go by. "I don't want to make the same mistakes I did before."

"Then figure out where you can make changes in your life. That's all you can do, son. But don't let her slip through your fingers if you love this woman."

His father had given him plenty to think about.

"You ready to head back?" Tyrone asked.

"Yeah, but go easy on your old man this time."

Tyrone chuckled, and they took off at a slow jog.

CHAPTER 33

"*H*ey."

"Hi." Ella stared at Tyrone, standing outside in the doorway.

"I came to get my things," he reminded her.

"Of course. Come in." She widened the door. She'd been so overwhelmed by his appearance, she'd forgotten why he was there.

"Sorry to come by so late. I just got off."

"It's fine." She led him into the living room where the plastic tub containing his neatly folded clothes and other items was located.

"You could have dumped everything in a plastic bag." He rubbed the back of his neck. He looked beat.

"That would have been rude." She shook her head and closed her arms around her waist in a defensive move to keep from reaching for him and comforting him.

"How have you been?" he asked.

"Okay. You?"

"Making it."

"I saw the other two officers survived the shooting."

"Yeah. Tough bastards." He laughed shortly.

"And the officer who died, how's his family?"

"Doing okay. The precinct's been real supportive."

"I'm sure his widow and the family appreciate the help."

He nodded. His gaze landed on the boxes stacked against the wall. She and her assistant had started packing personal items, but the movers would arrive after the new year and pack up everything else. "When do you move into the new house?"

"After the first of the year."

"Are the girls excited?"

Ella nodded. "The topic of a puppy came up again."

"Oh really?" He chuckled, and the warmth of his smile and the warmth of his laughter twisted her insides. "Are you finally going to get them one?"

"I don't have much of a choice. I don't know anything about dogs, so I'll have to do my research."

"Labs are good for kids, and they like the water. With the pond and plenty of space to run around, the dog and the girls will be happy."

"Labrador retrievers. I'll keep that in mind." Ella rubbed her elbow.

They stared at each other for a few seconds, and then Tyrone shook his head. "I better get out of here. Thanks for, um…" He picked up the plastic tote.

"Sure, no problem. I'll get the door for you."

They went back into the hallway, where Sophia, wearing her pajamas, came walking toward them.

"Hi, Tywone." Both she and Hannah had difficulty pronouncing the letter "r," and it was adorable the way they said his name.

"Sophia, what are you doing up, sweetie? You're supposed to be asleep," Ella said.

"Are you spending the night?" the little girl asked. She padded over and rested her head against Ella's hip. Obviously still sleepy, she rubbed her eyes. Ella placed a gentle hand on top of her head.

"No, I—" He glanced at Ella and swallowed before returning his attention to Sophia. "Not tonight, sweetheart."

"What's that?" Sophia pointed at the tote.

"Sophia," Ella chastised her.

Tyrone didn't seem to mind. He smiled indulgently at her daughter. "Your mommy was keeping a few things for me. I came to pick them up."

"Oh."

"She looks like she's about to fall asleep standing up."

"Probably." Ella lifted Sophia into her arms, and the little girl rested her head on her shoulder.

"I'm sleepy, Mama."

"I know. I'll take you to bed in a minute," Ella whispered. She looked at Tyrone, catching the pained expression on his face before he glanced down at the tote as if he could no longer bear to look at them.

"I'll see myself out," he said huskily.

"I'll walk you to the door."

"You don't have to."

"Just let me. Please," Ella said quietly. She pressed her lips together to keep them from trembling.

He took a deep breath, his chest heaving up and down, and led the way to the front door. Somehow, he maneuvered it open. Once outside, he turned to face her. "Thanks again."

"No problem."

He didn't move, and neither did she.

"You're a good woman, Ella."

"Don't."

"It's true. You deserve the best."

I had the best.

"I'm sorry we couldn't make it work. I just…" He gazed down the hall, his jaw going hard.

"I know." Falling in love was easy. Staying together was the hard part.

Ella took a tremulous breath and folded her arms under

Sophia's bottom to hold her more securely. "Take care of yourself, Tyrone. Please be safe out there."

"Always. Good night."

"Good night."

Neither of them moved, until finally she broke the spell of their locked gazes and stepped back. She closed the door, and it clicked shut. She stood staring at it for the longest, wishing he'd come back and ring the bell, say he'd made a mistake and they should try again. Try harder. Have another do-over.

She closed her eyes and took a deep breath. "It wasn't meant to be," she whispered.

Blinking back tears, she walked to the girls' room to put Sophia to bed.

* * *

ELLA UNLOCKED the door to her new home and led Reese and Malik inside. "This is it," she said, turning in a circle in the foyer.

Malik nodded his head, surveying the entrance. "Nice."

They strolled to the kitchen in the back, and Reese rested an ice-filled metal pail with a bottle of champagne and three glasses onto the island.

"Ready for the grand tour?" Ella asked.

Reese rubbed his hands together. "Let's do this."

Her parents had already seen the house, but Reese was the first of her siblings to check it out. Simone was out of town at a charity function, and Stephan had hopped on a plane right after Christmas and flown to Brazil for a few days, but should be back in time for New Year's Eve dinner with the family. She took them through the house and explained all the work she anticipated having done. By the time they made their way back to the kitchen, she'd become excited again about the prospect of renovating her new home.

Malik hopped up on the island. "What about in here?" he asked.

221

"Upgrades for sure." She wanted top-of-the-line appliances for the chefs and for herself, since she anticipated learning to cook.

"How's everything else going?" Reese asked. A concerned frown took over his brow.

Reese was the more sensitive of her younger brothers. Stephan enjoyed courting trouble and welcomed the spotlight that came with being young and rich. Reese, on the other hand, tended to hang in the background, though like Stephan, he had his fair share of female companionship.

"Everything else is fine. The girls are good. I'm good."

"Yeah?" A look passed between him and Malik.

"Did you want to ask me something?" Her gaze jumped from one to the other.

"Still no word from Tyrone?" Reese asked gently.

Overwhelmed by despair, she clenched her hands into fists and staved off the raw pain that ripped through her at the mention of his name. She'd stayed up plenty of nights thinking about him, hoping he'd call, wondering if she should call.

"I'm not thinking about him. I don't think about him. He made his decision. His career is the most important thing in his life. He told me so."

"I'm sorry. I shouldn't have brought him up. I don't know, I liked the guy. I thought he'd last."

"I did, too. But apparently, I wasn't enough to make him want to stick around."

"Don't say that. You're a good woman."

Wrong choice of words. With a soft cry, Ella pressed her palms to her face and burst into tears. Emotion broke free, like from a dam, choking with its intensity. Tears streamed down her face, tears she'd been determined not to shed but let loose under the overt concern from her brother.

"Aw damn. I'm sorry. Me and my big mouth." Reese put an arm around her shoulders.

"No, it's fine." Ella swiped away the tears with the back of her hands. "It's just that he said the same thing to me the last time I saw him. Said I was a good woman." Both Malik and Reese looked at her with pity in their eyes. "But that still wasn't enough to keep him from walking away." More tears flowed from her eyes, and she hid her crumpling face behind her hands.

Reese pulled her in tighter. Looping an arm around his torso, she rested her temple against his chest.

"We should beat him up," Malik said.

"I don't want you to beat him up." Ella sniffed.

"We can hire people to beat him up," Reese suggested.

"No, and he's a cop and he has a gun."

"We'll hire people with guns," Malik said.

Ella laughed through her tears. "No, you won't." She took a shaky breath. "I'll be fine, guys. Eventually."

Reese rubbed her back. "You're smart and pretty. Any man would be lucky to have you. Hell, I probably know a few who would kill for a date with you."

"The *last* thing I need is a date." Ella stepped out of the circle of his arms and rubbed her eyes. "I've got plenty to keep me busy with the girls, work at SJ Brands, and getting this house into the condition I want." She swallowed hard, unable to let go, unable to forget. "I thought he was the one, you know? The way he fit in with the family and bonded with Hannah and Sophia. They asked me about him the other day, wanting to know when he'll be coming for a visit. I told them he was very busy because I didn't know what to say. I didn't want to tell them he'll never come back, so I'm hoping eventually they forget and stop asking before I have to give them the bad news." Then they'd be just as devastated as she was. Ella released a cleansing breath. "Anyway, forget him. I bought a new house that I'll be moving into soon."

"Exactly. You'll have so much going on, you won't have time to think about Tyrone," Malik said.

Ella nodded, though she knew that wasn't true.

"We need to have a party after the new year, to celebrate your new place. Call up some friends and get everybody together." Reese flung an arm across her shoulders again.

Malik smoothed a hand down his beard. "I like that idea. Like a housewarming."

"Exactly. What do you think?" Reese asked, looking down at Ella.

"I like the idea, too. Once I'm settled in and everything is exactly the way I want, we can do that." She hadn't entertained in a while, and she'd already envisioned entertaining in the great room.

"Cool."

"All right. Time for champagne and the mini-celebration before the housewarming celebration." Malik hopped off the island and removed a Swiss army knife from his pocket. Using the corkscrew, he popped open the champagne and poured three glasses. They each took one.

"Tell me again how smart and pretty I am," Ella said.

"You're the smartest and the prettiest. His loss, Ella," Reese said.

"Yeah, his loss," Malik agreed.

My loss, too.

"You guys are the best." Ella hugged Reese's torso with one arm and held up her glass. "What are we toasting to?"

"Your new home and all the parties we're gonna have here," Reese said.

"Here, here!" Malik said.

"Sorry, guys. You're not turning my family home into a pseudo bachelor pad." Ella laughed at the mock disappointed frowns on their faces. "There's something else I want to toast to." She smiled through the aching of her heart. "Let's toast to new beginnings."

Her cousin and brother smiled.

"I like that. New beginnings," Malik said.

"New beginnings," Reese said.

They clinked their glasses together.

New beginnings.

CHAPTER 34

"*H*annah, Sophia, get in here, please." From the kitchen, Ella heard the girls laughing and playing in the adjacent room.

They'd only been living at the new place a couple of weeks, and there was plenty of work to be done. She could have waited until the renovations were completed, but she'd been too anxious and moved in early. Contractors had redone the floors, repaired the roof, fixed the holes in the walls, painted, and the kitchen redesign came next. Two designers arrived next week, one for the kitchen and the other for the rest of the house. For now, they used the furniture they'd brought from the penthouse.

Simone and Cameron bought the second house from Ella, and renovations started over there in a few weeks. She was excited to have her sister living next door and her brothers only a few miles away. Her family life was going well. Romantic life, not so much.

She still hadn't heard from Tyrone. She missed his company and his touch and had hoped they could still talk occasionally. She'd been tempted to call but didn't want to bother him.

Bottom line, they'd move too fast too soon. Next time, she

would go slower and date a man from her social circle. Only millionaires and billionaires need apply moving forward.

Ella rested her hands on her hips. "Hannah, Sophia, get in here, I said." She spoke in firmer tones this time.

They ran in, Sophia leading the way and her shadow behind her.

"You girls need to put away your toys so when Tracy arrives, she can get you ready for when your father comes by to pick you up."

Ella met Wayne's new girlfriend last week, and they were taking the girls to dinner so they could get to know the new woman in his life.

Ella heard the front door close, and seconds later, Tracy walked into the kitchen. "Hi, Miss Brooks."

"Hi, Tracy. I was just telling them they needed to put their toys away before you came."

Tracy smiled uncertainly, coming deeper into the room. "I brought a surprise with me. I hope it's okay."

Tyrone appeared in the doorway, holding a large white box with a red ribbon tied in a bow on top. The smile fell off Ella's face, and her heart stopped.

He wore a red Atlanta Falcons skull cap pulled so low, his thick brows were almost hidden. His face looked freshly groomed, and even from here she could smell his cologne.

Hannah and Sophia screamed excitedly and ran over to him. "Tywone! Tywone!"

"I buzzed him through the gate with me," Tracy explained.

Tyrone placed the box on the floor and enveloped the girls, one in each arm.

"You're not busy anymore?" Sophia asked, flinging an arm around his neck.

"Not as busy as I used to be." He cast a quick glance at Ella.

What did that mean?

"I brought something for the girls. I hope you don't mind."

"A pwesent?" Hannah's eyes widened.

"I don't mind." Dumbfounded, Ella could only manage a few words. His unexpected appearance had taken her by surprise, and she wished she were dressed differently instead of wearing faded jeans and a too-large sweater that draped off one shoulder.

Tyrone lifted the lid off the box and carefully removed a black Labrador puppy. The puppy looked at them with black, baleful eyes.

The girls gasped and started cooing at the dog. Sophia immediately took hold of him and rubbed her chin against his head. "Is it ours?" she asked, her voice wobbly with emotion.

"Sure is." Tyrone glanced up at Ella, who'd hardly taken her eyes from him since he arrived. "I hope that's okay. I didn't think about what I was doing until I had actually gotten here, and then I realized this might be a bad idea."

"It's a good idea. I told you I'd been wanting to get them a dog."

"Is it a girl puppy or a boy puppy?" Sophia asked.

"Boy," Tyrone answered.

"Mama, I wanna hold him," Hannah said, sticking out her bottom lip.

"Sophia, let your sister hold the puppy," Ella said.

"Be careful," Sophia warned, apparently now an expert in the art of puppy-holding.

Biting her lip to concentrate, Hannah took the dog and held him close to her chest. "He's so soft," she whispered. The dog nudged her chin with his nose and she giggled.

"What's his name?" Sophia asked, petting the puppy's head.

"No name yet. You get to name him." A grin spread across Tyrone's face, and Ella's heart clenched a little tighter. Why was he here?

"Scwuffy."

Hannah nodded vigorously in agreement. "Yes, Scwuffy."

"Er, you can take some time to think about it," Tyrone suggested.

"Scwuffy's his name. Hi, Scwuffy." Sophia kissed him on the head.

"Guess that settles it, then," Tyrone said.

They watched the girls love on the puppy for a few minutes, then Tyrone stood. "Can we go somewhere and talk?" he said to Ella.

"Sure. Tracy, could you get the girls ready for when their father comes by? Take Scruffy with you. I'll be up in a bit."

"Sure, Miss Brooks."

Ella led Tyrone into the solarium on legs springy from nerves.

"I still can't get over this room." He tugged off his leather jacket, eyes trained on the sky through the glass ceiling.

"It's my favorite one in the house." Ella clasped her hands together. "I'm sorry, can I get you something to drink?"

"No." He stood there, staring at her with intent eyes that made her weak in the knees. "I missed you."

She laughed hollowly. "You have a weird way of showing it. You picked up your belongings after Christmas, and I haven't heard from you since." They were more than halfway through January now. She thought for sure she'd hear from him around New Year's, but no calls or texts came through. It was then that she accepted they were truly over and she should move on.

"I wasn't ready to get in touch. Not until I took care of a few things."

"What things?"

"Before I tell you about that there's something I need to say to you first." He sat on the arm of a cushioned chair. He paused for a moment, arranging the words in his head. "Actually, there's a lot I could say to you right now, but the main thing I want to say is that I'm sorry for acting like a complete jerk. My ex and I used to argue all the time about my schedule, and it left a bitter taste in my mouth. I felt like she didn't understand me or my needs."

"I wasn't trying to be difficult."

"I know. When Nyla cheated on me, that hurt. A lot. And my ego was bruised. Here I was, a detective with the Atlanta police," spending a minimum of twelve hours a day solving crime, and I didn't know my wife was sleeping with another man right under my nose. My best friend. When you started in on me, some of that old resentment and anger came back."

"It wasn't just your schedule. I was worried about you, and you blew me off, like my concerns didn't matter. *I couldn't reach you.* I didn't know if you were lying in the street..." Her voice turned hoarse, and she couldn't finish the thought. He'd become so important to her, the thought that he could have been shot had filled her with terror.

"I had turned my phone to silent. The last thing you want is the phone to ring in a tense situation or when you're closing in on a suspect."

"Why didn't you say so at the time?"

"I was pissed. Annoyed. Being a fool. Felt like the woman in my life was trying to take away something I loved, again. Which brings me to the second reason I came by." He took a deep breath. "I'm no longer a police detective. I quit. Turned in my badge at the end of the year."

"You *quit*?"

He nodded.

"Are you working now? What are you doing?" She had a million questions.

"As a matter of fact, next week I start at the Cordoba Agency. I reached out to Cruz, and he was still interested."

She searched his eyes, seeking the same passion she'd seen when he talked about his work as a public servant. "Is this what you want?"

"They have access to technology and resources that I didn't have at the police department, and they're not limited by the same rules." His head tilted a little to the side. "I thought you'd be happy."

"I want *you* to be happy." She meant that. Even if they weren't together, she wanted the best for him.

"Well, I'm not happy, cause I don't have you in my life. I miss you and Hannah and Sophia."

"That's sweet, but I don't want you to give up the career you love because of me." He might resent her later, and then what? They'd be right back where they started.

"I'm not giving anything up. I'm still going to be helping people, but not in law enforcement. In some instances, my hands were tied as a cop, but I can use the connections I made over the past thirteen years to work on cases with Cruz and his team. I talked to him about extending their services beyond helping the wealthy, and he liked the idea. We'll do pro bono cases, like attorneys do, to help people who can't typically afford such a high-end service."

"So you'll be helping people, but in a different way."

"Exactly. And, since I'll only work forty to forty-five hours a week max, I get more time to do volunteer work if I want. Or, spend time with the people I care about." His eyes didn't leave her face. "I wanted everything to be in place before I approached you again. I didn't want to half-step."

"You have everything figured out."

"I think so."

"What's next?"

"You. Me. Together. Forever." A smile lifted the right corner of his mouth.

Ella lifted her chin. "How do you know I haven't met someone already? You've been MIA for weeks. Maybe I wasn't waiting around for you."

"Aw damn. So now I gotta kick somebody's ass." He shrugged. "I'll do whatever I have to." He stood. Holding his hands behind his back and looking at her intently, he edged forward. "Whatever you need me to do, whatever you need me to say, I'll do it."

She edged back, afraid to reach out and touch him, in case he wasn't real. "I'm going to speak my mind all the time. I'm not going to be quiet because you're annoyed or think I'm a nag."

"Good. I like my women feisty. Ready to scratch another woman's eyes out if she gets too close."

The corners of his mouth twitched, but she swallowed her laughter.

"Are you sure you know what you're getting yourself into with me?"

"I think so. Let's see...private jets, mansions, a lifetime of free beer—that's for my dad, by the way." He took two steps closer, and she stepped back into the glass wall. "You and your lovely daughters."

"So you're okay with everything I come with?"

"Yeah. If you're okay with everything I come with." He bent his head so their lips were close together.

"You'll have to deal with my impossible ex," she said softly, gazing into his eyes.

"*Or*, maybe he'll have to deal with me." He pressed his lips to her exposed shoulder, and she briefly closed her eyes, savoring the caress she thought she'd never experience again. "This shoulder has been tempting me since I saw you." Another kiss to the crook of her neck and then one to the underside of her jaw.

Ella moaned and spread her fingers over his chest. He was real, he was here, and oh, he smelled good. Her tongue grazed the hair on his chin, and she nipped at his bottom lip with her teeth.

"So whose ass do I need to kick?" he asked huskily.

"Nobody's," she whispered, looping her arms around his neck.

Tyrone's face turned serious. "I missed you so much." He rested his forehead against hers and closed his eyes. They stood there, absorbing each other and re-establishing their severed connection.

"I missed you, too." Tears surfaced in her eyes, but this time they were tears of happiness. She thought she'd never see him again, thought she'd never hear his soothing voice again or experience his touch. Thought she would never again laugh at his teasing and have the pleasure of teasing him back. "But you're back."

"I'm back." Tyrone smoothed his hands down the curve of her spine to her bottom and pulled her against his body. "Forgive me?"

Ella peeled the skull cap off his head and ran her hand over his tight curls. She rubbed her cheek along the short hairs that blanketed his jaw and chin. "Yes." There was no other answer she could give.

"We're gonna make this work. I promise," he whispered.

She believed him, and her insides warmed with the possibility of what the future held.

EPILOGUE

*S*uper Bowl Sunday in Texas turned out to be much more exciting than Ella ever imagined. She was never a football fan, but Tyrone's excitement became her excitement and the trip had turned into a family affair. She, Tyrone, Clinton, her daughters, as well as all her siblings—except Stephan at the moment—and Cameron were together in a luxury suite at the NRG Stadium in Houston watching the Atlanta Falcons beat up on the New England Patriots. Tracy had also come along and brought a friend with her.

At Tyrone's request, they all dressed in Falcons gear to send positive vibes to the team, and as far as he was concerned, it was working. The Falcons led in the third quarter with a score of twenty-eight to three. Tyrone had taught Hannah and Sophia the dirty bird, and the girls were adorable with their Falcons T-shirts and Falcons ribbons in their hair, doing the celebratory dance with Tyrone and Clinton after the last touchdown, joining in the excitement that wound through the stadium and the other spectators.

"Come on baby, let's do this!" Tyrone yelled down to the field, clapping his hands.

"Let's do this!" Sophia yelled.

Hannah echoed the same cry.

On a bar stool near Ella, Simone shook her head. "He's really into this, isn't he?"

"You have no idea," Ella said.

Stephan strolled in a few minutes later, wearing a plain white T-shirt and jeans. Not a single falcon in sight. She should have known he'd be contrary.

Tyrone must've sensed his presence because he turned around and stared at Stephan, his eyebrows snapping low over his eyes.

Ella hopped off the stool and pressed a hand to her brother's chest. "Where are your clothes?"

"What, you mean Falcons gear? You were serious about that?"

Ella placed her hands on her hips. "Look around you. You're the only one not dressed in support of the team."

He glanced around, caught Tyrone's eye and gave a head nod, but Tyrone didn't respond or smile. He muttered something and nudged his father, who in turn cast an annoyed look at Stephan.

"Are you guys serious?" Stephan asked his sister.

Simone snickered. "You see I have mine on, don't you?" She pointed at her Falcons T-shirt.

"I seriously doubt the fact that I'm not dressed in support of the team will make any difference. It's the third quarter, and the score is twenty-eight to three. Obviously, they came to win."

"Why can't you ever play along?" Ella asked.

"Oh, I don't know, because I'm unique. Because I'm a leader, not a follower." He thumped Ella on the forehead, and she swatted away his hand. He went across the room and sank into the leather chair between Cameron and Reese.

Tyrone looked at Ella, widening his eyes, as if to ask, *what happened?*

She shrugged her answer, and he shook his head in disgust.

"He's too worried," Simone said. "There's no way the Patriots can catch them now."

"True." Ella nodded and hopped back up on the stool.

* * *

AFTER TUCKING the girls into bed in the adjoining hotel room where Tracy was also sleeping with them, Ella quietly closed the door. She padded into the bedroom of the suite and found Tyrone in the same position she left him in, propped up against the pillows on the bed, staring across at the wall. Sullen, utterly destroyed, as if he'd played in the game himself. Sadly, the Falcons hadn't scored again, and the Patriots won in overtime with a score of thirty-four to twenty-eight.

"They played as hard as they could," Ella said, not sure what else to say. Silently, he looked at her and then returned his attention to the wall.

"I'm going to change and get ready for bed."

Still no response.

In the bathroom, she put on a silver nightie with lace edging on the bodice and hem. She let out her hair and brushed the strands until they shined, then fluffed her hair so it fell in full waves around her face. She opened the door and stretched a hand above her head on the doorjamb, posing with one hip at a jaunty angle and let the spaghetti strap fall off one shoulder.

"How about a consolation prize?"

His face came alive. "You're no one's consolation prize. You're the Lombardi Trophy of prizes."

"I have no idea what that means, but I'm pretty sure it's a compliment, right?"

This time, a full smile crossed his lips. "It is. The Lombardi Trophy is what the winning Super Bowl team receives."

"Then I'm special for sure."

"Come here," he said, pulling his lower lip between his teeth.

Ella sashayed to the bed and threw one leg over his lap and sat back on his thighs. "I'm sorry about the game."

"Please tell your brother Stephan I'm not speaking to him."

"Honey, come on. You know the loss had nothing to do with my brother."

235

He crossed his arms over his chest. "What was the score in the third quarter?"

"Twenty-eight to three."

"When did Stephan show up?"

She tilted her head to one side. "Tyrone."

"When did he show up?"

Ella let out an exasperated sigh. "The third quarter."

"Was he wearing the appropriate clothes?"

"Honey—"

"I'm asking a simple question. Was he wearing the clothes that I specifically requested everyone in attendance wear for Super Bowl Sunday?"

"No, he was not."

"Exactly."

Ella trailed her finger down the middle of his long-sleeved shirt. "Does that mean you're not in the mood tonight?"

His eyes followed the movement of her hand down his body. "I don't know. What did you have in mind?"

"Something to make you feel better."

"So you think you can just come in here and have sex with me and it'll make everything okay?"

The trailing finger ran over his belt buckle and the swell against the zipper in his pants. "That was the idea."

He chuckled. "Well if that's what you think, you're right."

She smiled and leaned forward, kissing him first on the cheek, then the nose. "My poor baby," she whispered. She kissed his soft, delicious mouth, and Tyrone cupped her bottom and squeezed until she was pressed flat on top of him, grinding her hips. They both moaned at the same time.

Ella pulled back. "Just so you know, I'm sure Stephan is sorry." She didn't know that but thought it might help.

"Just so you know, Stephan isn't invited to our wedding. I'm dead serious."

She froze, staring into his eyes. "Wedding? You're willing to get married again?"

"Aren't you?"

Ella nodded, smiling. Before him, she hadn't considered the possibility, but he'd changed her mind. She no longer shied away from the thought of marriage. She embraced the idea, ready to wade into the unknown with Tyrone at her side.

"Whew. For a minute there, I thought you didn't want to buy the cow because you're getting the milk for free."

She giggled. "Maybe in your case we should say buy the bull because I can get the sperm for free."

They both wrinkled their noses.

"Ew," Ella said. "Never mind, let's stick to milk and cows."

"Good idea." He laughed, and they kissed again.

She stroked his jaw. "I really am sorry about your game. I know you were looking forward to a championship."

"That's okay. They'll get another chance to get it right."

"Like us."

"Yeah." He rolled her over onto her back and whispered, "You said something about making me feel better?"

"Why, yes, Mr. Evers, I sure did."

"I'm an emotional wreck. Might take all night to lift my spirits."

Using only his teeth, Tyrone pulled the strap of the nightie off her shoulder, and she giggled. But the giggles turned to gasps when his mouth closed over her nipple, and soon there was no more talk of football, or championships, or cows.

More Brooks Family and Johnson Family

Get ready for Lindsay, the woman who makes Malik Brooks give up celibacy, in *Wild Thoughts*. Coming soon. Add the book to your Goodreads shelf now.

Find out how Simone Brooks and Cameron Bennett met and fell in love, in A Passionate Love.

Read how Oscar Brooks and Sylvie Johnson found their way back together in the short story, Passion Rekindled.

Check out the Brooks family cousins in the Johnson Family series —about a billionaire beer and restaurant dynasty based in Seattle. Meet Ivy, Cyrus, Trenton, Gavin, and Xavier in Unforgettable, Perfect, Just Friends, The Rules, and Good Behavior.

ALSO BY DELANEY DIAMOND

Royal Brides

- Princess of Zamibia

Brooks Family series

- Passion Rekindled
- Do Over
- Wild Thoughts (coming soon)

Love Unexpected series

- The Blind Date
- The Wrong Man
- An Unexpected Attraction
- The Right Time
- One of the Guys
- That Time in Venice

Johnson Family series

- Unforgettable
- Perfect
- Just Friends
- The Rules
- Good Behavior

Latin Men series

- The Arrangement

- Fight for Love
- Private Acts
- The Ultimate Merger
- Second Chances
- More Than a Mistress
- Undeniable
- Hot Latin Men: Vol. I (print anthology)
- Hot Latin Men: Vol. II (print anthology)

Hawthorne Family series

- The Temptation of a Good Man
- A Hard Man to Love
- Here Comes Trouble
- For Better or Worse
- Hawthorne Family Series: Vol. I (print anthology)
- Hawthorne Family Series: Vol. II (print anthology)

Bailar series (sweet/clean romance)

- Worth Waiting For

Stand Alones

- A Passionate Love
- Still in Love
- Subordinate Position
- Heartbreak in Rio (free to newletter subscribers thru 7/31/18)

Other

- Audiobooks
- Signed paperbacks
- Free Stories

ABOUT THE AUTHOR

Delaney Diamond is the USA Today Bestselling Author of sweet, sensual, passionate romance novels. Originally from the U.S. Virgin Islands, she now lives in Atlanta, Georgia. She reads romance novels, mysteries, thrillers, and a fair amount of nonfiction. When she's not busy reading or writing, she's in the kitchen trying out new recipes, dining at one of her favorite restaurants, or traveling to an interesting locale.

Enjoy free reads and the first chapter of all her novels on her website. Join her mailing list to get sneak peeks, notices of sale prices, and find out about new releases.

Join her mailing list
www.delaneydiamond.com

f facebook.com/DelaneyDiamond
🐦 twitter.com/DelaneyDiamond
ⓟ pinterest.com/DelaneyDiamond

95298820R00135

Made in the USA
Columbia, SC
08 May 2018